CITY OF TORRANCE

75th Anniversary

1912 - 1987

STORM CENTRE

Douglas Clark's winning team of Detective Chief Superintendent Masters and Detective Chief Inspector Green
are once again on top form, using their meticulous logic
and ingenious leaps of imagination to solve murders
committed by unusual means. (They have an uncanny
skill in making bricks without straw.)

Masters, still recovering from a gunshot wound sus-
tained in his last case (recounted in *Jewelled Eye*) is
invited by his Scotland Yard chief to do a spell of
lecturing at a police college. Lured by the prospect of
taking his wife and young son with him for what
promises to be a pleasant few weeks in the country, he
accepts. He has reservations, though; doubts which he
can't quite pin down. His suspicions are justified once
he arrives. The college has a tricky problem with the
local force over the disappearance, during a period of
five years, of two teenage boys.

Since the case is not his, Masters has to proceed with
the utmost discretion. He quickly assembles his famous
team of DCI Green and DCs Berger and Reed. Between
(and during) lectures they start work on the case. They
are in their element, having to treat the problem as
theoretical since they have no access to the local police's
files. But despite their lack of information they manage
to solve the case with a speed and brilliance which
dumbfounds both the college and the local force.

STORM CENTRE

by

DOUGLAS CLARK

LONDON
VICTOR GOLLANCZ LTD
1986

First published in Great Britain 1986
by Victor Gollancz Ltd,
14 Henrietta Street, London WC2E 8QJ

British Library Cataloguing in Publication Data
Clark Douglas, *1919–*
  Storm centre.
  I. Title
  823'.914[F]   PR6053.L294

  ISBN 0-575-03833-0

Typeset in Great Britain by Centracet
and printed by St Edmundsbury Press,
Bury St Edmunds, Suffolk

Chapter 1

WANDA MASTERS ANSWERED the door of the little house behind the Westminster Hospital.

"Not too early, are we?" asked Doris Green whose husband, Bill, stood behind her grinning. "This silly fool made me come at least ten minutes before . . ."

"You're never too early," replied Wanda. "Come in. I'm just straightening up a bit. George is in the sitting room. He's been playing with Michael and we've got stickle bricks hidden under every piece of furniture and under every cushion. I still haven't located them all. I know because I can judge the size of the heap from long association and I think there must be at least thirty missing."

"Get the great detective on to it," said Green.

"The great detective is watching television, as you can hear."

"How's his arm?" whispered Doris.

"No need to keep your voice low, love," said her husband. "George knew he was shot in the arm. It hurt him and there was a lot of blood . . . "

"Fool," snorted Doris.

"The arm is fine," said Wanda. "He's supposed to use it normally whenever he can to build up the muscle. He has to put it back in the sling when its gets tired, but the wound has healed very nicely." She turned from hanging up their coats. "Go in, William, and help yourself to a drink. What about you, Doris?"

"I'll help you, dear. That's if there's anything I can do to help."

"In this house, with a man and a child here all day!"

Doris smiled. "You love it."

"I do, actually. But those two are so untidy . . . come through to the kitchen. I've got a bottle of sherry out there."

Green joined Masters.

"Hello, Bill. Help yourself. Gin or beer. Whichever."

"Thanks. How's the busted pinion?"

"Fine, fine. I haven't to go across for them to look at it for another week."

"Good, because . . . "

"Because what?" Masters got up and switched off the set. "Because what, Bill? Is something going on?"

Green finished pouring the glass of beer before replying. Then, as he came to sit in the chair facing Masters, he said: "Anderson wants to see you."

"He can come whenever he wants. It's not what you might call a long way from the Yard to here. And he's been here often enough over the years."

"'Tother way round," growled Green. "He wants you to go to him."

"Any idea why, Bill? I mean I haven't even finished the three weeks sick leave granted me when I was shot. Then there's two weeks ordinary leave to come."

Green nodded. "That's what I told him, but he is the Assistant Commissioner Crime and so I couldn't be too blunt about it. Cheers!"

Masters grinned. "Whoever could suppose you blunt at any time, Bill? Any idea what it's all about? I mean, he was on the phone to me three or four days ago. . . . "

"No idea, chum. He called me in at about half past three this afternoon and suggested I came round then to deliver the message, but when I told him I would be calling on you tonight, he said this would be soon enough so long as you made it to his office tomorrow morning."

"He sounds as if he's in a hurry to see me."

"For what it's worth—and I could be mistaken—he seemed in a worry to see you."

"Agitated?"

"A bit."

"Then why in heaven's name didn't he phone me?"

Green shrugged. "Don't ask me. I'm only the messenger boy."

"And you really have no idea what it's about?"

"Not what it's about, but I've got some idea of how Anderson's mind works. He wants you for something and he's feeling a bit sheepish about calling on you while you're still on sick leave. So he'd like to get you there on his home ground to size you up. To see if you're fit enough to take on whatever it is he's got in mind. Not a very subtle character, our Edgar."

Masters grimaced. "Do you know of anything that's cropped up? We're not at the top of the out-of-town list, are we?"

"Permanently fixed at the bottom till you return. And no, there are no out-of-the-ordinary whispers going round. As you know, he can't officially send me off on anything on my own, but I've done a bit with Reed and Berger. All straightforward stuff, relatively. We even picked up a couple of villains who'd done a sub-post office yesterday. Bit of luck, really. The man in the shop noticed one of the stocking masks had got a hole in it at the side. Said he thought it had snagged on the earring the yob was wearing and showed a scar just on the jawbone."

"Somebody in the book?"

"There are large as life. We picked them both up and most of the loot. Some of it had gone, of course."

"Still, it was good work. Help yourself to more beer, Bill. There's another bottle there, I think, and I'll get some more from under the stairs."

"Ta. Like me to do the lifting for you?"

"Six bottles in a shrink pack? I reckon I can just about manage that."

Wanda and Doris joined them a few minutes later. "Supper in a quarter of an hour," said Wanda. "Just time for Doris and me to have another sherry, darling."

"Coming up." Masters moved across to the wine cabinet. "How are you, Doris? I haven't seen you for quite a long time."

"I stopped her coming," said Green. "Didn't want her upsetting the walking wounded."

"We stayed away on purpose, George," said Doris quietly, accepting her drink, "because we thought Wanda would have

7

her hands full with you and Michael. I told her that if she needed a baby-sitter of course we'd come over, but as you were here, she could go out and leave Michael with you."

"Actually," said Wanda, "we've had one or two nice afternoon walks with Michael. Down by the river and in the park. The weather has been really very good for March." She put her glass on the coffee table. "And how are things at the Yard, William?"

"So, so, love."

"Oh? Is there anything wrong?"

Green nodded towards Masters. "Your old man will tell you."

"Tell me what, George?"

"Anderson asked Bill to tell me he'd like me to call on him sometime tomorrow morning."

"Oh, no! Whatever for? Can't they leave you in peace for five minutes?"

"I've no idea what it's about, darling, nor has Bill. It could be just something he wants to have a word about. Like that cheque from Rutland."

"What cheque was that?" asked Green.

"Rutland sent a cheque for five thousand pounds as a thanks offering for finding Hopcraft. Anderson wanted to know what to do with it. Send it back or bung it in police charities."

"Anderson, my foot," snorted Wanda. "It was sent to you personally. You handed it to him."

"I'm not allowed to accept gifts, poppet."

"True," said Green. "A good thing, too. Down with bribery and corruption. What's for supper, love? It smells good."

"Bill!" expostulated his wife.

"Now what's up? Aren't I allowed to congratulate my hostess on her smells?"

"Now you're making it even worse."

"A pair or a brace or whatever of duckling," said Wanda, laughing. "They're quite small so we'll need the two."

"*A l'orange*?" demanded Green.

"No orange, no rice. Just straight, old-fashioned, roasted."

"Good," said Green. "That's how I like 'em."

"In that case, as you would yourself say, come and get it, because you're going to do the carving."

The next morning, soon after nine o'clock, Masters rang the Yard and asked to speak to Anderson. He wanted to know at what time the AC (Crime) would like to see him. Anderson's secretary took the call and told him that she had, in fact, a note on her pad to remind her to ring him. It appeared that her boss had instructed her to invite Mrs Masters to the meeting which, if possible, Anderson would like to take place at eleven that morning.

"You're sure he intends my wife should be there?"

"Definitely, Mr Masters. Mr Anderson asked me to arrange for a WPC to look after your son if you have to bring him with you."

"Thank you. I'll let you know if we need the services of the WPC and, indeed, whether my wife will be with me. I don't know her arrangements for the day. But I shall be there myself at eleven."

When Wanda heard the news, she asked: "What's going on, George? I'm not one of Edgar's little lambs, to be called to meetings of the CID."

"Quite right, poppet. I told his secretary that I didn't know whether you would be there or not."

"Oh, I shall be there. Out of curiosity, if nothing else, because whatever it is concerns me, obviously. More than the usual vagaries of your job, I mean."

"It would seem so. What about Michael? Shall you take him along and leave him to the tender mercies of some young WPC?"

"I may have to, but I think not. I'll try to get Mrs Howlet to sit in. Michael knows and likes her."

"Mrs Howlet being?"

"You know her. Molly Howlet."

"Ah! The one wot makes the pretty curtains and such."

"George, she's here at least once every week. She brings her hand-sewing and sits with Michael when I have to go out on adoption business."

"I never see her."

9

"Of course you don't. You're away when she comes. I'll ring her now. Could you clear the breakfast dishes for me while I speak to her?"

Mrs Howlet was agreeable to coming. At a few minutes to eleven, Masters showed Wanda into his office and then rang Anderson's secretary to say they had arrived and would await her summons to the meeting. A moment later, Green knocked and came in.

"Heard you were here, love," he said. "Couldn't believe my ears, at first. Are you going to wait for George, because if so . . . ?"

Wanda smiled. "William, I have been requested, nay summoned, to attend the councils of the high an' mighty. Even as we speak, Edgar Anderson is . . . "

The internal phone bell interrupted her. Masters answered it.

"Time to go, darling."

"There you are, William. The AC Crime eagerly awaits me. He is pacing the office carpet in avid anticipation. He is . . . "

"Out," said Masters. "And there's no need to feel nervous."

"Nervous? At meeting Edgar?"

"You were acting the goat, evincing signs . . . " He ushered her out of the room.

Anderson gave Wanda a little kiss on the cheek—as was his custom whenever he met her—before shaking hands with Masters, thereby indicating that the meeting was unlikely to be a serious affair.

"After I told Bill Green to give you a message, George, it occurred to me that what I wanted to discuss with you would affect Wanda as much as you, so I asked my secretary to invite her, too.

"I'm glad you could come, my dear, because I don't want you cursing me for suggesting that George should get back to work before he's fit or before the due date."

"And are you?" asked Wanda gently.

"In a sense, yes."

"I thought that might be it."

10

"It's not quite the way you think, my dear. But judge for yourselves. Quite briefly, an instructor at the College . . ."

"Police College?"

"Yes. He's the one who lectures about recent crimes and then sets the problems connected with them—you know what I mean, George, you've been through the course."

"Sillick did that sort of thing when I was there last."

"That's the chap. He's gone sick, and is likely to be out of action for six or eight weeks. So they want a temporary replacement. The point is they want an articulate man and one who is not only capable of lecturing and conducting tutorials etcetera, but one who knows half a dozen or so recent crimes—big ones—inside out, without having to spend weeks researching his material.

"We've been asked to help, and your name immediately sprang to mind as the best one to fill the bill. I know you've over a fortnight to go before you return to duty, but I just wondered whether a couple of months or so in the country might not be as good for you, or better than, coming back here at a much earlier date."

"It sounds quite lovely," said Wanda, speculatively, "but eight weeks away from home seems a bit of a tall order."

Anderson waved one hand in the air. "No, no, my dear, I haven't made myself clear. You would get one of the houses kept for permanent staff. You and young Michael could go with George if you wanted. Plenty of room. Three bedrooms. Ready furnished, of course. Not up to your standard, perhaps, but all mod cons in the kitchen and so forth. The armchairs are not all that good—issue type, you know, but all there, everything, bang in the middle of the country, and with spring about to come in . . . what do you think?"

"I think you're a darling for thinking of it for us," replied Wanda. "If George is happy about the job, then Michael and I will be very happy to go with him."

"Thank you, my dear. What say you, George?"

"It sounds attractive, sir, but despite the encyclopaedic knowledge of modern crimes you credit me with, lectures and materials like drops, maps, slides and so on have to be prepared if the students are going to get their money's worth.

11

And there will be checking and research even though you said not. To go into action at the drop of a hat will take some doing. Would I have a secretary or typist?"

"I don't imagine so. But you would have an office and . . . wait a moment. How good is your sergeant at this sort of thing?"

"Reed? He's a passable typist and, of course, his knowledge would complement my own if you envisage me using my own cases as studies."

"That is the idea, so that not too much research would be necessary. Look, how would it be if I were to send Reed with you? He'd get a cubicle in the single students' quarters and feed in the mess there. Would that suit?"

"It would make all the difference, sir."

"I can't promise he would stay all the time, but you could have him for two or three weeks."

"That ought to be long enough to get . . . how many lectures? . . . together."

"One major case a week, I understand. Two hours of it. That's a long time to talk, I know, but . . . "

"We would need that," said Masters. "To put the business over properly."

"I suppose so. And it needs to be done properly."

"What else, sir?"

"Tutorials—two or three students at a time. Essays to be set and marked. Quite a full programme, actually, but not as tiring as being here and going off on murder investigations, I'd have thought. You'd be at home every night and, indeed, at other times when you weren't actually dealing with students."

"When would we be expected to report, sir?"

"As soon as possible. Look, I don't want to pressure you into accepting, but there isn't much time to spare. Another replacement will have to be found if you turn it down."

"We would like an hour or so to talk it over, please," said Wanda. "We could go to George's office for that."

"Excellent. Then you could lunch with me."

Wanda shook her head. "I shall have to hurry home to relieve the baby-sitter and give Michael his lunch. And if we do decide to go . . . well, from what you say, Edgar, I shall have to start packing."

"Of course, of course. But don't forget that if George and Reed were to go down there, you could follow when you're ready and when the house has been opened up." He got to his feet. "I hope you decide to go. The country round there will do George good, and the job will give him a bit of variety."

They took less than a quarter of an hour to consult Reed and then to decide to take the temporary appointment that had been offered to Masters.

"When will you go?" asked Anderson when they had told him. "Tonight?"

"Tomorrow morning," replied Masters.

Anderson looked slightly disappointed at this reply, but did not press the matter, although for a moment or two both Masters and Wanda thought he was about to.

"Reed will drive the Rover," said Masters, "and Wanda will drive me in our own car. I don't think I should trust the arm yet."

"No, no, of course not. I'll let the Commandant know you will arrive before lunch tomorrow."

"If you will give me the Chief Instructor's name and phone number, sir, I can call him to get a better idea of what I shall need down there."

"You'll need a uniform, George. I know you only wear one about once a year, but every so often they dress for dinner in the mess. And you'll need a long frock, my dear. They have a guest night once a month."

"I was thinking more of tutorial materials, sir."

"Right. His name's Locke. You've got the College number. The switchboard will put you through. His official title is Deputy Commandant and Dean of Police Studies. Rank, I believe, is Assistant Chief Constable, but you can find that out when you get down there."

They returned home for lunch. Masters was very quiet as they ate.

"Darling," said Wanda, "I know you've been gypped of a

fortnight's leave and I don't like that, but weighed against two months in the countryside . . . it'll be almost like a long holiday and it will do you good and Michael and I will enjoy it. Woods and fields and a nine-to-five job. You are pleased aren't you?"

"Of course I'm pleased at the prospect, my sweet, and to be honest, I've always rather fancied myself as a lecturer or, rather, I've fancied having a stab at it. Otherwise I wouldn't have agreed to go."

"But?"

"I'm not quite sure. Didn't it strike you that Edgar Anderson was in a hell of a hurry to get us down there?"

"You, certainly. But he explained there's a yawning great gap in the tutorial staff which somebody is wanting to fill very quickly, and if he couldn't say you had agreed somebody else was going to offer very quickly. It's quite a plum little job in its way."

Masters nodded and buttered another biscuit. "Agreed, my sweet. But all Anderson had to do was to phone through to say I had accepted, and that would stop other candidates. What, in fact, he was after was to get me down there in person without a moment's delay. You saw him when I said we would go tomorrow morning—which is very short notice for you, after all—rather than tonight as he suggested. He was just about to insist I went tonight, and then thought better of it. Probably because you were there."

"I did notice that," replied Wanda slowly, "but I put it down to his natural wish for hustle. You seem to be interpreting it in another way."

"I'm thinking about it. You could be right. But this evening or tomorrow doesn't make a ha'porth of difference to the academic duties I'm about to assume."

"True. But was the need for hurry initiated by Edgar, or was he acting as a dutiful intermediary and passing on whatever the College Commandant had stressed?"

"I can't see Anderson playing the role of dutiful intermediary to anybody." He put his knife on his plate and looked across at Wanda.

14

"I could be getting highly fanciful, my darling, but I am beginning to get the feeling that I have been duped."

"We," she corrected. "I was there, too, and agreed to Edgar's proposals."

"That alone is suspicious," said Masters. "I know we are trying to humanise the force and all that, but whoever heard of a wife being called into the consultations concerning her husband's next appointment?"

"Be fair," counselled Wanda. "Don't jump to unfounded conclusions, George. The conditions were abnormal, remember. The job at the College is a temporary attachment, not a real appointment. And it is one which isn't, strictly speaking, CID work. And you are on sick leave, from which they cannot recall you without your agreement. As the attachment concerns me, too . . . well, I read it as Edgar hoping to get my backing, on the grounds that the break would do us all good, whereas he had some doubts as to whether you alone would accept two months away from Michael and me. I thought the idea of including me in the decision making was rather sweet of him, even though he was counting on my support to sway you."

Masters grinned. "Sweet is hardly the adjective I would use to describe Anderson. But although I agree with every word you've said, there is just the possibility that your argument supports my feeling of having been conned in some way."

"How do you make that out?"

"My going off for a couple of months can't be to Anderson's liking. In fact, it could be a nuisance to him to have one of his senior investigating teams out of action for so long. So I could understand it were he to accept my probable absence rather grudgingly, even allowing for the fact that the last drop of the milk of human kindness has been wrung out of him in the interests of my well-being. But he was not grudging. He was avid to get me away. He even sought your help to swing it. I'm wondering why."

She smiled. "Darling, I think your pride has been hurt because Edgar thinks he can manage without you for five or six weeks longer than he is obliged to."

15

He grinned back. "There could be something in that. But when I ring the Dean of Police Studies this afternoon I shall try to discover if there's more behind this than Anderson let on to us."

"Be careful what you say. Don't give him the impression that you mistrust Edgar, just in case you've got it all wrong and there's no ulterior motive behind it. You may believe Edgar went about it in a funny way, but that could just be that he mishandled the situation slightly, while acting from the best possible motive."

Masters helped himself to more cheese. "You know, poppet, I would believe that a little more readily had Anderson called here to put his proposition to us. Then it would really have seemed like the nice, cosy little domestic arrangement he would wish us to assume it was. But to send a semi-official summons to attend at his office, via Bill Green, then to invite you up to the official sanctum . . . it all smacks of wanting to get me out on a job he desperately wants me to take on, but which he couldn't order me to go on because the quacks say I'm not yet available for duty."

Wanda frowned. "His willingness to send Sergeant Reed with you?"

"That, too. With the demands on his available manpower being what they are, I cannot believe he would be willing to let me have Reed for any length of time at all unless he envisaged I could have a need for him in an investigative capacity." He took a bite from the biscuit and after clearing his mouth, asked: "I wonder what he would have said if I'd asked for the services of Bill Green and Sergeant Berger, too?"

"If nothing else, such a request would have shown you'd rumbled him or, at any rate, that you reckoned there was something more in the wind than a lecturing job."

"Milk now," said Michael, who had come to the end of his lunch and felt it was time that his personal needs were attended to.

"Just a moment, darling, and I'll get it for you. Let me wipe your chin first . . . there, that's better. George, there's an egg custard in the fridge . . . "

16

"Misled you?" asked Locke. "I think not. Not seriously at any rate. If he has, I think it would be a sin of omission rather than commission."

"Meaning what, sir?" asked Masters, changing the phone from one hand to the other.

"The job is not purely that of lecturer, Mr Masters. We want your advice and help. I'll explain briefly. A couple of days ago I had cause to call on the Commissioner. During our conversation he told me that you had recently introduced a new tactic in investigation. He explained to me that you had used what I believe you call a moderator—a senior detective officer from another force—to put you and your team through a prolonged grilling session during a particularly important case. In an effort to wring out every fact and idea from those involved. The Commissioner would tell me nothing of the case except that it was highly intractable and one which had to be brought to an acceptable conclusion. He told me that the method you had adopted had been highly successful. Am I right?"

"Absolutely right, sir. I recommended to the Commissioner that it should be considered for adoption as a standard procedure, in cases which warranted it, of course."

"Excellent. Now we, down here at the College, have been under some pressure from the Home Office to introduce—as part of our senior staff course—an element of training in inter-force co-operation. For some time now we have been wanting some idea, such as your moderator scheme, to use as the basis for that element. When I heard about it, and indeed that you were unfit for more active duties, I seized the opportunity to ask if you could be released for a couple of months to fill the gap left by one of my tutors who is ill, so that we could have you here and—quite unashamedly—pick your brains."

"I see, sir. I shall be glad to help."

"I thought you would. After all, it's your baby. But I don't think Edgar Anderson would know anything of this. I asked the Commissioner to get your agreement and then, if you were willing, to send you down here at the first possible moment. I imagine the Commissioner urged the need for haste on the AC Crime without giving him all the details. So I think it is safe to say Anderson did not mislead you as he didn't know everything we hope you'll be able to do for us. That's all."

"Thank you, sir. Shall I be able to see you tomorrow?"

"At half past two. You won't want to be involved in moving house with one arm in a sling, but I understand you'll have your sergeant with you. Leave any heavy work to him while you come and talk to me. Can do?"

"That sounds an admirable arrangement, sir. Do I report to the quartering office like a student, or is there some other arrangement for staff members?"

"Poke your nose into my outer office in the main block. My secretary will have everything laid on for you. I'm sure she'll have arranged to have your house opened up for you and all that sort of thing."

"Thank you, sir."

Wanda came downstairs a moment later. She had been listening on the bedroom extension.

"Happier about things now, darling?"

"Very much. Locke seemed a reasonable bloke."

"I liked him. As much as one can by judging from a phone call. Now, darling, I must get on. Are you fit enough to get the cases down from the top of the wardrobe?"

The day was bright, if a little cold. The early flowering shrubs and trees still carried a little of their pink and white blossom, but for the most part it lay in carpets on the pavements and lawns. The lilacs were showing a hint of new green while daffodils and crocuses bloomed in great clumps in many of the gardens.

"If it stays like this it will be lovely in the country," said Wanda, who was driving their own Jaguar. Masters, not yet considered fully fit to drive, sat beside her, while Michael sat behind, strapped in his baby seat, fastened midships, with soft parcels and bundles on each side of him.

"Lovely for walks and, one hopes, picnics, in the fullness of time," replied Masters, whose main function appeared to be to keep his son amused so that Wanda shouldn't be distracted.

"You are looking forward to it, George?"

"Immensely," replied her husband, who was half-turned in his seat to pay closer attention to Michael. "We're going to have a good time, aren't we?" he said to his son.

"Time," said Michael.

"I'm glad of your support. Look at that big red bus. Lots of people in it."

"Big bus."

"Any sign of Reed?" asked Wanda. "We didn't arrange to travel in convoy but I thought he might try to keep company."

Reed was driving Masters' official Rover.

"He said he would go on ahead. He must have got in front by some route best known to himself, because I haven't seen him pass us."

"What's his hurry, darling?"

"He seems to be under the impression that you and I are unlikely to be able to deal with the inventory."

"What inventory?"

"For the quarter, my sweet. Everything is listed and signed for. You know the form. Twelve cups, twelve saucers, none chipped. One cruet comprising salt, pepper, mustard and one spoon."

"I hadn't realised that."

"Everything down on paper. And we hand it back exactly as we got it."

"Everything? A cot for Michael?"

"Yes, with bedding."

"What happens if things aren't quite right when we leave?"

"If you've lost the sitting room carpet or the washing machine, you pay for it."

"Damage? Not that I think there'll be any because we're very careful."

"They allow for fair wear and tear. If Michael spills orange juice on a chair cover, we pay for it to be cleaned. If you chip a cup or break a plate . . . well, there's a system of points. Briefly, it is that each week you are credited with, say, ten points, each of which is worth five pence. If you break a plate worth eighty pence, that's nearly a fortnight's worth of points gone. The plate is replaced, of course. With any luck, we'll leave there not having used any points, but it's as good a way as any to account for wear and tear among crockery and the like. Soft furnishings are simply adjudged to be worn out and are then replaced, as long as they haven't been ill-treated. Such things as cigarette burns on furniture are definitely frowned on and come expensive—for repair or repolishing."

"So Reed will be inspecting everything to see it is in good order, is that it?"

"That's it. As I said, he thought to relieve you of the chore of taking over and doubted my ability to do it conscientiously."

"Meaning he has a poor opinion of your attention to detail?"

"Something of the sort."

Wanda laughed aloud. "I don't think his action was prompted by any such thought. He knows that you get grumpy doing fiddling little jobs like that when you can't see any good reason why you should be saddled with them."

"I get grumpy?"

"Yes. As for attention to detail—that matters, that is— Reed would swear you were the greatest attentionist in the business."

"There's no such word, is there son? No such word as attentionist?"

"Then there ought to be," said Wanda. "There's an attender . . . "

"Which among other things means one who pays heed or attention."

"I mean it differently. Anyhow, I've coined the word."

"A very good word, too. Try it out on Bill when next you see him."

"Talking about seeing William," said Wanda, "we shall have to invite the Greens down for a weekend fairly soon. I spoke to Doris last night and she sounded decidedly envious— in a nice way."

"We owe it to them," said Masters. "If ever anybody has been a tower of strength, those two have ever since we've been married."

"Right. Perhaps after we've given ourselves a week or two to settle in . . . is it right at the next roundabout, George?"

It was a few minutes short of eleven o'clock when they turned off towards the College grounds.

"There's the Rover, on the left," said Masters.

Wanda had to negotiate perhaps twenty yards of track that ran between trees to draw in alongside the Rover.

"It's a very nice house, George. Oh, I do like it, sitting here among the trees. It's just been put down here. No fences or gates or . . . it looks as if it was just snoozing there, enjoying its freedom." She looked to right and left. "But you can see the neighbours through the trees, so it's not lonely."

"Very nice," agreed Masters, undoing his seat belt. "I'll find Reed if you'll unstrap Michael."

Reed opened the front door before Masters reached it. "All here, Chief. I've checked everything, but I wouldn't sign the inventory."

"Something wrong?"

"Light bulbs. Whoever was here last must have saved up a load of duff ones and swopped them for the good ones. I told the quartering bloke that you'd sign sometime after the bulbs had been replaced. He said he'd send the maintenance man over. I'm waiting for him to come."

"Thank you. Everything else all right?"

"All in working order, Chief. I hope Mrs Masters won't mind, but I've taken the jar of coffee out of the box of groceries she put in the Rover. The kettle's boiling, so if you'd like elevenses it's all ready."

"Nothing we'd like better," said Wanda coming up with Michael. "There's a thermos of milk and a packet of short-bread in the box, George. If you'd find those while I make the drink. . . . "

They were sitting over coffee when there was a knock at the back door. Reed got to his feet. "This will be the maintenance man with the bulbs. His name is Rimmer, Chief, if you'd like to see him. Ex-sergeant."

"You attend to him, Reed, please. You know where the bulbs are to go."

Reed went to the door.

"Eight bulbs," said the man grumpily. "I don't know why you couldn't have fetched them yourself seeing you've got a car. Where do you want 'em?"

"Where they're supposed to be. In the light sockets."

"You're not expecting me to put 'em in for you, are you?"

"Sure thing. Put them in and test them. What if one of those doesn't light, or the circuit's blown a fuse?"

Rimmer didn't like the idea.

"They're new. You can see. Still in their covers."

"And how many have you dropped on the way over?"

"Cheeky young bastard!"

"Watch it, chum. Let's get those bulbs in and tested."

"I haven't got my steps."

"You can stand on a chair."

Grumbling, Rimmer followed Reed around, inserting and testing the bulbs. When they arrived at the bathroom, Reed said: "I hope you've got a hundred-and-fifty watt one for here. The Chief likes to see what he's doing when he's shaving."

"He can have a hundred and lump it."

"I asked for a hundred-and-fifty."

"He can have the same as everybody else. If the Commandant can make do with a hundred, so can this bloke."

"I think you've got things wrong, Rimmer," said Reed, curtly. "The Commandant is only the Commandant. My Chief is DCS Masters, and what he wants, he gets. You can put the hundred in now, but before you go off tonight I want to see a hundred-and-fifty in there."

"Haven't got any. Not allowed to issue them. They use too much electricity."

"Don't try that one on me. I told the quartering officer and he made no objections. And if you haven't got one, get one. Smartish."

"I'll have to see about it. I can't go getting odd bulbs just because some smart arse likes to see his physog in the morning. We buy in bulk. Sixties and hundreds."

"Two things," said Reed grimly. "First, get that bulb or else. Second, don't ever let me hear you speak like that again about Mr Masters. He eats old-timers like you for breakfast."

"Get out of it. He's coming to lecture, int'e? Lecturers aren't proper coppers. All say an' no do. There isn't one of 'em who's felt the collar of a villain like I have."

"I'll give you a word of advice, Rimmer. It's this. DCS Masters has taken in more murderers than you've had hot dinners. And when he takes them up they stay taken up. Banged up. So don't run away with the idea that Mr Masters isn't a proper copper."

"Banged up? He hasn't had any hanged though, has he? That's what we had in my day. That's what I done. Helped to put 'em on the trap where all murdering villains should find themselves at eight o'clock one morning."

"Just get the bulb," said Reed wearily, "and save your reminiscences for somebody else."

"This Masters," said Rimmer, "he's from the Yard, is he?"

"He is."

"One of the fancy boys then. Fancies this, fancies that an' fancies himself no end. A hundred-and-fifty to shave by! Who the hell does he think he is?"

"Out!" said Reed. "Leave the chair where it is. You'll be wanting it again when you fetch the big bulb. You can find your own way out—by the back door."

"I don't know what was going on," said Masters, "but from the sound of it, you and ex-Sergeant Rimmer weren't seeing eye to eye over something. We're not upsetting the hired help already, are we, Reed?"

"You couldn't upset that grumpy old sinner any more than he is already, Chief. A request for a decent-sized bulb is merely more proof to him that the world has gone to the dogs."

"Pity, that. Has he any recipe for restoring things to rights?"

"Yes, Chief. Hanging. Anybody who asks for a big bulb for the bathroom deserves topping."

"I see. One of the old school, eh? Ah, well! I think we could unpack the cars now."

"You leave that to me, Chief."

"I can earn my keep, Reed. It only takes one hand to carry a case."

Chapter 2

MASTERS WAS SHOWN into Locke's private office precisely at half past two by a middle-aged secretary who had kept him waiting a minute or so until the electric clock on the wall registered the exact time arranged for the meeting.

Though irritated by this seemingly pointless punctiliousness, Masters was gently amused by it. So much so that he was smiling when he saw Locke for the first time.

"You must be some chap," said Locke, coming round his desk when the door had been closed. "You're the first person Gertie's ever caused to smile."

"I could have been a little put out, being kept there unannounced when it was clear you had no visitor, sir, but she's a bit of an anachronism, isn't she, and I rather like that. Makes for variety."

"As a matter of fact," replied Locke, "I think she does it for my benefit. She thinks I like to snooze in my chair for a bit after lunch, so she takes great care not to disturb me before the stipulated time. She credits me with the ability to have forty winks and then to wake up—presumably aroused by some internal alarm clock—precisely at the moment when I should be about my business. She's wrong, of course, but she did surprise me snoozing one day some years ago and has been extremely solicitous ever since."

"How very considerate of her."

"Come on," said Locke, drawing up a chair. "Sit down. How's the arm, by the way?"

"Almost better, thank you, sir," replied Masters, taking the seat. "I am supposed to have one more, final examination in a few days time. I may have to go back to London for it, or perhaps you've got a resident quack who could give me a clean bill."

"I'm sure we can fix that for you. Now, before we begin, I

24

think I should tell you that the senior members of my staff call me Bobby—for obvious reasons—and invite you to do the same. In return I shall call you George. All right?"

"Very friendly," said Masters. "Do you actually play golf?"

"Everybody asks me that. Never had a club in my hands in my life." Locke leaned back on the high backrest of his desk chair. "First off, let me tell you what I propose you should do in the ordinary curriculum. Six cases—all your own. Ones you can put over in great detail, starting at the beginning and going through to the end. It's a bit like story telling, but it is criminal history. Varied cases, please. I know something of your track record, so I am aware that you have taken on a great many medical problems, but there are plenty of others so you should be able to get a good mix. Then, lessons arising. You can set essays based on your lectures or provide synopses in the way of lecture notes, but I don't just want straight essays. I want supplementary questions designed to test grasp of method, alternative courses open to the investigators and so on. Remember, where you may have taken leaps in the dark, many of our students will have to try to arrive at similar answers to yours by more routine or mundane routes. This you must instil into them, otherwise some could become dispirited in the future at not being able to emulate some of your *tours de force*. Then, there are definite lessons you must emphasise and illustrate with examples. Team work, for one, accuracy in reporting for another, attitudes of officers towards suspects for a third and so on. As I say, illustrate and emphasise, and re-iterate *ad nauseam* We are not seeking to provide Staff College solutions for all cases, but we can set standards and suggest frameworks for investigative procedures."

"What ranks will my students be?"

"For those lectures, both senior and junior courses."

"There will be other lectures for senior students?"

"Some. But as I mentioned to you over the phone, we are seeking to introduce this new element of inter-force co-operation into the curriculum. Nothing is concrete yet. But I propose that you should address the senior course on this subject. My own staff will attend. Then, if possible, I should like a demonstration of your moderator tactic. A full and complete one. Quite how we can lay that on, I am not sure. I don't suppose we could recreate the actual case in which you used the idea?"

Masters shook his head. "I'm afraid not, Bobby. It was classified as Ultra Secret and was instigated by the Home Office."

"One of those, eh? Nothing will ever come to light?"

"All the records we kept were destroyed within days of the case being completed."

"Satisfactorily?"

"Entirely so, I believe."

Locke regarded him shrewdly for a moment or two. "Except for a bullet in the arm?"

Masters stared back innocently. "I feel sure you are aware of how I came to collect the bullet. The case was publicised quite widely in the press and in the Commons."

"Quite," said Locke drily. "Where the Home Secretary gave an unprecedentedly full account of an operation that just happened by chance."

"Just so."

Locke sat up. "Then that is out for demonstration purposes."

He got to his feet and went to the door to ask the secretary to send in a tray of tea. He moved to the window and stood gazing out at the drive and a nearby flower bed. With his back still to Masters, he said quietly: "How long would the average moderator session take—on an intractable problem, that is?"

"If it were really intractable, I would guess at a full working day as a minimum."

"There are a number of intractable cases at all times, up and down the country."

Something in his tone alerted Masters who wisely made no comment. Locke swung round on him. "Would you say we could borrow the unclosed file of such a case and use it as the basis for a demonstration?"

Masters was slow in answering. Then, for some reason he

was himself not quite sure of, he asked: "For demonstration purposes, or in an effort to solve the problem?"

"The former, though the latter, were we able to achieve it, would be a bonus, wouldn't it?"

Masters nodded. "It would, but such a result would be so unlikely, in my opinion, as to be discounted even as a possibility. My idea was to grill the men actually on the job, in the area where they were investigating and where they knew every yard of ground, the name of every person involved and so on. To try to produce an answer from people who had simply mugged up the reports would be useless, because the moderator battue is meant to drag out what the reports do not contain—the impressions that cannot be transferred to paper, the memories jerked to the forefront of minds by other facts, the likely results of possibilities . . . but I needn't go on. I think you know exactly what I have in mind. But it seems you could be proposing a sort of superior investigating court, divorced from the men on the ground."

"An idea which you think would be useless?"

"Quite useless."

There was a tap at the door and the secretary carried in the tea.

"Thank you, Gertie, we'll pour out for ourselves."

Locke busied himself with the tea. As he handed Masters a cup, he asked: "Has my suggestion annoyed you, George?"

"Nothing for me to get annoyed about. As I said, I don't consider it possible for a session in one of your training rooms to come up with the solution to a crime in, say, Lancashire—given that the crime is one which has defeated the local police in that area."

"I thought I detected a change in your manner. If not annoyance, wariness perhaps. Increased wariness a minute or two ago."

"Perhaps. When you started talking about unsolved crimes."

"Why then? I ask, because I sensed the same wariness in your voice yesterday when you rang me. A hint that the AC Crime might have misled you—to use your own word."

"There were certain straws in the wind that led me to

27

suppose I hadn't been given the full story. Mr Anderson's anxiety to get me down here so quickly. In fact, his inviting my wife to the Yard to help him to persuade me to come here should I show an unwillingness to do so. Several clues of that nature."

"In other words, you sensed that Edgar Anderson might be conning you."

"He's not normally a devious man in his dealings with us."

"So you did think he was conning you."

"If you wish to put it that crudely, yes. On reflection, I did."

"He wasn't."

"I'll take your word for it."

"He was the one who was being conned."

Masters set his cup down on the desk, but made no comment.

"I have been interested to see how sensitive you are to atmosphere, George. From the tiniest of hints, you apparently suspected a con took place in the AC's office yesterday morning. It did. But it wasn't the way round you thought it was."

"Are you suggesting that I somehow, for some purpose of my own, pulled the wool over the AC's eyes?"

"No, no, no. You had nothing to do with it. Edgar was conned by the Commissioner, at my insistence."

Masters frowned. "My wife suggested yesterday that Anderson could be acting the part of a dutiful intermediary. An idea I pooh-poohed at the time. Now you tell me Wanda was right."

"If Wanda is Mrs Masters, then I am. Edgar acted the part of the honest broker. By that I mean he was not told everything, but I suspect he relayed to you everything he had been told."

"Am I to learn the reason for this . . .?"

"Tomfoolery?"

"Yes."

"Let's get Edgar Anderson out of the way first. I told you I had called on the Commissioner a day or two ago. I suspect I don't have to tell you that I don't make a personal call on him when I find I need a temporary lecturer. Our meeting concerned something much more serious. More of that later. For the moment I'll confine myself to telling you that I put the problem before the Commissioner, and to save you guessing, I'll just say that when I say problem, I mean just that. Not a criminal case for which I was seeking the help of an investigating team from the Yard because, as you know, we here at the College are not responsible for policing an area or investigating crime. We are an enclave within the Central Southern Counties area and are, for all practical purposes, just a normal civilian institution.

"As I said, I put my problem to the Commissioner not to seek active help, but guidance, if you like. He heard me out and we then had a long discussion about the problem. The upshot of our talk together was that he said there was one man he thought would be able to advise me and whom he would like to lend me. You! George Masters. Unfortunately, he said, you were on sick leave after being wounded and had also been given a fortnight's ordinary leave to help put you back on your feet. The doctors would not allow him, the Commissioner, to haul you back for active duty.

"It was then I asked whether giving advice could be regarded as active duty. The reply was that if you were ordered here, it would be considered as such. The only way to get you down here was to get you to agree to come, and in order to get you to agree, there should be some inducement. Not, I hasten to add, because the Commissioner believed you would need to be bribed from leave, but because he thought he owed it to you.

"It was then that I mentioned the fact that I had a vacancy for a temporary tutor. I asked if two months' light duty would be an attractive recompense for missing two or three weeks leave—which would have been followed by an immediate return to normal duty. When I explained that there would be a pleasant furnished house for you and your family, out here in the countryside, the Commissioner said that he thought the odds would be about even. So I asked for you to

29

be sent down here, should you agree to come, at the first possible moment.

"And that is what Edgar Anderson was told by the Commissioner. To offer you the two months here in exchange for your leave. No mention was made of my problem. As far as Edgar knew, it was a straight swop, but he was instructed to do his utmost to make you accept and then to get you down here without any delay. That, I believe, is more or less what he did. He had no time to call on you that afternoon. He tried to phone you but got no reply . . . "

"I was walking with my wife and son."

"So the house was empty. He got hold of a colleague of yours and asked him to bring a personal message, which I believe you got. In the meantime, Edgar had the bright idea of involving your wife. If she thought the temporary attachment in the country would be a good thing for all of you, the business would be as good as settled. That is how it happened. Edgar got you down here as soon as possible. But he knew nothing of the reason for your coming other than the fact that you were to lecture.

"I sensed something had not gone quite according to plan when you rang me yesterday, hence your questions about being misled."

Masters had been filling his pipe. As he took out his matches, he said: "And yet, knowing nothing of the second, and probably more serious, reason for my coming here, the AC Crime offered to let me bring Sergeant Reed with me. I find it hard to understand why he should make such a concession if he thought all I was to do here was to deliver half a dozen lectures."

"Ah! One of his instructions was to let you bring somebody—Reed was not specified—were you to raise any question or objection about not being fit enough to do the job. That was, chiefly, to help ensure your acceptance—or perhaps that of your wife—but the Commissioner realised that such a helper could be of value to you, not only to help prepare lectures, but to act as a hewer of wood and drawer of water should the help and advice I am proposing to ask for assume any practical facets. Please believe me, George, when I say

30

Edgar Anderson did not mislead you. If anybody did, it was I, when we spoke yesterday. I did not give you the full picture because I was not prepared to do so over the phone. I was a little perturbed to hear you had doubts, but all I could do then was to exonerate Edgar. As for the Commissioner ... well, I went to him for help and advice. He felt I needed it so badly that he set out to do the best he possibly could for me—and that was to make sure you came here."

"Did the Commissioner think I would bilk at giving you verbal help with your problem?"

"Not a bit of it. But he said that knowing you, the help might not stop at advice, and he was not prepared to order you here without giving you a free hand. So you had to be persuaded to come of your own free will. The help you give can be as limited as you wish it to be or consider it necessary to provide—now you're here."

"I see. A free hand, I think you said?"

"That was the Commissioner's stipulation, to which I readily agreed. But ... "

"Ah! I am to be hedged about."

"Not by me. But you will see what the difficulties are or could be when I tell you my problem. And that problem—as far as I am concerned—involves the College. Nothing more. I am also to assure you that I am speaking with the Commandant's agreement and authority."

Masters grinned. "In that case, Bobby, fire away."

"Before I begin, would you like me to send for your sergeant? If you think he ought to be briefed ... that's the way you work, I believe?"

"When on a case, yes. But you have assured me this isn't a case in the ordinary sense of the word. A problem is how you have defined it."

Locke shrugged. "Fair enough, George. I want to start about five or six years back. A little later in the year than this, when the trees were in full leaf, the weather was warm and sunny and the kids were running about in T-shirts and jeans. A young lad, just fourteen, was on his way home from playing in the woods with his pals. He was a bit of a tearaway and a known nuisance. He'd been taken up for breaking the

31

glass bulkhead lights on lamp posts, damaging a car, nicking a bike and so on. He lived with his parents in a small house about two miles from here. Anyhow, as I said, he was on his way home about four o'clock in the afternoon. He'd thumbed a lift as far as a roundabout about a mile from home and was set down there, where he at once began to try to get another lift going his way. He was seen there by several witnesses.

"The point is, George, he never reached home. As you can imagine, the local force pulled out all the stops and spent months trying to find out what became of him. The road along which he was trying to thumb a lift is not a terribly busy one—not at four o'clock on a working day anyhow. Naturally, the locals really went to town to discover what vehicles had been along there at the vital time. To cut a long story short, one of them was a rust-red DAF with a left-hand drive."

"Foreign, in other words."

"Yes."

"Was it traced?"

"Yes. To here at the College. As you know, we take foreign police officers as students. At that time we had a Dutch Inspector on the junior course. He had come over in his own car."

"A rust-red DAF with a left-hand drive?"

"Quite. Now I said that car had been traced to the College. But it had taken some days for the locals to satisfy themselves that it was a DAF and then to trace it to here. I don't have to tell you how vague some witnesses are and how long it takes to establish solid fact. The point is, that by the time the locals got round to visiting us, the Dutch Inspector had gone back to Holland, taking his car with him.

"You can see the difficulties, can't you? There was no evidence against our student. A rust-red DAF had passed along that road. Nothing more. Nobody could approach the Dutch authorities to even question the man on such a flimsy pretext. Diplomatically, it was a non-starter. Nobody could regard him as suspect in any way, and although questions were asked here to try and establish his movements on that day, not one hint of his implication in the crime came to light. But the point is that every other car the locals heard of as having passed down that road was traced and examined and the drivers eliminated from the investigation."

"All except the DAF, which was never inspected for particle transfer, bloodstains and so on?"

"Right. And the Dutch Inspector was never interviewed although, as I said, we made an attempt to trace his movements."

"With an inconclusive result, I think you said?"

"Totally inconclusive. By that, I mean he was not attending a lecture at the time the lad disappeared, which would have ruled him out completely, but his name was signed in at the squash courts for the hour from four to five."

"No partner to vouch for him at that time?"

"There appeared to be. That sounds vague, and is meant to be. The questions were being asked, very indirectly, as you can imagine, so as not to give a clue as to what we were after. And they were being asked late in the day. Squash buffs use the courts daily. If they've played against the same man a dozen times in a month, it is fairly difficult to remember details of dates and times a few weeks later. Another student we had here thought he had played our Dutch friend at that time on that day. But he couldn't be sure because there was nothing to fix it in his mind. It wasn't a ladder match or anything like that. However, in fairness to the Dutch Inspector, I should tell you that our PT man, who is responsible for all sports facilities and court bookings, is sure the squash court was not left unused at the time. The demand for them is so great, that an empty court would immediately draw attention, and I can believe that he would have noticed a gap at a prime time such as the hour between four and five. As against that, however, the wife of one of our tutors was walking back up the road to the College—the one which passes your house—and she is certain she saw the rust-red DAF being driven away from the College towards the main road at twenty to four that day. She is certain of the day, because she was returning from a dental appointment."

Masters tapped out his pipe. "So what's your problem, Bobby? The case is still unsolved. One of your students could

33

have been a possible. Nothing more than that, and as you said earlier, you are not responsible for policing this area. So why the worry? Apart from the slim chance that the College is involved in some way?"

Locke didn't give a direct answer. Instead he continued his narrative.

"The leaves were on the trees then, and the undergrowth thick and heavy with full growth. The job of searching for the body was an impossible one because when the local force came to add up the extent of woodland and heath round here, the answer came out as hundreds of square miles. Dogs couldn't work through the gorse and brambles. Helicopters couldn't see. The only real answer was to wait until the autumn and the leaves had fallen. Then the search started again."

"Abortive?"

"Completely. Not a sign of the lad's body."

"I expect steps were taken to ascertain whether he had just gone off to London to live rough with some group of homeless or junkies?"

"Every possibility was tried. He had disappeared."

Masters began to refill his pipe.

"I still can't see your problem, Bobby."

"You will. Have you been keeping your eyes on the papers and official reports lately?"

"As little as possible. No official reports, because I've not been at the Yard for the last three weeks, and with this arm as it is I've found so much difficulty in holding newspapers that I've tended to give them a miss. I've spread the odd one on the dining table and glanced over it, but I can't remember seeing much to draw my professional attention."

"Then you will have missed the reports of another lad going missing a mile or two from here."

"Another lad? Same age?"

"Thirteen years old and another tearaway. This one had been before the juvenile court for a bit of tyre slashing. Outside a house where there was a wedding reception. He'd shoved a knife into all four tyres of the groom's car that was waiting outside to take him and his new wife on honeymoon.

34

One of the guests had seen him but had not thought much about it at the time as it was to be expected that that particular car would be receiving a bit of attention while the party was on. It was only when the jokers came to tie on the old boots and tin cans a short time afterwards that the tyre slashing was noticed for what it was. Of course, the kid got away with it—they always do these days—despite the fact that he'd been in trouble some months earlier for bullying younger children at school into handing over their dinner money.

"But that is by the way. His parents both go out to work and they didn't give him a key—didn't trust him I suppose— so he couldn't go straight home after school. He'd gone to a friend's house to watch a video nasty until the friend's father got back from work and packed him off. About a quarter to six that was, ten days ago. Just getting dark.

"He had the best part of a mile to go. He was seen turning on to a not very busy road—not a main one—which runs past a playing field. A middle-aged woman had been walking her dog on the field, and the lad had frightened her by drawing a stick along the upright railings just behind her. She said the noise had made her jump and the dog had strained at its lead. According to her evidence she had called him a dirty young bastard and he had cheeked her back in language the good lady didn't like repeating. But she'd had a good look at him. In fact she'd seen him about fairly often.

"And that was the last that was seen of him. But the locals did the same exercise as before and tried to make a complete list of all cars that had gone along there at that time. Several motorists responded to the appeal. They were able to give a fair bit of information. One of them listed a Volvo hatchback, stationary, half way along the length of the playing field railings. He couldn't be sure of the colour because the light was so bad, but he got the impression it was metallic green. He didn't pay it all that much attention but he thinks it had a foreign number plate and what he calls a foreign GB plate, but he can't remember what the letters were."

As he stopped, Masters grimaced. "I take it you don't want me to spoil your story by guessing the end?"

Locke grinned ruefully. "It's that obvious, is it?"

"I think so. You have a Dutch, silver-green hatchback Volvo on the College car park belonging to a student who was here on a junior course as an inspector five or six years ago, and who has now returned as a superintendent to attend the senior staff course."

Locke nodded glumly. "Quite right. What do I do about it?"

"You are asking my advice?"

"Yes."

"Then you must proceed strictly in accordance with the law of this country. Have the local police been informed that a vehicle such as the one they are trying to trace is here?"

"Yes."

"And?"

"They have inspected it and found nothing out of the ordinary. The soil particles and dust and so forth are exactly the same as one would expect to find in this area. And, of course, nothing has been found belonging to the youth to compare anything with. All his clothing is missing with the body. Certainly no blood, and no fingerprints belonging to the boy."

"Does the car show signs of having been wiped over inside?"

"The owner is accustomed to keeping it impeccably clean, so it's not surprising that the dash and windows had been wiped, but when the locals looked it over there were prints—his and those of at least two other people—in various places. None anything like those of the missing boy."

"Was the owner aware that his car had been examined?"

"Yes. We camouflaged it by having all the hatchbacks in the place examined."

"Was he quite amenable?"

"Most. He offered the keys quite happily."

"And where was he at the time the boy is supposed to have disappeared?"

"He says he was in his quarter taking a bath at the time."

"Any confirmation of that?"

"He was attending a lecture until half past five, and he was definitely in the bar by a quarter past six."

Masters grimaced, but said nothing.

"And the car?"

"He says he didn't take it out all that day."

"But you don't believe him?"

"That's just it, I do. He is a thoroughly likeable fellow and, one would have said, honest. But there's a girl clerk here who thinks she saw it leaving the College grounds when she set out to cycle home. She leaves at half past five, so I should say the time she saw it—if she saw it—would be about five thirty-five."

Again Masters made no comment. After a pause, Locke went on: "The locals want to pull him in for questioning. I've said that though his name could well be in the frame, they have no solid fact to justify any such rash action. They point to the coincidence of his presence here on both occasions. My point is that they got no evidence against him the first time, so that end of the coincidence falls flat; and they've got nothing solid against him on this recent business."

"Apart from two car sightings."

"Quite. Now I agree with you about proceeding according to the laws of this country. But there's another side to this. The diplomatic side, if you like. In the interests—if not of international relations, then of this College as a recognised world centre of police co-operation—I don't want the locals to put a foot wrong. I don't want them to move without being sure of their facts. A coincidence doesn't offer enough grounds for causing trouble, unless and until some other shred of evidence is produced to support any move against our Dutch visitor. So far, I have managed to hold the locals off, but I shall not be able to do so for ever. I believe they will get no further with this present business than they did with the first disappearance."

"Tricky," said Masters. "If they go bald-headed for your student, a senior officer from a friendly country, of course there will be trouble, unless they can prove their case against him."

"That is my problem, George. The one I went to consult

37

the Commissioner about. The one he said you might be able to help me with, and the reason for hurry. And don't be too hard on the Commissioner. He can't send his people to investigate a case here without a request for help from the local Chief Constable. The local CC has not asked the Yard for help, nor will he, in my opinion. The only course open to us was to bring you to the College where policemen are two-a-penny and let you work or advise or whatever you decide to do, here, on the spot."

"I see the point," replied Masters slowly. "In essence, what is needed is an investigation parallel to that of the locals, conducted from the safe anonymity of the College."

"My view exactly. I wondered whether you thought it possible to conduct such an investigation, because if anybody makes a bog of this, we can say goodbye to intakes of foreign students, and I want to avoid that at all costs."

Masters laughed.

"You think that's funny?"

"Not your sentiments, Bobby. I was just imagining some of the comments in foreign countries if they were to hear we had made a hash of it and couldn't solve the case when we've got a whole College full of detectives on the spot. It wouldn't be a very good advertisement for our training, would it?"

Locke replied: "Can you do anything about it? I mean just sit here and think the thing through. If you had any bright ideas, I could feed them to the locals as sort of titbits of professional gossip among the students which might be of use to them."

"I would prefer not to work by proxy," said Masters. He suddenly seemed to come to a decision. "Have you an outside line I could use?"

"Lift the phone up and ask for one. Then you can dial whatever number you like."

"I'll call Edgar Anderson."

"To tell him he was conned?"

"Not quite."

"Would you like me to leave you so that you can make the call in private?"

38

"No need for that. Now, just to be sure about things, you did say I was to be given a free hand."

Locke nodded. "Within normal bounds and bearing in mind you must neither upset the locals nor damage the reputation of the College."

"Thank you." Masters picked up the phone.

"AC Crime."

"George Masters speaking, Mr Anderson."

"Hello, George. Safely installed?"

"More or less, sir."

"What can I do for you?"

"Listen for a minute or so. It's this way. There's a job for me that you don't know about. Not a case. The locals haven't called us in. But Mr Locke has a problem actually within the walls of the College. He has asked my advice about it, and the only real help I feel I can provide is to try to solve the business for him. It's tricky, because it concerns a senior officer from a foreign country. . . . "

"What's he done? Pinched the issue spoons?"

"It's slightly more serious than that, sir. As far as we know, he has committed no crime, but by a series of mischances involving one thumping great coincidence, he has been guilty of putting himself under suspicion in a double murder case. The locals are investigating the murders. Mr Locke has asked me to extricate his senior officer from the fix he appears to be in, because the locals are making handcuff noises and by so doing are likely not only to make a professional police blunder, but a diplomatic one, too."

"How do you propose to go about it, George, without getting in the locals' hair?"

"By disguising it as a Staff College exercise," said Masters with a laugh. Then: "More seriously, sir, I've been given the story by Mr Locke, and I think I can see one or two avenues. . . . "

"I'll bet you can. But you're supposed to be on sick leave."

"I propose to play armchair detective, sir." He looked across at Locke and winked. "I have already told Mr Locke that no matter what happens, this case must be dealt with according to British law and police procedure. He, of course,

39

agrees, so we shall tread warily, but apparently the Commissioner agreed that I should come here for this purpose, among others, and agreed that I should be left with a free hand."

"Well, you're there for two months, you must do what you can, George. Is that what you rang to tell me?"

"That, and to ask if I could borrow Bill Green and Sergeant Berger for a short time."

"This sounds as if, in spite of what you've said, you're going to mount a full investigation."

"No, sir, but I'm not totally fit, remember. I can't even drive. And I do think Bill Green needs a short holiday. He can stay at this lovely house I've got. If he brings Mrs Green they can walk in the woods, visit the nearby pubs, meet a few local rozzers by chance—while on holiday—and get into conversation with them. Just idle chit-chat. You know how these things happen, sir."

"You're acting the tit, George."

"Never more serious, sir."

"Right. I'll tell Green immediately."

"And Berger, please, sir. Bill will need somebody to drive him down—in an unmarked car, of course."

"Right. Anything else?"

"Tell Bill Green either Wanda or myself will ring him at home tonight and we'll expect them in the morning."

"I'm a fool for playing along with you, George. Give my regards to Wanda."

"Fairly painless," said Masters as he put the phone down. "As you heard me say, DCI Green and his wife will stay with me, ostensibly on holiday. I took it for granted you could quarter DS Berger in single student accommodation."

"Nothing easier."

"Thank you." Masters looked at his watch. "Four o'clock-ish. I'll be on my way if there's nothing more at the moment."

"Nothing I can think of, but this door is always open to you."

"Gertie permitting?"

Locke grinned. "As you say. And, George, thank you for what you're doing."

"Nothing to thank me for yet."

"Oh yes there is. Your willingness to help."

Masters shrugged. "I was beginning to get a little bored, anyway." He got to his feet. "Ah! I nearly forgot. What's the Dutchman's name?"

"Robbert Andriessen. Here, I'd better write it down for you. Double 'b' in Robbert. He's a Chief Super, by the way." Locke handed the slip of paper over.

"Just one more thing. Why, after the suspicion aroused on his first visit, did you accept Andriessen back for a second course?"

"What reason had we for refusing? We take places with them, they take places with us. More of theirs come here than ours go there, of course, because of their greater ability to speak our language than ours theirs. They propose their students. The places are, I believe, much sought after. We'd have to have strong reasons for refusing anybody. Andriessen did well when he was here last, so we couldn't suggest he wasn't bright enough. And we could hardly tell the Netherlands' police authority that we suspected him of murder. Besides, as I told you, he's a likeable man, as I hope you will agree after meeting him."

"Did he apply to his bosses for a vacancy, or did they send him?"

Locke looked up at Masters. "I hadn't thought of asking that question. The answer could make a difference, couldn't it?"

"It could, but I wouldn't set too much store by it. My guess is that his authority suggested it, but he would have to agree."

"I expect you're right."

"Right. Now I really am going. I shall keep in close touch."

As Masters left Locke's outer office and walked along the short length of corridor towards the main door of the administrative block, a door opened lower down the passage and a middle-aged man put his head out. Then he emerged completely.

"DCS Masters, sir?" he called.

"The same," replied Masters, turning to face his questioner.

41

"I'm Inspector Woolgar, sir. Quartering officer."

"What can I do for you, Mr Woolgar?"

"First off, sir, if you wouldn't mind, you could sign your inventory now the bulbs have been renewed."

"Right. Down there?"

"Yes, please. The small back room on the right."

As Masters signed the two large double folded sheets—one for Woolgar and one for himself—Woolgar said: "I hope you won't take this amiss, sir, but I have to mention it to you."

"Have I contravened some College bye-law?"

"No, sir. Not you. I've had an official complaint about your Sergeant Reed from Sergeant Rimmer."

Masters looked up. "The maintenance man?"

"Yes, sir. I've had to mention it. Rimmer has complained of Reed's behaviour this morning."

"When he came to renew the bulbs?"

"Yes."

"I'll hear about it, but I warn you I was present, and I can't remember anything in excess of what one might expect between people of the same rank when one has patently failed in his duty."

"That's what I suspected, sir. Rimmer is an old nutter. He's quite clever at his job, doing the minor electric jobs round the quarters and even in the lecture rooms. But he gets ideas. . . . "

"What sort of ideas?"

"I suppose you'd call them obsessions, sir. You know the sort of thing. Nothing's as good now as it used to be, whether it's electrical goods, people, behaviour, football or the weather. And he gets so het-up about present-day short-comings that he begins to fall down on the job."

"So you want me to forget about the complaint now you've done your duty by Rimmer in mentioning it to me?"

"That's what I think should happen, sir."

Masters looked at Woolgar. "Just as a matter of interest, did Rimmer get the correct instructions about what was wanted in my quarter?"

Without replying, Woolgar opened an A4-sized Stationery Office ledger. "The job book, sir. Everything that either of

42

the maintenance men or the cleaners have to do is entered in here. We have to do that to keep track of materials and stores and also so that when they've finished one job and I'm not handy they can see exactly what they've got to get on with next." He pointed to an entry three or four from the bottom of that day's list. "There you are Mr Masters. Eight bulbs for your quarters. Seven one hundreds and one one-fifty to be delivered and installed before lunch. There's Rimmer's signature. All there in black and white. He only read you wanted eight bulbs and he didn't bother to note one had to be a big one. That's what I mean when I say he falls down on small things."

"Thank you. I see you said he had to install the bulbs. He didn't want to do that, and I think the slight animosity which arose between Reed and Rimmer was occasioned by that—and the wrong-sized bulb, of course."

"I guessed as much, sir."

"Is that the end of it?"

"You can leave it to me now, Mr Masters. Thank you for signing the inventory. I hope you and Mrs Masters will enjoy your stay with us. It's quite a nice quarter you've got and we'll always be happy to help if anything goes wrong."

Masters thanked Woolgar and left the office to make his way home.

"Darling," said Wanda as he walked into the sitting room, "you've been gone a long time." She turned to the two women who were sitting in the fireside chairs. "Mrs Highett, this is my husband, George. Mrs Locke, my husband, George. Darling, Mrs Highett is the Commandant's wife and I suppose you can guess Mrs Locke is the Dean's wife. They very kindly called to welcome us."

As Masters shook hands with the two women he thanked them for their gesture in coming to make Wanda feel at home at the College.

"I'm sorry to be so late back," he said as he straightened up after shaking Mrs Locke's hand. "The Dean and I had a lot to talk about."

"I'm sure you did," said Mrs Highett. "My husband and Bobby Locke seem to have been quite excited at the prospect

43

of your coming here, Mr Masters. It appears you have something of a reputation even among your own kind."

"It's the usual business," replied Masters. "One is lucky enough to be given the right job at the right time on a few occasions and before one can turn round one is saddled with a bubble reputation."

"Maybe," said Mrs Locke, "but you were literally at the cannon's mouth quite recently, I believe. How is the wounded arm?"

"Mending nicely, thank you. As you can see, it is out of the sling now."

"A cup of tea, darling?" asked Wanda, anxious to get the conversation away from the personal prodding and probings which she knew her husband hated.

"Thank you." He sat on the sofa beside his wife and accepted the cup she handed to him. As he smiled at her, she said: "I'm afraid I've a confession to make, George."

"Ah! Which skeleton is going to come to light now?"

"I've lost my set of keys to the Jaguar."

"Is that all? I thought you were going to say you'd broken an issue tumbler or something equally serious."

The two visitors laughed.

Wanda said: "But it is so annoying. I had them when we arrived, obviously."

"Reed and I must have had them when we were unpacking the car," reasoned Masters. "So if it is locked now, one of us must have done it, which means we should have the keys."

"But it's not locked," wailed Wanda, "and Sergeant Reed hasn't got the keys. He's looked everywhere for them. . . . " She turned to him. "Unless you have them in your pocket?"

"Not guilty," said Masters. "I have my own, of course." He produced his key-ring. "But I certainly haven't got yours. Don't worry about it. They'll turn up, and until they do, you can have mine."

"That's the best idea," said Mrs Highett. "I've known of several key-rings that have gone missing over the years. It always amuses me to think that we have so many policemen here and things like key-rings get lost. But they always turn up eventually. At the quartering office, usually. People find

44

them and return them there. Just let Inspector Woolgar know, Wanda, and I'm sure that if you don't find them among the wrapping papers or your son's toys, he'll have them for you in a few days."

"Oh, I'm sure it will be all right. We can buy new keys if there's a dealer somewhere near, but I feel so foolish about it."

"Where is Reed?" enquired Masters.

"Looking after Michael. They're playing hunt the keys. It seems Michael likes the game, so at least the loss is not without its useful side."

Masters put his empty cup on the coffee table. "Let's not worry about the keys, poppet. As you say, we can get another set." He turned to Mrs Locke. "I encountered the Dean's secretary this afternoon."

"Gertie? She's a dear soul, really, but so unbending. She even frightens Bobby. He daren't be a moment late in getting to his office, you know."

"Or early, I should imagine. She kept me waiting until the sweep hand on the clock got round exactly to the appointed hour."

Mrs Highett joined in the conversation which became general for the next quarter of an hour and then the two visitors rose to go. As Wanda saw them out Masters heard them issuing invitations to tea and other social functions, including a bridge party. He went in search of Reed.

"Any luck with the keys?"

"There's not a sign of them anywhere in the house or grounds, Chief. I'm sure I saw Mrs Masters put them on the kitchen worktop when we first arrived, but I've not seen them since, so I can't retrace their movements, as it were. Nor can Michael. He's helping."

Masters picked up his son. "You haven't found mummy's keys then, feller?"

"No keys," said Michael, "Tea now."

"Mummy will be here to give it to you in a minute."

"Bread and butter, cake, milk," said Michael.

"I don't know what the menu will be, old chap, but I'm sure it will be something good."

"Anything for me, Chief?" asked Reed.

"To eat? Help yourself."

"I meant workwise, Chief."

"I see. Yes. Lots. What's your programme for this evening?"

"Nothing laid on. I'll go over and get supper in the mess, of course. After that—perhaps a drink."

"Have you moved in?"

"Yes, Chief. I've taken care of all that side."

"Hang on until Wanda comes back . . . ah, here she is."

"Did you want me?"

"Michael would like his tea and I'd like to know what we're doing about dinner."

"Catch as catch can, darling. All out of tins, I'm afraid. I had intended to go shopping, but I was held up because I couldn't find the car keys and then our two visitors arrived."

"There's bound to be a supermarket open for another hour or so," said Reed. "If you'd like me to whip into town and get you something."

"Good idea," said Masters. "And get enough for three. I'd like to talk to the two of you over the meal."

"What's it to be?" asked Reed.

He and Wanda had a small discussion, while Masters entertained Michael. When he'd handed over the child to his mother, he took out his wallet to supply Reed with money. "Bring in a litre of reasonable plonk, a bottle of Amontillado and a shrink pack of beer as well. That should cater for all tastes until tomorrow. When you get back, dump them here, go over and change or whatever it is you want to do, and then get back here as soon after seven as possible."

"Right, Chief."

Masters wandered into the dining room to join Wanda who was feeding Michael on Marmite soldiers.

"Can I talk, or will that upset the proceedings?"

"The way this young man is wolfing his food, he won't have any time to notice whether you talk or not."

"He seems a bit hungry."

"He's late. He should have had this half an hour ago, and

46

I daresay he's worked up even more of an appetite running round with Sergeant Reed."

"Very likely. Poppet, you heard me say I want to talk to you and Reed over supper."

"Yes." She handed Michael another finger of bread. "All about the lectures, is it?"

"That—and other things."

"Oh? Like what?"

"My inviting Doris and Bill down here."

"We said we'd do that."

"Officially, I mean. Tomorrow morning."

Wanda said nothing for a moment or two as she poured out a beaker of milk for Michael. Then: "I don't know that I like the sound of that."

"You don't mind Doris and Bill using the spare room, do you? I thought you'd like them to join us. I can make other arrangements for them, of course."

"You know I don't mind them coming, although I'd have preferred a day or two in which to settle in before having visitors. However, that's beside the point. It's the reason for their coming that's worrying me. You said officially."

"Yes. I had to get Edgar Anderson's agreement."

"And that means there's an official reason for their visit. And that in turn means a case." She turned from attending to her son to look at her husband. "This was supposed to be in the nature of a holiday, George. A rest cure, in fact."

"You're quite right, and although I haven't actually got a case on my hands, there is something of a problem to be sorted out here in the College."

"A very big problem if you need William down here to help you."

"And Berger."

"The full team. Are you sure it isn't a case?"

"I will explain over dinner. I want Bill and Berger down here to do the legwork, while I get on with my lecturing."

"Cake, darling?" Wanda asked Michael.

"After you've put Michael to bed, we'll ring Bill and Doris."

"George, I really am feeling very cross about this. I take it

47

that your feeling yesterday was right. Edgar Anderson did con you after all."

"As a matter of fact, he didn't. He was the one who was conned."

"Edgar was?"

"Yes. By the Commissioner. Edgar was just told that they needed my help and advice down here as soon as he could get us to agree to come. Up to a point that was true, but he gathered the help and advice were all to do with academic courses."

"But there was something else."

He nodded. "Bobby Locke has explained the problem to me and asked me to help."

Wanda wiped Michael's chin with the napkin. "I hope you won't be overtaxing yourself, George. You really do need a change and a rest."

"I know, poppet, and this sort of atmosphere would suit me down to the socks. Just for a couple of months. In fact, I'm feeling better already. The air is so much less debilitating than that of London. But about the Greens. Would you like me to see if there's another vacant quarter they could have?"

"Of course not. Not if Doris is coming. If it were William alone, he could go into single quarters, but if you feel you need Doris here. . . ."

"Camouflage, poppet. As I said, there's no case. So the Greens are coming as guests."

"Meaning you are trying to fool somebody. Who?"

"The police, darling."

She stared at him. "You're trying to fool your own colleagues?"

"Something of the sort."

"Now I know why you smelt something fishy about the offer of this attachment."

At about seven o'clock, after Michael was safely in his cot and apparently unperturbed by the thought of sleeping in a strange room, Masters rang Green.

"What's going on, George? All Anderson has told me is to

present myself to you tomorrow morning, with Doris and Berger in tow."

"I'd like to wait to give explanations because the business is fairly complicated and by trying to condense it for you I could give the wrong impression."

"Understood. Just one thing."

"What's that?"

"In spite of what you haven't told me, I suss this business is definitely under the rose, as you'd say."

"Quite right. You and Doris are coming here on holiday."

"And Berger?"

"He's a bit more difficult to explain away, but it will be put around that I propose to mount a moderator show and as one of the very few people who has experienced this method of working—together with you, Reed and myself, it would seem reasonable to have him here."

"You mean that though I'm supposed to be on holiday I shall have to work?"

"Shall we say you'll be roped in because you're here."

"You're a devious bastard, George."

"Thanks."

"Anything else?"

"Wanda would like to speak to Doris."

"Put her on. I'd like a word with her myself, just to pass on a few words of warning about the man she's married to. The word 'con' springs to mind."

"It's funny you should say that."

"You mean you're admitting it?"

"I'll tell you tomorrow. Here's Wanda."

It was obvious from the one side of the cosy chat which followed, and which Masters overheard, that Doris Green was delighted at the prospect of coming to stay at the new house. If Wanda had any reservations about the visit she hid them extremely well and the talk about what clothes to bring and the good points of the house and the surrounding countryside sounded decidedly amicable and to the liking of both women.

In the middle of the conversation, Reed arrived to join them for supper. He and Masters had already helped themselves to a drink by the time Wanda joined them.

"Sherry," she said, "and make it a large one."

"Something wrong?"

"Yes, me."

"What's the trouble?"

"I'm a bit miffed with myself for saying it was a bit soon for Doris and William to visit us. They are so obviously looking forward to it and we owe them so much that even to think their coming might be anything of a nuisance is uncharitable to say the least. I'm sorry, darling. I shouldn't have been anything less than happy at your arranging for them to come."

Reed handed Wanda a schooner of Amontillado. "Excuse me, Mrs Masters," he said, "it's not really my business, and I wouldn't contradict you about whatever you think you owe Mr and Mrs Green. But I can tell you this, that if you do owe them anything, the odds are even. You see, ever since you and the Chief got married, you've given them something to think about that they like thinking about. They've sort of adopted you and you've befriended them and it's made a difference. Take it from me, ma'am, they're different people now. Happier, if you like. More . . . more extrovert I suppose the trick cyclists would say. And as for it being too soon to come, well, any housewife I've ever known would want a day or two on her own in a new house to get things straight and settled before she had visitors to stay. What you may have said about it earlier is no cause for regret. You were feeling upset at losing the car keys and don't forget you've been under a lot of stress recently with the Chief getting wounded and being in hospital. You may not think it, but experiences like that take it out of you and so anything the slightest bit out of the ordinary can assume the proportions of . . . well, of being a nuisance when ordinarily they wouldn't."

Reed reddened under their gaze as they continued to stare at him for a moment or two after he had finished speaking. Then Wanda said quietly: "Thank you, Sergeant Reed. That's one of the nicest things that's ever been said to me in the way of a rocket. I'm very touched that you should even think in those terms and excuse my shortcomings so logically."

"Good show, Reed," said Masters. "I want to thank you, too, for what you've just said, because I couldn't have done it. Have another drink."

They sat down to supper a little later. Reed had brought in sausages, oven-chips and frozen green beans, with ice cream to follow, so they did very well. Even so, what they ate seemed to be unimportant as they listened to what Masters had to say. He recounted all he had learned from the Dean and then invited questions.

"One thing is worrying me, Chief."

"What's that?"

"It sounds to me as though the Dean is insisting that DCS Andriessen is not guilty and he's wanting you to protect him from the local force. I agree that the locals don't appear to have much of a case against this officer, but at least I think they're right to put his name in the frame. How can Mr Locke be so sure they're wrong and that Andriessen is innocent? If there's no evidence to point to anybody other than him, there's nothing to clear him of suspicion. I don't think you can take on this business accepting that this chap is innocent. You've got to keep an open mind, and that means keeping him in mind as the villain."

"I thought that, too," said Wanda.

"You're both right," said Masters. "Absolutely right. Mr Locke is strongly of the opinion that Andriessen is innocent and he bases that opinion on his knowledge of, and liking for, the man, as well as the fact that, despite the coincidences of his presence here on both occasions and the car sightings, the local force can bring no definite evidence against him."

"But that's not right, Chief," expostulated Reed. "You can't say a man isn't a killer just because you like him. Nobody can judge that. And the coincidences may not be evidential facts against him, but they are hints that he is implicated, and there doesn't appear to be a hint of a hint against anybody else."

"Quite right. If you'd taken any other view I'd have been disappointed in you. That is my own attitude towards the

51

problem. But with Mr Locke there are other factors. First off, he's not a practical detective, he's an academic. A theorist, if you like. He can teach and teach well all the right things, but it doesn't mean that he can put into practice what he preaches, because he's never had to—at least not in the heat of battle as we do almost daily. It's a common enough phenomenon."

Reed nodded. "I've heard Bill Green talk about that, Chief. During the war, early on, he went with his battery to that training place at Larkhill, and he said there was an Assistant Instructor in Gunnery there who gave them hell. He knew every nut and bolt on a gun, every movement they should make, every signal, how to lay the guns and so on. He had all the drill books and manuals off by heart. Then, out in the desert, when Bill Green had been promoted to sergeant, who should turn up one day as a replacement sergeant on the next door gun but this chap who'd snarled and ranted at them in training. According to the DCI, this chap was hopeless. Absolutely lost. The squaddies on his gun had it in action, laid and fired before he knew what he was about. And he never did come to terms with it. He had to be sent back. But Bill said the pasting he'd given them on Salisbury Plain was what had made those gunners as good as they were in action."

"As good an illustration of my point as you could have," conceded Masters. "And there's one other factor affecting Mr Locke's judgement. Two factors, to be precise. For want of better terms, we'll call them PR and diplomatic. The PR side deals with keeping the morale of this College very high and maintaining its good name as a first class establishment because the whole of the police forces of Britain rely upon it to provide the superlative training which alone can raise and keep raised the standards of policing within the kingdom. The diplomatic factor concerns overseas students. Each of those students is an ambassador in his own way. Good relations between various countries are helped by their visits here and their treatment during training. Also, international police co-operation is enhanced by the good work of the College. If we can contact officers who know the way we work—and they us—it must be of benefit to the forces of

52

individual countries as well as to institutions like Interpol. Mr Locke is very conscious of his responsibilities in this area, and so he is more than anxious that the locals should not put a foot wrong concerning this senior officer from the Netherlands. I think this colours the Dean's thinking as well as the other matters we have discussed, and it has helped him to come to the conclusion that Andriessen is innocent, or must be treated as such until a cast-iron case can be made out against him. And made out against him, I should add, without recourse to taking him in for questioning or any other overt move towards him."

Reed sat back in his chair. "I still think you shouldn't take it on, Chief. Even if you let Mr Locke think you agree with him about Andriessen's innocence while actually keeping an open mind on that score, you can't operate with your hands tied behind your back."

"Meaning what, Sergeant?" asked Wanda.

"Meaning not being able to approach the suspect, Mrs Masters. It'll be like trying to play ludo without throwing the dice."

"I see what you mean." She turned to her husband. "George, this case really is a non-starter."

"Poppet, I have already told you it isn't a case."

"I know. It's a problem."

"What's the difference, Chief?" asked Reed.

"Quite a lot. We would have a case to solve had we been called in by the locals. But they have not called us in, and so they are investigating their own case. Here, within the enclave of the College, the Commandant and the Dean have a problem. Their problem is to preserve the integrity of their institution in the face of difficulties created by the locals' investigation of the case. The problem is a result of the case."

"That sounds as if they had no faith in the ability of the locals to solve the case, Chief. In fact they're expecting the locals to make a boob."

"Quite right. They wouldn't express it in those terms, of course. They would say that the locals still have an unclosed file on a murder or disappearance which happened five or six years ago. All the signs are—so the College authorities will argue—that this present case will also remain an unclosed file, because there is no reason to suppose that the locals will succeed in a case exactly similar to one in which they have already failed. But, in the meantime, while grasping at straws in their efforts to succeed, the locals may do untold damage to the reputation of the College and a senior police officer from the Netherlands."

"Only if Andriessen is not guilty, Chief."

Masters smiled and shook his head.

"No?"

"Think it through, Reed. As soon as Andriessen is taken in for questioning, the finger of suspicion will be pointed at him. There are countless cases similar to this where lurid articles have been written about a suspect being questioned for hours by the police when, at the end of it all, the suspect has had to be released. Why? Because he is innocent? Very likely. Or because, so the buffs will have it, the police knew he was guilty but couldn't get the final bit of evidence to nail him? Whichever, genuinely innocent or innocent because he can't be proved guilty, that man is considered guilty by impli- cation—or however you like to put it. The Dean knows that once the locals start to question Andriessen the damage will have been done, whether the man is guilty or not. They want to avoid this at all costs, and their wish is bolstered by the fact that they believe him innocent."

"How can you stop the locals taking him in if they want to, Chief? There's only one way to do that, isn't there? And that's to find the villain—if it's not Andriessen. But you can't do that because you're not investigating the case. The locals are doing it for themselves, and they're not going to like your being here, let alone if you start feeding in their trough." Reed shook his head. "I still think you can't take it on, Chief."

"When you say take it on," asked Wanda, "what exactly do you mean?"

"Trying to solve this problem without upsetting the locals, without access to the reports and files of the first case as well as the present one, and without the help of a thumping great squad of men to search and to get out and about and ask questions. What the Chief is proposing to do is like finding his way across an unfamiliar room in the dark without so much as touching any of the furniture. Because as soon as he touches a bit the whole house will fall round his ears."

"Graphic imagery," said Masters with a grin.

"Yes, but is it true?" asked Wanda.

"More or less."

"Then Sergeant Reed is right. You've taken on a hopeless task."

"A difficult one, certainly, and one I am by no means sure we can bring to a successful outcome. But we've rarely taken on a difficult problem and been sure of success at the outset. Such is not the nature of our work. A builder can be given the trickiest of building plans, but he knows that if he follows his instructions to the letter the edifice will rise just as the architect originally envisaged it. Nothing like that happens with us. The only instruction we get is that we must not fail for want of trying. In other words, whether the problem seems hopeless or not, we have a bash. And I want to have a real bash here, because I value this College and the work that it does. I am, myself, an alumnus."

Wanda said sweetly, "Darling, I think you're trying to pull the wool over our eyes."

"How can you say that?"

"Do you really want me to spell it out?"

"Yes, please, Mrs Masters. I would like to know how you think the Chief is fooling us."

"Not fooling us, exactly, Sergeant Reed. Just not giving us his real reason for taking on this problem that you so rightly insist is hopeless. Mr Locke is not the only one to doubt the ability of the local force to bring this double tragedy to a successful conclusion. Two young lads, mere boys, have disappeared, probably done to death, possibly after undergoing unspeakable acts of savagery or depravity. Nobody likes the idea of the perpetrators getting away with it. Least of all my husband. We have a young son, remember. However, he can do nothing unless he is required to take the case. So it would be left in incompetent hands with—in his opinion—little likelihood of a satisfactory outcome were it not for a quirk of fate. That quirk was the chance which enabled Mr Locke to ask for the help of my husband in solving a problem. A problem which offers him a very slender opportunity, but still an opportunity, to apply his mind—together with the not inconsiderable help you other three can give him—to a business about which he, himself, feels very strongly. At first I was very much against his taking on this so-called problem, just as you were. But as I came to realise his true reason for wanting to try to help, I began to change my mind. Now, I must say that he has my full support in what he is about to attempt—namely to find the killer of two young boys."

"Thank you," said Masters quietly. "I didn't realise my motives were so apparent."

"They weren't, darling. You did a damn good job of fudging them over."

"You had me fooled, Chief," said Reed, wrily. "And I've spent all this time trying to head you off."

"And very useful our conversation has been," said Masters, "even though you haven't managed to deflect me. I think we've cleared the air quite a lot and I now have things plainer in my mind than when we sat down. I like that. It helps with straight thinking and planning."

Masters rose from the table. "Come along, Reed. You're not on duty first thing tomorrow, so we can have another drink before you go."

As he lay in bed with Wanda in his arms an hour or so later, Masters said: "Did you have to bare my soul in front of Reed?"

"Why not, darling? It did no harm and he appreciated it. Besides . . . "

"Besides what?"

"I thought I'd better tell him that rather than give him the real reason why you were so adamant about it."

"What real reason?"

"The fact that the Commissioner told Bobby Locke you were the only officer who could pull it off. That flattered your ego."

56

"Flattered my . . . you little . . . "

Wanda murmured contentedly as he drew her closer to him.

Chapter 3

"WILLIAM, HOW NICE to see you." Wanda kissed Green's cheek.

"Before you did that I'd made up my mind to say a few words to your old man. But you've made my day, so I won't spoil it by putting the boot in."

"He's fooling you," said Doris, kissing Wanda in her turn. "Ever since Mr Anderson told him we were to come down here he's been acting the giddy goat. At least ever since he got home last night. We'd done our packing and were just going to bed when the silly fool asked me if I knew where his spanners were. Of course I fell for it. I told him and asked him what he wanted them for. He said to unfasten the kitchen sink because I'd forgotten to put it in one of the bags."

"Four bags she's got," said Green.

"Why not when we were coming by car?" She turned to Wanda. "One of them's got a lot of magazines in. When you said it was a nice house but not homely because it hadn't any books and things lying about I thought I'd bring my old copies of *Homes and Gardens* and a few paperbacks."

"Lovely."

"It'll look like a dentist's waiting room in there," said Green. "Where's his nibs?"

"In his office, with Reed. They're preparing lecture notes on one of your old cases. I can get through to him on the phone if you'd like me to tell him you're here."

"Not to worry, love. We'll have our mid-mornings in peace."

"Bill!" expostulated his wife.

"What's up?"

"You can't ask people to give you coffee. You have to wait to be asked."

"Come inside," said Wanda. "It's all ready. You, too,

58

Sergeant Berger. Just put the cases in the hall, please. They can go up later." She turned to Doris. "Michael is in the dining room with his toys. It makes an ideal nursery because they supply one of those expanding gates for the doorway. I put cushions round the table legs, just so he wouldn't hurt himself if he were to fall against them. George put the chairs on the table."

"I'll look in on the little love."

"Don't be long. We'll have coffee and then maybe we can put him down for an hour's sleep."

As they sat down, Green asked: "When will George be back, love?"

"I'm not expecting him until lunchtime. He's preparing notes for a lecture for tomorrow morning. Sergeant Reed is making drops for another lecture, I believe, and I know George is hoping to use Sergeant Berger with his camera to get some slides for illustrations."

"For tomorrow, Mrs Masters?"

"Oh, no. Not for tomorrow. He proposes to give an introductory lecture, I believe. He said it would be of a general nature and intended to make the students think about basics. Would that seem right to you, William?"

"I reckon so. George is the sort to have it all planned and he's got the gift of the gab."

"Bill, that's unkind," said Doris, rejoining them.

"Well, he has."

"You're talking to his wife. There's no need to insult her."

"I wasn't insulting her. George could get up and speak to this lot here for a month of Sundays and never repeat himself. It's a gift he has, as I said."

"And he knows his stuff," added Berger.

"I was about to say that, too," said Green. "And I'll tell you something else. It's a good job he has got the gift of the gab because he doesn't work to your set routines. Don't forget he has flights of fancy, and describing flights of fancy to a classroom full of coppers is going to take some doing if they're to understand what he's on about."

Wanda smiled. "I understand exactly what you're saying, William. I am wondering myself how he is going to describe

59

his own thought processes when it comes to telling students the reasons for some of his leaps in the dark. I know you've always described him as jammy, William. . . . "

"Only in the nicest possible way," said Green through a mouthful of biscuit. He swallowed what he was eating and went on: "Talking of explaining, I reckon George has got a lot of that to do to us. Not a case, he says. A problem. What sort of a problem? Arithmetical? Financial? Can you tell us, love?"

"He has explained it to me, William. I think he would rather have waited until you arrived, but I was getting a lot of wifely concern about his coming down here for a rest and then accepting a case, so he thought it better to appease me. But I don't think I'd better try to explain, lest I give you the wrong idea."

"He managed to convince you there was a difference between a case and a problem?"

"Yes."

"There you are," Green said to his wife. "And I get clobbered for saying he's got the gift of the gab. Any bloke who can put one like that over on an intelligent girl like Wanda doesn't only have to have the gift of the gab, he has to be a contender for a Nobel Prize in misrepresentation. I tell you . . . "

"You can save it for later," said Doris. "We're going to see if Michael would like a little sleep."

"Glad to see you, Bill."

Green lowered the newspaper he was reading and looked up at Masters from the depth of an armchair.

"Pleased to hear it," replied Green. "I thought you'd forgotten you'd arranged for us to come."

Masters sat down and took out a tin of Warlock Flake. As he carefully separated a leaf for rubbing, he said: "Sorry not to be here when you arrived, but I have to keep up the pretence of doing what I am ostensibly here for."

"Pretence?" queried Green, putting the newspaper on the floor. "Ostensibly? They're funny words to be using. They suggest some undercover job."

"Quite right. Or at any rate the part of the job you and Berger are down here to help with is."

"You told me it wasn't a case. Something about a problem, you said."

"I'd better explain. By the way, where are the ladies?"

"Gone off in your car with the young shaver to do some shopping. They said they'd only be gone half an hour and then they'd be back to put a cold lunch on the table."

Masters applied a match to his pipe. When it was drawing satisfactorily, he said: "We might as well have a drink, Bill. There's still something left from the small stock we got last night." He got to his feet. "If you've nothing better to do this afternoon, you might get Berger to take you off to buy more. Particularly beer."

"If I've nothing better to do?"

Masters was pouring the last two bottles of beer. "That's what I said."

"I don't get it." He accepted the glass of beer. "You drag us down here at a moment's notice and then start talking as if there was no reason for our coming."

"Oh, there's very good reason, Bill." Masters sat down. "Cheers!"

"Cheers! What reason?"

"I want us to carry out an investigation in parallel with the local force."

"A sort of competition? Tug-of-war?"

"Not quite. They're to know nothing about it."

"You're raving, George. First off you say you're not on a case and now you're suggesting we undertake a totally unethical investigation unbeknown to the legitimate force in whose area we find ourselves."

"Within the College, Bill. Listen, and I'll explain."

Masters spent the next ten or twelve minutes giving Green the background and explaining why he maintained he was out to solve a problem and not undertaking a case.

Green listened patiently and then drained the last of his beer before speaking.

"I'll say this for it, George, it's novel. Nothing like this has ever come my way before."

61

"The point is, Bill, can we help?"

"Now you're asking! On the face of it, I've got to say the chances are slim. But then I don't know how you propose to go about it."

"That's a matter for discussion, Bill. I'd like the two sergeants to be present, and I shall be busy for the first part of the afternoon, so will Reed. If you and Berger could join us in the office they've assigned to me at about four o'clock, we could have a couple of hours before dinner. That's why I said if you'd nothing better to do until then, you could lay in some drink."

"It'll be a pleasure. There's no more beer here now, is there?"

"Sorry. Sherry, gin or white wine."

"I'll have a slug of gin. Leave the sherry and wine for the girls."

Masters got up to do the honours. As he did so, there was the sound of a car pulling up to the house. "Here they are," he said.

Green got up to look out of the window. "Wanda told me she'd lost her car keys. It's a mystery where they could have got to."

"Reed covered the ground pretty thoroughly but couldn't unearth them. They'll turn up sometime."

Masters handed Green his gin and tonic. "Berger, I take it, is settled in?"

"After coffee. He'll have found Reed by now."

"Good."

Wanda and Doris came in with Michael.

"Hello, darling. I'll have a glass of white wine. I'll have it while I give Michael his lunch. If I get that out of the way first . . . " She picked up her son. "Come along, young man. Fish pie for lunch. We've just got to heat it on the stove and then there's stewed apricots."

"Fish, fish, fish," chanted Michael as he was carried off.

"I'll have wine, too, please George," said Doris. "I'll take Wanda's and mine through and sit with her."

As the two men settled down again, Green said: "I've been thinking, George. There's no reason why we shouldn't meet this Andriessen is there? Socially, I mean. It sounds as if there's a bar in the mess which he uses. I'm allowed in—as a visitor—aren't I?"

"Of course you're allowed in. And I agree it's a good thing to cultivate Andriessen."

"Suss him out over a pint."

"Quite. We may get no information from him, but we can at least learn what sort of a chap he is. Bobby Locke says he's thoroughly likeable."

"Anything else you've got in mind, George?"

"How would it be if I got Locke to have some sort of little party and invite some of the locals for a drink?"

"Meaning the senior CID men responsible for investigating the disappearance of the lad?"

"We might just be able to bring the conversation round to cases and they might just give us an idea of things."

"I like it. Will Locke play?"

"It's his problem."

"Is he more likely to be worried about his pocket than his problem?"

"He shouldn't be. He'll get an entertainment allowance as Dean. Anyway, I'll sound him out."

"On another level, George, couldn't Reed and Berger do something like that? They ought to be able to chat up some DS or other who's attached to the case."

"We'll explore that, too. In fact, we'll try everything we can think of."

The two sat silent for some time, then Green again opened the conversation. "How's the arm, George?"

"As you can see, I no longer have it in a sling. I'm to go to the resident quack here for a new dressing in a couple of days' time. That will probably be the last. Why do you ask?"

"I was just thinking that an arm in a sling is a good starting point for professional gossip. A ready made opening gambit. The sort of thing somebody can ask about and then you can get in with some question about how they're getting on with their search for the missing youth."

"You're getting crafty in your old age, Bill."

"I've got to get something if we're to do anything here, George. It has me worried."

"Don't be."

"You're that sure of success?"

"No. But when we get going, Bill, we try. Really try. And if we fail after doing our utmost, well I feel sure we shall at least have some lines of thought to pass on to Bobby Locke. He should be able to pass them on as his own if the locals get too importunate over Andriessen."

"To put them on the right lines, you mean?"

"It's a possibility, isn't it? As I said, I'm not sure of success, but I'm pretty sure that between the four of us we'll at least get a few ideas. You've had a few just sitting there for the past seven or eight minutes."

Green nodded and again lapsed into silence. After he'd finished another gin, Doris put her head round the door. "Lunch is ready. French bread, sliced ham and salad stuff. Everybody to make their own sandwiches."

"Typical," grumbled her husband.

"How do you mean, 'typical'?"

"Nothing to do but work, nothing to eat but food," said her husband. "Now you want us to have nothing to eat unless we work at the food as well as for it."

"Silly ass. I don't know what you're going on about, but I do know one old saying, and that is that every word hinders a bite. If you talk much more you won't get anything to eat."

Before leaving for his office after lunch, Masters asked Green to brief Sergeant Berger while the two of them went off to buy a supply of drink and whatever else Wanda might ask them to bring in. So it was that, when the team foregathered in his office at four o'clock, Masters was satisfied they were all aware of the problem facing them.

They sat round his desk, Green lounging in the low-slung visitors' chair and the two sergeants on the government-issue varnished oak and rexine uprights.

"First of all," said Masters, "let us define the problem. Quite simply, it is to throw some light on the disappearance of two youths, one five years after the other. It is not to prove

64

the innocence of Mr Andriessen, but it is to try to forestall any attempt by the local police to embarrass the College, its staff, and international relations in general, by involving Mr Andriessen without due cause. What that amounts to is either to find the villain or alternatively to suggest lines of investigation that may give the locals more facts or theories on which to base a reasonable approach to Andriessen or whoever it is whose name appears in the frame.

"Our investigations are to be clandestine. Nobody apart from Mr Locke is to know of them and certainly not any member of the local police force."

"Are we allowed to talk to people?" asked Berger. "To ask questions, I mean, Chief?"

"Yes. But such questions have to be cloaked in some sort of camouflage net. They are to come up during a chat, never in anything resembling an official interview. I don't think I have to explain that further, but I would remind you of the oblique technique."

"What's that when it's at home?" grumbled Green.

"You can't ask a leading question. That would be too obvious. But you can make a leading statement to provoke reaction."

"Example, please, Chief."

"Easy," growled Green. "If I came up to you and asked if you wore red underpants, you'd want to know what business it was of mine. But if I came up to you and made the statement that nobody ever wears red underpants you'd immediately reel off a list of about eighteen chaps who do, just to prove me wrong. So, if I were looking for a villain who, I knew, had a fetish for pillar-box red, well, I'd have at least eighteen suspects to think about."

"Got it," said Reed. "And if there's no response of that sort, you assume the bloke you've addressed has nothing to tell you on that particular point."

"More or less," said Masters. "But it's a very inexact science, so you may have to try the same tactic again elsewhere if you think the point is worth pursuing. Now, we'll push on. We've defined the problem. The next thing is to collate what we know."

"Five or so years ago a youth disappeared and has never been found either dead or alive.

"Three weeks ago the same happened to a second youth and, so far, he too seems to have disappeared into thin air.

"Both incidents occurred within a mile or two of the College.

"Both happened latish in the afternoon.

"On each occasion there was, resident at the College, a CID officer from the Netherlands.

"On the first occasion a rust-red DAF motor car was seen in the vicinity of the place where the youth was last sighted. On the second, a metallic green Volvo was seen. Both cars, according to witnesses, were foreign cars. Both cars are said to have been seen leaving the College grounds approximately half an hour before the boys were said to have been last seen.

"On his first visit here, Andriessen owned a rust-red DAF. On his second, a metallic green Volvo.

"The local police were not in time to inspect the DAF belonging to Andriessen before he took it back home to Europe. They have, however, inspected the Volvo and have found nothing in the way of fingerprints, or even of dust and particle transfer to suggest that the second missing youth had ever entered it. This evidence, however, is inconclusive because the clothing the boy was wearing at the time is not available for comparison, and Andriessen is said to keep his car clean and polished, both inside and out, at all times.

"That is all we know about the case, gentlemen. We are now faced with our problem. Was Andriessen involved in these disappearances or not?"

Masters sat back and waited for contributions from the other three. Berger, who had been making notes, was the first to speak.

"Your fifth point, Chief, was that on each occasion Andriessen was resident here at the College. I don't think that can stand on its own. I expect there are quite a number of people who were living here on both occasions."

"That's right, lad," growled Green. "It won't stand on its own. There'll be plenty of regular staff who were here each time, and it could be that some students, foreign and British,

66

were here on both occasions. Not necessarily on the same courses as Andriessen, because they're split and they overlap and so on." He looked across at Masters. "There should be records that Bobby Locke can make available to us. I think we should get a list out of all who were here five years ago and are here now."

"I'm in agreement with that. Berger, it was your point. I'll leave the search to you. I'll make sure the necessary records are available for you."

"Right, Chief."

Reed came in.

"Chief, I've been having a think about this chap Andriessen. If he'd abducted a youth and presumably killed him five years ago, would he come back here again? I'd have thought he would have fought tooth and nail to avoid it, just in case there might be a nasty surprise waiting for him on this side. He couldn't know there wouldn't be, and most of these chaps on the continent have a healthy respect for the British police. In his position—if I'd been guilty—I would definitely assume I was under suspicion—suspicion that hadn't been voiced because I was safe in Holland where the British couldn't get at me to ask the questions needed to pin the guilt on me and so make me subject to extradition.

"And very senior police officers like Andriessen can always find a good excuse for not doing anything they don't want to do—at any rate if it's to avoid running the risk of a life sentence in a foreign jail."

"I think what you have said, Sergeant, is definitely a point in Andriessen's favour. But I suspect you hadn't finished everything you'd got to say about this aspect of the problem."

"Not by a long chalk, Chief. You could argue against what I've just said by saying Andriessen is some form of nutcase that gets its kicks out of abducting and murdering young lads, so that when the chance came again to travel to England where he'd had a bit of fun five years earlier—and got away with it—he jumped at the opportunity. Now he's had another bit of fun."

"It's a point of view," said Green.

"But is it?" asked Reed. "If Andriessen is that sort of nut, would he wait five years between his bits of fun? He couldn't have known very long before he actually came here the second time that he'd be coming. A few months probably. So what has he been doing in the meantime. Have youths been going missing in Holland in his police area? Oughtn't we to find out? Because if there have been no incidents over there, it speaks in his favour."

"Very, very good point," said Masters. "If the Netherlands authorities publish police statistics, it ought to be quite easy to discover." Masters turned to Green. "Bill, will you phone the Yard tomorrow to ask if we get such statistics from foreign countries each year? If not, would you speak to Anderson personally and get him to request the published figures from our embassy in the Netherlands. Not from the Netherlands embassy in London. We don't want them to start wondering what we're about."

"Will do," said Green. "But there's one point Sar'nt Reed didn't mention. Andriessen is the equivalent of a DCS. Detective Chief Supers are responsible for investigations into the likes of youths disappearing and being murdered. If he has been having his bits of fun, as Reed calls them, he's in a pretty good position to see the guilt is not pinned on himself."

"That's true," agreed Reed, "but it doesn't matter in the sense in which I've been talking. The cases, whether they've been solved or not, will still appear in the records, won't they?"

"Let's hope so, lad."

"Continuing the same line," said Masters, "we've got to appreciate that pathological killers—Reed's nutcases—often get very self-confident. If Andriessen is guilty, and has got away with it on a number of occasions, he could think he would get away with it as often as he liked to try it on. So if he has been operating successfully in the Netherlands, he could well believe that he was still fireproof over here, despite his killing five years ago. However, those statistics should throw further light on that point."

"So what's Reed saying?" demanded Green. "If Andriessen is not a pathological crocodile he wouldn't have made a second visit here if he were guilty?"

"More or less. But it doesn't hold water put just like that, Bill. What you've just said suggests that whether completely pathological or not he could be implicated. Reed has simply stated that a one-time killer would not come back. He has asked us to try to establish whether there is evidence to show whether Andriessen has been around when other similar cases have happened. If there is not, then we chalk up a plus-point fo Andriessen."

"Got it."

"Have you any points to make, Bill?"

"Yes. You didn't put it in your list of facts we know, but you have told us that Andriessen only had the time between leaving a lecture and appearing in the bar—three quarters of an hour, wasn't it?—to have abducted the second boy, if he did abduct him, that is. Actually, Andriessen says he didn't go out at that time because he was having a bath, and the time before, five years ago, according to Bobby Locke he was playing squash at the time the lad was last seen. This seems to me an area I should look at very closely, with young Berger's help. I know people have said they saw him in his car at the vital times, but even if they did, I can't help thinking there's something wrong in that area. I mean, George, Andriessen couldn't have jumped in his car and said to himself I think I'll go out and abduct a boy and be back for a drink in three quarters of an hour. Nobody could have known there'd be a boy handy for abduction. And then, where could he have taken the lad in that time? I know you can knock somebody on the head anywhere, but it takes time to get the body to a hiding place that hundreds of searchers won't find pretty quickly."

"You want to busy yourself with that aspect, Bill?"

"Yes, please, because it needs looking into. There was three quarters of an hour between the end of Andriessen's lecture and his appearance in the bar. Knock five minutes off each end—for leaving the lecture room and getting to the car in the first place, and for parking and walking back to the bar on his return. That leaves thirty-five minutes. Knock off another five for minor transactions like getting the lad into the car and then later, killing him and getting him out again.

69

Half an hour left. I want Berger to time how long it takes to get to where the locals think the lad could have been picked up. Allow five, say, for getting there . . . "

"And another five back," said Berger.

"What does that leave? Twenty minutes. Ten minutes each way. Well, I know you can travel a hell of a way in ten minutes. But only on roads. If you leave the roads, ten minutes is nothing. I assume this lad wasn't killed on a road and just rolled into a ditch?"

"I think you are safe in that assumption, Bill. His body would have come to light before now if that had been the case, even without the intensive search."

"So I'm going to concentrate on that area," said Green. "Among others."

"Which others?"

"The ones you're just going to tell me about."

Masters laughed. "I haven't made sufficient contribution to the pool yet, is that it?"

Green took out his crumpled packet of Kensitas. "That thought hadn't occurred to me," he admitted, "but knowing you, I didn't reckon we'd get away without you having your pennyworth."

"In that case . . . look, we already have enough to be getting on with and I don't want to overburden anybody at this stage. But I would like to add a thought or two."

"I guessed as much."

"It seems to me that the locals are obsessed by the coincidence of Andriessen's presence here on both occasions. Because of their attitude, I feel that we are falling into the same trap.

"Had Andriessen not been here at the moment, I think the locals would not necessarily have thought that the killer was the same in both instances. Five years is a big gap. I think that we should consider the possibility of two killers. Once we do that, each case becomes individual and can be considered as such. That means that we can not only regard each one as separate, but treat them in a more normal way than we appear to be doing. The advantages of this approach could be twofold. If we were to solve the recent case, that

70

would be that one dealt with and then, should it become clear that the two are linked, it would mean that both had been dealt with.

"So why not regard this second case as one entirely in its own right? I don't say one has totally to disregard the first. Indeed much of what we have already decided to do embraces them both. But don't disregard any pertinent facts or ideas that appear valid for one and not for the other."

"There could easily be two killers," agreed Green. "And pal Andriessen could be one of them and somebody else the other. There are various combinations here, George."

"Just so. That is why I don't want us to be blinkered as the locals appear to be. So, gentlemen, let us look at each case individually. Now, if we had been called in to handle a single, similar case, we should go about trying to discover if the victim had an enemy. Somebody who hated his guts. I told you that both these lads were known tearaways having vandalised and damaged the property of others. I can imagine the feelings of the owner of a new, shiny motorcar who discovers that a youth has just done a great deal of wilful damage to the paintwork."

"He'd feel like murder all right, Chief."

"Quite so. And that is one of the acts both these lads were known to have done. What about vandalism they may have indulged in that the police didn't know anything about but the owner of the vandalised property did? There's a widespread feeling in this country these days that young offenders—sometimes guilty of devastating crime—get away with it all ways: first because the police don't catch them or, if they are caught, the magistrates are so soft or our laws so liberal that nothing is done by way of retribution.

"But all that is by the way. What I'm really saying is that there could be those who live around here who might wish those lads harm. Then there are others—perverts of various sorts—who molest young people from a very tender age upwards. The really small ones can't fight back. These young lads, in their early teens, are capable of resisting. And when they do put up a fight, then is the danger time. They have to be silenced. There could be some of those perverts about,

71

gentlemen. Don't forget the group who took a very small boy in Brighton and abused him so shamefully. There are lots of cases like that. Either or both of these cases could be among them."

"There's a hell of a lot to think about," said Green. "And I've no doubt at all that there'll be more hints and ideas coming up every day."

"I hope so," said Masters, "because that is generally a sign of progress in a case." He looked at his watch. "I think we've talked long enough, gentlemen, so if nobody has anything more he wishes to say at this moment, I propose to call it a day. Bill, I leave it to you and Berger to do what you can tomorrow morning. Reed and I have a long session in a lecture room, so we won't be available till after lunch. After that I don't think we appear again until next Monday, do we Reed?"

"That's it, Chief. The first of the cases."

"We should have time to work that one up fairly comfortably as well as help you others. Right, gentlemen, thank you for your time. That's it for today."

When Masters and Green reached the house, they were met by Wanda who had a scarf tied prettily over her hair, working gloves on, with a duster in one hand and a tin of spray polish in the other.

"Hello, sweetheart," said Masters, kissing her on the tip of her nose. "What's this, a Dorcas meeting?"

"Doris and I have been sorting things out a bit."

"So I see," said Masters, peering into the sitting room. "You've changed the furniture round."

"To make it more cosy. I think our predecessors here had a television set in that corner and all the chairs were lined up like rows of cinema seats."

"Futiles," said Green. "Nine penn'orth of hot hand at the back."

Wanda looked puzzled.

"*Fauteuils*," said Masters, explaining. "Double seats for courting couples at the back of cinema pits."

"*Fauteuils* if you were lucky," said Green. "Futiles if you

72

weren't. I know I never had any luck when I used to take Doris. She'd never . . . "

"Bill!" said his wife adamantly, coming out of the dining room, apparelled very much like Wanda.

"What's up, love?"

"What you were talking about."

"I was only going to say you'd never let me buy you a box of chocolates in case the papers rustled."

"Get out with you," said Doris. "You couldn't afford chocolates. *Black Magic* were ninepence a quarter in those days."

Wanda laughed and linked her arm in that of her husband. "Doris has been a tower of strength. We're in much better order now. You'll have to put up with the smell of lavender, but we felt we had to polish everything."

"I don't find it unpleasant."

"Good. Oh, by the way, would you have a look at the window in Michael's room. I can't get it open."

"Stuck with paint as like as not," said Green. "If you shift it, George, grease the ways with a bit of soap. That'll ease it."

"Right."

"You," said Doris to her husband, "can look after Michael for a few minutes while Wanda and I get things ready for putting him to bed and straightening up in the kitchen."

"Nothing I'd like better. Where is he?"

"Playing on the dining room floor. Take him into the sitting room because I want to lay the table."

Masters and Green went about their allotted tasks.

About ten minutes later, as Masters was coming downstairs, he saw Wanda listening outside the sitting room door. When she heard him she lifted a finger to her lips to enjoin quiet. He stood beside her to listen.

"Now ain't I a'going to be a re'glar . . . " said Green.

"Toff," said Michael.

"A'riding in me carriage and a . . . "

"Pair."

"Top hat on me . . . "

"Head."

73

"Fevvers in me . . . "

"Bed."

"An' call myself the Duke of . . . "

"Barnet fair."

"With aristamacranna round the bottom of me . . . "

"Coat."

"A Piccadilly windy in me . . . "

"Eye."

"Only fancy all the dustmen shouting in me . . . "

"Ear."

"Leave us . . . "

"In your will before you die. Oy!" gabbled Michael.

Masters looked at Wanda and grinned. "All good stuff," he whispered.

"Seems a pity to break it up," she agreed. "What is it? Old music hall song?"

"I imagine so."

They entered the room. Michael was being bounced up and down on Green's knee. By now the chosen verse was "Ride a Cock-horse".

"Time for bed now, darling," said Wanda. "Say goodnight to Mr Green."

"She had a wart on the end of her nose," said Michael as his mother lifted him.

"Who had, darling?"

"The fine lady on a white horse."

"Really?"

"Rings on her fingers and bells on her toes and a blooming great wart on the end of her nose. What's a wart?"

"A big sort of bump, darling. Not very nice."

"Poor lady."

"Yes, poor lady," agreed Wanda as she made for the door.

"Goodnight," said Michael seraphically over his mother's shoulder.

"I must say you have a way with children, Bill," said Masters.

"Never had anything to do with them till yours came along," replied Green. "We like each other," he added simply.

"You deserve a drink," said Masters. "By the way, thanks for stocking up the cellar."

"I had to consider my own likes and comfort, too, you know."

"Of course. Still . . . what's it to be?"

"Oh, gin, please. George, I think we should try to meet Andriessen as soon as possible. Would Wanda mind if we were to trickle across to the mess after supper to see if he is in the bar?"

"I don't think she'll mind. She'll have Doris here and I suspect she is as anxious as we are to get this problem solved as soon as possible."

"What about it, then?"

"Why not? It's only two hundred yards away, so if Andriessen is not there we shall only be gone about ten minutes. If he is . . . an hour at the most I'd have said."

"You think we should meet him?"

"Most assuredly. There's no reason to work blind if we don't have to."

"How does it square up with Bobby Locke's wish to keep him clear of suspicion or investigation?"

"Your suggestion was that we should simply talk to him, not discuss the disappearance of the boy."

Green took out his battered packet of cigarettes and selected one carefully, drawing it out between the nails of his thumb and middle finger. When this operation had been accomplished, he said: "I know I suggested that we should try to meet Andriessen. I still think it's the right thing for us to do. But on second thoughts . . . " He paused to strike a match and light the cigarette before continuing. "What if he is guilty? Won't the fact that two jacks from the Yard seek him out, accidentally on purpose, put him on his guard? Guilty men are wary, and he could easily jump to the conclusion that we are up to something. If he comes to think that, we could have lost a trick or two."

Masters nodded his agreement with this thought before saying: "That's if he's guilty, Bill. What if he isn't?"

"He won't get any ideas about us."

Masters shook his head.

75

"No?"

"Put yourself in his place, Bill. He knows the lad has disappeared, because everybody round here does. Everybody in the kingdom except me does, if it comes to that. He must also have heard of the first disappearance five years ago. Don't forget he didn't leave here until several days after the newspapers carried the reports of the lad's disappearance.

"Now, if we can be struck by a coincidence, so can he, if he's anything of a policeman, that is. He will be able to see that he could be under investigation. Not at first, maybe, but he will have realised it by now. Don't forget, his car was one of those examined by the locals. There's just a possibility that he has heard about the rust-red DAF that figured in the first case. He was asked about his movements at the vital time in the recent case—not in isolation, of course—but there are enough straws in the wind to indicate that he isn't totally in the clear. And, as I said, a senior policeman is likely to be very alive to nuances.

"So, in reply to your statement that if he is not guilty he won't get any ideas about us, I should say we can't count on it, Bill."

"Not when he's confronted by a bloke with your reputation, you mean?"

"That's not quite what I meant. I can see no reason why Andriessen should ever have heard of me. We're quite well known to the various English forces because we get out and about to work among them, but reports of our doings are unlikely to be—literally—noised abroad."

"You really believe that?"

"Of course. Otherwise I wouldn't have said it. How much do we know of the work of our counterparts in other countries? The same will apply in reverse."

"Not in this neck of the woods," said Green. "The place is well aware you are here. Your recent wounding is a talking point. The sergeants tell me people are buttonholing them to ask about you. Andriessen must, by now, be aware of who you are and what you've done. That's why I said that your tackling him could make him uneasy whether he's guilty or not."

Masters got up to renew the drinks. "Are you suggesting you should go along to see him without me, Bill?"

"Not on your Nelly. I reckon you've got to show your face, George. Not just to Andriessen, but to everybody who might like to see you. If I go alone, they'll think you've sent me there for some reason. No, we go together, or not at all."

Masters handed Green his drink.

"And play it off the cuff, Bill. We won't force it."

"Agreed. Ta! Here's tears!" He raised his glass to indicate the decision had been reached.

A few minutes later, Wanda and Doris joined them and asked for sherry. They were no longer dressed for housework, and the little circle was complete for that pleasant period that is the run-up to dinner time.

"Bill and I are going across to the mess after supper," announced Masters.

Wanda, knowing that her husband was not in the habit of leaving her in the evening unless work demanded it, accepted the information without protest. Doris, however, demanded to know why, on the first night of their visit, her husband should be hauling their host away from hearth and home.

"The beer's cheaper in the mess," said Green. "They buy it wholesale, you see, and the mark-up isn't as big as in pubs and off-licences."

"That's rubbish and you know it," retorted Doris. "You're just going out because there isn't a television here to watch."

"Got to see a man about a dog," said Masters, sucking his pipe stem reflectively.

"I'm surprised at you, George. You're as bad as Bill."

Masters sat forward. "A Dutchman."

"You'll be telling me next he's got clogs on."

"It's right, love," said Green. "A real little Mister Baggy-Britches."

"Are you telling me the truth?"

"I think they are," said Wanda. "Not that I know much about it, but when George told me about this problem they've got, he mentioned a DCS Andriessen from the Netherlands."

"That's the one," said Green.

"In that case," said Doris, "when you go, don't be long about it. Remember which day you go on."

"Talking of remembering," said Wanda, "I'd better see how the potatoes are doing."

There was a fair number in the mess when Masters and Green arrived soon after nine o'clock.

"Not my ideal spot," said Green. "A bar full of nothing but policemen."

"There are at least two women here," said Masters.

"Makes no difference, they'll still be cops. What's it to be George?"

While Green got the drinks, Masters looked about him to see if there were any familiar faces in the crowd. He recognised one man playing brag at a table in a far corner, otherwise everybody else was unknown to him, though he reckoned he could pick out the half-dozen or so foreign officers present. He was wondering if there should be some way of telling if any of them was from Holland—the clogs Doris had mentioned came into his mind—when Green handed him his drink.

"Sorry, George, they wouldn't allow me to pay for them. They had to go on a bar chit with your mess number on it. I signed for you."

"I didn't know I had a mess number."

"One three five. Easy to remember."

"Thanks. I pay at the end of the month I suppose."

"Unless you get Bobby Locke to authorise a number for me."

Masters sipped his drink. "Which one is Andriessen, do you reckon? If he's here, that is."

"Impossible to tell."

A heavily built man came up to Masters. A blond giant, as tall as Masters and as square as Green.

"I'm the uniform Super from the South East Force," he said. "Name of Craig. Archie Craig. Our ACC has spoken about you on several occasions. You pulled one out of the bag for him once when he was DCS in East Midlands. He still doesn't know how you did it."

"How do you do, Mr Craig. This is my colleague DCI Green who is also SSCO at the Yard."

Craig grinned. "Mr Fillingham's mentioned you, too. Says you've got a memory like an elephant and a turn of phrase that would melt a crowbar."

"Thanks," said Green. "How is Caspar Fillingham these days? Still dribbling down his chin when he gets het up, or has he had his china clappers fixed like I told him?"

Craig laughed heartily. "You see, you remember. Yes, he still dribbles a bit. But it isn't his teeth as I understand it. Apparently he's got over-active glands in the mucous membrane round the outside of his gums, so he produces a lot of spittle outside his teeth which he can't swallow without opening and closing his mouth like a goldfish. If he forgets, he runs over."

"Bad luck, that. What happens if his missus puts a mouth-watering bit of dinner down in front of him? Does he drown?"

"Lord knows. But as I was saying, he's always on about you people and how you baffled him even though he listened to the trial and the continuation of evidence was all there. He'll be tickled pink when I tell him you've come to lecture us, Mr Masters."

"The case . . . " began Masters.

"He said his people had got bogged down in mistaken identities and you showed them how the trick had been worked."

"Ah, yes. I remember now. Would you like a drink, Mr Craig?"

"I came over to invite you to have one. Finish that off. . . . "

"Ta!" said Green, handing over his tankard. "I'm a guest here, so I can't stand my corner, otherwise I would oblige. But as I've always said, Freeman's is the best ale you can get and being here proves my point."

Craig put the glasses on the bar and gave the order. "Why are you here, actually, Mr Green?"

"Holiday," said Green laconically. "His nibs here, and his missus, have got a nice quarter for a month or two, so they invited me and my missus down for a few days for the good of our health. And talking of good health . . . " He raised his refilled tankard.

"Cheers. You're gazing about, Mr Masters. Are you looking for somebody in particular."

"I'm looking to see how many I recognise. There's just one, I think. He's in the card school at the moment. But I understand I'll be lecturing to some foreign students, too. I was trying to identify them. There must be five or six here by my reckoning."

"That'd be about right. The coloured one is from the Caribbean, the brownish one from Delhi, there's an Aussie here, too, and . . . let me see . . . yes, that chap in the blue shirt is Norwegian, the one talking to him is a Dane, I think, then there's a German talking to the woman—she's a Chief Inspector by the way—the one in the yellow sweater is from Brussels . . . "

"No Swedes or Dutch?" asked Green, as though only mildly interested.

"Definitely no Swedes. But Dutch . . . yes, there's Andriessen, he's from the Netherlands. You'd soon get to know him. The bar had to lay in a stock of special gin for him. Yellow stuff. See, he's got it in his hand."

Masters grinned inwardly. Of course. How to tell a Dutchman in a bar. Hollands gin, Bols, Primrose, Geneva . . . He was brought back to earth by Green asking if there were any other lecturers present.

"Only two," replied Craig. "They live here permanently, you see, so I suppose they're more housebound than us temporary residents."

"Here, Archie, lad," said Green, as if struck by a sudden thought. "If you're going to keep his nibs company for a bit, I think I'll wander about. You never can tell, I might see somebody I know who'll buy me another drink."

Recognising Green's tactics, Masters turned his back on the room and leant on the bar. Craig sided him, and the two were soon deep in a conversation which was mainly shop, interrupted by the need for Masters to order a refill for them both. Shortly after this, a newcomer joined them and then a fourth strolled in and spoke as he bought his drink. Masters realised that at this hour in the evening there could be a little rush of custom at the bar as students who had been studying decided to come for a drink before closing time. He found himself the centre of a little knot of interested strangers, most of whom knew something of his previous exploits and all of whom had heard of his most recent, much publicised, case which had culminated in his being wounded. They seemed anxious to talk about much of what he had done and how he had gone about it, but he did his best to head them off with the excuse that were he to answer their questions at that time he would be pre-empting what he had to say in his lectures. It came as a relief when Green came and rescued him.

"One of our foreign friends would like to meet you, George. In the interest of international relations I think you'd better have a word."

Making his excuses to those round about him, Masters followed Green across the room to where a biggish, round-faced man with short-cropped hair was standing alone.

"Detective Chief Superintendent Andriessen of the Netherlands," said Green, introducing him.

The two shook hands.

"I've been telling Robbert that the Yard has given you a sort of sabbatical, George. Just for a couple of months."

"Not quite a sabbatical, eh?" asked Andriessen. "Not when you have to come here to work."

"A few lectures," replied Masters. "Mostly concerning my own work and as, like most people, I can go on talking for ever about myself, I shan't have too much preparation to do."

"That cannot be so. You have a reputation for exact detail, Mr Masters. You will need to have it all ready for your own satisfaction."

"I have my detective sergeant with me to do the spadework."

"Spadework? Digging?"

"In a sense, yes, in so far as he will be digging up facts and figures for me, but I meant the actual physical preparation of anything I may need."

"I have it. Spadework. I will remember the word."

"Very much like the dull routine of police work."

"Yes. I understand. But I am told you do not employ routine. You are unorthodox, yes?"

"Only because the cases we are called to investigate are usually ones where too much routine is unlikely to provide the answer. The cases themselves dictate the method to be adopted."

"I understand this. You have a saying about the long arm of the law. It can reach everywhere, but the hand at the end of the arm does not always know what it is to pick up. Yes?"

Masters grinned. Green said: "Bang on, Robbert."

Andriessen laughed. "I have hit the coconut, yes?"

"Yes. The hand often needs a bit of extra guidance before it can make the right choice."

"And you have not been asked to give the much-wanted guidance to the hand that is trying to pick out who has abducted the boy close to the College?"

Masters glanced at Green before replying. Andriessen noticed the hesitation. "You are here for that purpose?"

"No. Definitely not. The local police have not seen fit to ask for our help, and unless they do ask, we cannot interfere. But I hesitated before answering because Bill Green and I were discussing what little we have heard about the case earlier this evening. But we have none of the facts, nor have we seen the files, so we were unable to reach any conclusions."

"I am suspected," said Andriessen, simply.

"You are? Why?"

"This is the second time a youth has been abducted. Five years ago it happened, too. I was here five years ago and I am here now."

"So what?" said Green. "I expect at least a dozen people would be here both times. Staff, tutors, workers . . . probably far more than a dozen."

"It is said my motor cars were seen. My DAF five years ago and my Volvo now."

"Seen where?" demanded Masters. "Surely not at the scene of either crime, because as I understand it, the local police do not know exactly where this last boy disappeared. I suspect the same applies to the first case."

"In the vicinity. On the roads where the boys would be."

"And were they?"

"No. You must understand I did not know about the first case until now. I went home before my DAF was found. It is only now when I have come back that I have learned of this. And now my Volvo was seen."

In his excitement, Andriessen's command of English was slipping a bit.

"You said your motor cars were not on the roads at the time of the disappearances, Mr Andriessen. Surely you can prove that."

"I cannot. When one is having a bath one is alone. One has no alibi."

"Are you talking about the second case?"

"Oh, yes. I cannot remember from five years what I am doing at any time."

"Quite. But what you have told me is not sufficient evidence for the local police to suspect you. Naturally, they would have you in mind, because of the sightings of motor cars. But beyond that they cannot go without harder evidence. Have they examined your motor car?"

"Yes. With others."

"With what result?"

"They found nothing, but they were suspicious because the car had been cleaned."

"Do you clean your car a lot?"

"I do. I have a pride. My wife, she insists it is cleaned very much."

"You're married?"

"With two little daughters. I have them with me." Andriessen took out his wallet. In it were two or three snaps. He handed one to Masters. A coloured shot of a flaxen haired woman, buxom and smiling, holding miniature replicas of herself by each hand. "My three ... how would you say it? Pretty things?"

"That's a very good description," said Masters, handing the photograph to Green. "It's a fine family you've got there."

"You have children?"

"One small son. A toddler."

83

"Nice," said Green, returning the photograph. "They must be missing you while you are away."

"And I miss them. We all write letters each day."

"Well," said Masters, "please don't get too worried about any suspicions the local police may have about you. As I said, I know very little about the case, but without more evidence to go on I don't think they can do very much about you."

"They will wish to question me, yes? To take me to their police station?"

"Not unless they know something more than you have told me."

"There is nothing more. I would have said to the Commandant that I will go to their station and answer their questions, but my wife and my daughters . . . the newspapers and the television, they would get to know. How do they say it? A man is helping the police with their enquiries. He has been inside for five hours. He is a Detective Chief Superintendent from Holland. How it would seem to my wife? Our newspapers would say the same as yours."

"Don't volunteer to go to the police station," counselled Masters. "The publicity would be devastating to you and your family. However, if you feel you must confront the local police, ask the Commandant to invite them here to speak to you. In the privacy of his office."

"You advise me to do that?"

"It would take the wind out of their sails," said Green. "To be invited to interview you, I mean."

"Do I do this?"

"I don't advise it," said Masters firmly, "not unless, as I said a moment ago, you feel compelled to meet them. Don't let them think that you have the fact that you are suspected in your mind. To some people, particularly when they are at their wit's end in a search for evidence, it would be an indication that you have a guilty conscience."

"I will take your advice."

"Do more than that," said Masters. "Promise to come to either Bill Green or myself if you get into any trouble, or are worried, or think of something you would like us to know.

We have nothing whatever to do with this case, but we are policemen, and it is every policeman's duty to interest himself in justice and the law."

"Are you saying you will help me?"

"Only you can answer that, Mr Andriessen."

"I do not understand what you are meaning."

"Should we do anything in this case—remembering that it is none of our business officially—it will be to help the local police find the proper answer. That means helping to discover the guilty party as well as protecting the innocent."

"I understand now. You are saying that only I know if I am guilty or if I am innocent."

"Absolutely right. You, in your own country, would take exactly the same attitude. You would help the innocent to the utmost of your powers, but you would also do what you could to discover the criminal."

"That is right. Your attitude is very correct. However, I should like to say to you that I know nothing of these affairs."

"And we shall believe you, unless something happens to make us think otherwise."

Andriessen smiled. "It is the good way. You say innocent until proved guilty. There are those who do it . . . do you say, in reverse?"

"The reverse way, yes. We shall meet again Mr Andriessen, and I can assure you that though we are not investigating this case, we shall take as much interest in it as we are permitted. But I must ask you not to tell anyone of our interest, because if it were to come to the ears of the local detectives they would have cause for complaint, and I would be guilty of contravening professional ethics."

"I understand. I shall say nothing. But you English, you have your little rules which are pleasant to know about, but which sometimes get in the way of what you could do for better work."

Masters smiled. "Maybe so. But at least this particular little rule enables you to talk to us privately, whereas if we were all one big force, none of us would be approachable in this way."

Andreissen shrugged. "I am happy about it. I am now happier than before. Thank you."

"Think nothing of it, Robbert," said Green airily.

"We sat up for you," said Wanda, "though you've been gone much longer than you thought you would be."

Masters kissed her upturned face. "That's because we struck oil, sweetheart. Bill did the initial survey and then things went our way."

"Can you tell us how?"

"It's difficult to be dogmatic about this," said Green, "but both George and I reckon we've been talking to an innocent man."

"Mr Andriessen?"

"The same, love. He's a nice, family bloke, with two smashing little girls. Real little blonde Dutch dolls."

"Wouldn't that alone argue against . . . "

"Not entirely, darling," replied Masters. "There are ambivalent characters around, but it is certainly a point in his favour. However, the man's whole demeanour was that of an innocent man. I know I'd be the first to argue that nobody can judge guilt or innocence simply by taking part in a conversation, but a man who has to argue his case in an alien tongue in a foreign country is at a serious disadvantage, I'd have said."

"So would I," said Green. "But he came through it white as white in my opinion."

"I'm glad."

"So are we, love. It's no joke being asked to help prove a guilty man innocent."

"Mr Locke was certain of his innocence."

"True, love. But George and I like to judge for ourselves. Bobby Locke, being a Dean of Studies, hasn't had quite as much practice at it as we have."

Doris asked, innocently: "Do you and George go round assessing everybody all the time? If so, Wanda and I hadn't better get up to anything."

"It doesn't apply, my dear," said Masters. "It's a question of on parade, on parade, off parade, off parade. We just don't

86

operate in the same way at home. So if you and Wanda have any little subterfuges . . . "

"Oh, I'm sure we haven't."

Masters laughed. "In that case, you're not the women Bill and I thought you were."

Chapter 4

MASTERS MOUNTED THE podium in the small lecture room the next morning at nine o'clock.

The room was supposed to hold thirty-five people and Masters had been expecting something less than this number. As it was, the room was overcrowded, with some people occupying chairs that had been moved in for the purpose. Locke and three or four others whom Masters took to be members of the academic staff were seated level with the podium facing inwards from the side wall.

He looked round slowly, with a faint smile. Then:

"Ladies and gentlemen, these sessions of mine are mere substitutes for the real thing so, please, even though I may from time to time cast a few pearls, remember that as a stand-in lecturer I am little more than a promising hysteric (laughter) wondering how he came to be here.

"The purpose of my lectures will be twofold. First, practical detection and second, co-operation between forces. As time goes by we shall, I hope, discuss both subjects in some depth. Before doing so, however, and as a preliminary to both aspects, I propose to touch on a number of general points so that we shall all understand each other later on."

"Promising hysteric or not," whispered the man sitting next to Locke, "he's got no notes with him."

Masters paused a moment to look around the room and then suddenly pointed to an officer sitting behind one of the front row tables.

"You, sir. Please continue to look at me, straight in the eye. That's right. Now, tell me, what colour are the socks you are wearing this morning? No, don't look down. What colour?"

"Grey—I think."

"Grey, you think. Are you agile enough to stand on the

88

table, using your chair as a mounting block? Yes, please, get up, and raise the bottoms of the legs of your trousers just a few inches so that everybody can see."

There was a ripple of amusement at the display. The officer held his pose for a moment and then descended.

"Thank you. How many of those present would describe the hosiery just modelled as grey or even 'grey I think'?"

"Nobody?" Masters pointed at one of the three women present. She was sitting some way back in the classroom. "You, madam. Are you wearing lipstick?"

"Yes, sir."

"What colour?"

"Coral pink."

"That sounds very definite. Not, 'Coral pink, I think'?"

"No."

"Excellent. Is your lipstick in the handbag you have with you? No, no, don't open it to see."

"Yes."

"Better still. Do you often wear that particular shade?"

"Always. Well . . . mostly."

"For how long have you favoured it?"

"How long have I been wearing it you mean, sir?"

"Yes. For months, years? How long?"

"At a guess I would say five years, probably sir."

"We'll accept five. Please tell me, without looking at it, the shade number or colour code on the bottom of the lipstick container."

The woman bit her lip and reddened.

"Have I stumped you?"

"Yes, sir."

Masters looked round and picked on a young-looking CID officer. "You, sir. Please tell me why I am on a winner as far as lipstick is concerned."

"Well, sir, first off, Inspector Collis didn't know the number, so whatever it is, you've won the guessing game."

"Good. And?"

"And what, sir?"

Masters glanced round. "Anybody, please?"

A grey-haired officer replied: "even if there isn't a shade

number there you'll have won a point because she didn't know there wasn't one."

"Thank you. Exactly what I wanted to hear." He turned to Inspector Collis. "May we please know in which way I won?"

The little lipstick tube came out of the bag. "'HN 154', sir."

"Thank you, Inspector Collis. The lesson to be learned from these games is that even a highly trained CID officer cannot remember the colour of the socks he put on scarcely two hours ago, and Inspector Collis, who has freely admitted handling that tube of lipstick every day for five years cannot remember a simple number such as HN 154. Yet she, too, is a trained observer."

"I dressed in the dark," said the discomfited CID man, with a grin at Masters.

"Then, sir, you are even more at fault. You guessed, instead of frankly admitting you did not know. But your attempt to play the percentage game is another useful lesson which we shall come to shortly."

Masters eased one buttock on to the wing of the upright desk on the podium.

"I have not yet been here three days, but I have listened avidly to all those of you I have been lucky enough to talk to. I have received a warm welcome, for which I am grateful, and have undergone a good deal of questioning, for which I am equally grateful. Not because I particularly enjoy answering questions, but because they have shown me the way many of you feel about the way I act and think.

"Some of you apparently believe I am here to preach heresy because you regard me as an unorthodox operator who pays scant attention to the basic principles of investigation laid down here and at other training establishments. Nothing could be further ·from the truth. What I am here to say is that those basic principles are vital and common to all of us. In addition, all of us have it within ourselves to add a personal and extra dimension to what we are taught. We build on the foundation we lay down here and we make the best possible use of whatever bricks and mortar come to hand thereafter.

"Just briefly, let us think of an incident centre. I have been accused of never using one. The reverse is the truth. I always use one. Probably not a pretty set-up in a church hall with phones and files and officers cross-referencing reports. Those are excellent when there are large bodies of investigators to control or the reports of a widespread house-to-house to collate. But though they will yield valuable information on times, dates, names, car numbers and all such verifiable facts, they rarely produce a complete answer, no matter how efficiently run. What goes into an incident centre comes out of it, just as with a computer. But just consider a moment. If within this room—where is gathered, possibly, the biggest slice of investigative talent in any one place anywhere in the world at this moment—we cannot be sure of the colour of a pair of socks put on two hours ago or the number on a lipstick used every day for five years, just how accurate is the information that is fed into an incident centre going to be?

"So often, ladies and gentlemen, you have to use young, raw, inexperienced officers to go and ask your questions for you. I would not wish to belittle the evidence they gather or their intelligence, but I would doubt their ability to draw out of untrustworthy witnesses every fact we should hope to get. That is my only point. Witnesses are not reliable, just as police officers have failing memories and faulty powers of observation as we have seen today. So, to make up for any deficiencies in our basic principles, we have to add something extra. Something personal, something idiosyncratic, something unorthodox if you like.

"My unorthodoxy lies, quite simply, in training my team of four people to work in exactly the same way as those manning an incident centre. A mini incident centre. It takes time, training, and even a judicious choice of personnel to achieve what I have done. But that is my way of working. Others may have a different approach, but whatever their chosen method, it must be sufficiently flexible to meet the needs of many different types of investigation. My incident centre has that flexibility. Many of our cases are, as you know, out of London, so we must be small enough to travel, but we can, if the need arises, add to our numbers from among the local personnel who have asked for our help.

"I have worked up a special way of reporting. Everybody involved in a case, of whatever rank, is told everything. At the end of every day, or at lunchtime or whenever, everybody involved reports directly to everybody else who is involved. If I, as the DCS in charge of a case, borrow a WPC merely to act as guide in some unfamiliar town, that WPC becomes part of the team and has to play her part. She has to report in public and she is reported to. Whenever necessary we use notes, of course, but we have attempted to perfect total recall. I want my Detective Sergeants to talk to me, not to do a reading test. No notes contain the fact that a woman when interviewed took out a handkerchief and wiped her eyes, but I expect to be told that, and that her husband likes sweet coffee but uses tablets in preference to sugar."

Masters looked round. "Some of you are smiling, some look sceptical. Ladies and gentlemen, within a few days I shall be telling you how we successfully solved a case of murder by knowing that a man used saccharin tablets in his coffee instead of sugar. Perhaps that will drive the point home more effectively than I appear to have managed to do so far."

Masters grinned. "Don't be embarrassed at my unorthodoxy, please. I am using it to illustrate what I wish to convey. Maybe some of you will have heard an accountant defined as a man who stays aloof from the battle and then, after the ceasefire, attacks the wounded. We are similar. We don't attack the wounded protagonists, but we do rob them. By the time we arrive, the battle is usually over, the crime has been committed. We rob the corpse of every fact it can yield and then we turn to the other participants and hold them to ransom for every fact, clue, hint, nuance or motive that we can squeeze out of them. Then we use what we get for our own purposes. Those facts, etcetera, could include a report that a man uses saccharin in coffee or—dare I labour the point?—that a man was wearing fawn socks instead of grey or a woman couldn't tell the number of her lipstick.

"So, we aim for total recall of all detail, and verbal reports are made to everybody, just as if they were being filed in an incident room ledger for people to come in and read.

"Then, each evening, we brainstorm. Again, it involves everybody, not just the senior officers on the case. Everybody present is expected to participate. The most difficult thing is to make people not accustomed to brainstorming speak up and overcome the fear of feeling foolish. Nothing, no matter who says it, is ever foolish at a brainstorming session."

Masters suddenly turned to his left to face Reed who was sitting in the corner of the room, behind the podium.

"Sergeant Reed."

"Yes, Chief?"

"The witness you interviewed this morning who said he was wearing grey socks, but was wearing fawn, and then tried to excuse his wrong answer by saying he dressed in the dark. What about him?"

"There's something fishy about the chap, Chief."

Laughter.

Reed ploughed on.

"If you ask me, Chief, we should consider several things about him. First off, his claim that he dressed in the dark can't be true. By the time he got up at half past seven it was already daylight, and we know that his bedroom couldn't have been dark because his missus insists on sleeping with the curtains open."

"What do you deduce from that?"

"That if he did dress in the dark, he was up much earlier than he claims he was, or else he was sleeping with a woman, not his wife, who likes the curtains shut overnight."

Laughter. Reed paused for it to die away.

"Either way I reckon we've got him, Chief. If he got up while it was still dark, it would have to be for a good reason, like going out to clout the dead bloke over the head. The quacks say he died about five o'clock—as near as they can say. It was still dark at five."

"Is that it?"

"No, Chief. Quite a bit more actually. Say he made the mistake about the colour of his socks not because he dressed in the dark, but because he actually did put grey socks on earlier, went out to clobber his man, and then came back and changed his socks and shoes. He'd have to, Chief, because the long grass between his house and the location of the body was wringing wet. So he changed both socks and shoes and forgot that the second pair of socks was fawn, not the grey he originally put on. I reckon we should look through the dirty linen basket there before anybody washes them. And look at his shoes. There's a patch or two of soil about the area. If he's cleaned his shoes, have forensic look at his shoe cleaning kit for traces of similar soil."

"Good point."

"I reckon it is, Chief, because if that's not what he did, then he at least had somebody other than his missus in his bedroom with him."

"The Collis woman?"

"Yes, Chief. I had my doubts about her as soon as I called at the house. She was wearing the wrong colour make-up. She's very dark, Chief, but had this pale pink on her lips, the sort of thing you'd expect a blonde to wear. So I reckon Collis was there, and not the wife. Moreover, Chief, I reckon she'd lost her handbag—which we ought to look for—because she had to use the make-up on his wife's dressing table."

"Which you reckon was wrong?"

"Yes, Chief. Of course Collis will claim she's been using that shade for years, but if we could send a couple of WPCs round the two local chemists' shops, we might learn different."

"So Collis was in it with him?"

"I don't say she actively helped to kill the chap, Chief, but I think she could have been aiding him. We could find out if Collis always sleeps with the curtains drawn shut. It would be a pointer. And that would help to explain why we haven't met the wife. We'll probably find she's disappeared, Chief, as opposed to just having taken a trip to London for the day as we've been told."

Masters stopped Reed there, with a word of thanks, and turned to the class. He picked out another CID man. "You, sir. Was that all nonsense?"

The man referred to looked bewildered. "I've got to say it wasn't, sir, but I can't believe it."

94

"What in particular can't you believe?"

"Not the sergeant's suggestions, sir, but the fact that he could make them. If his piece wasn't rehearsed beforehand . . . "

"Which I assure you it wasn't. In fact I did not even tell Reed that I would call upon him, and I certainly knew nothing about grey and fawn socks and coral pink lipstick before entering this room."

"That's just it, sir. Inspector Collis and Chief Inspector Dooley entered this room as innocent students and now they're almost in the dock on a murder charge."

"Wrongly?"

"I would have said so, yes."

"So you propose to ignore completely any relevant point Sergeant Reed made?"

"No, sir."

"So their names are still in the frame?"

"Yes, they've got to be."

"So Reed was not talking total nonsense?"

"What he said has to be proved or disproved."

"Worthy of further investigation, in fact?"

"Yes, sir."

"To keep the investigation moving?"

"Yes, sir."

"Very well. It is the end of the working day and you don't want to send anybody out at so late an hour to test Reed's suggestions on the ground. You are brainstorming. It's your turn to speak. What do you say?"

"Nothing, sir. I know nothing about this crime."

"No? A man died at five o'clock in the morning across a field from where the Dooleys live. He was killed by a blunt instrument. You are beginning to suspect Dooley. The woman, Collis, has entered the scene. You are DS Smith, and at this point you have to contribute. Anything."

The student began slowly. "Is Collis married? If so, where's her husband? We haven't been able to identify the dead man. Could he be Mr Collis? We ought to check that. Or to see if there is any known connection between him and Dooley and Collis. . . . "

"Or?"

"Or what, sir?"

"Or between the dead man and Mrs Dooley."

"Oh, yes."

"Think, please, all of you. The demand of the prospect of having to contribute to brainstorming gradually causes every member of the team to think about his case at all times. He doesn't just do the job he's told to do. That's training, gentlemen. However, we'll leave that case now, and return to where we were before Reed gave us his thoughts on the matter. Just remember this . . . "

Masters picked up a piece of chalk, and on the board behind him drew two precisely similar rectangles. "Those are boxes of chocolates, ladies and gentlemen. Very similar. In fact neither has the edge on the other for weight, taste, quality, price or availability. You are faced with the task of promoting and selling more of box A than your competitors can sell of box B. How do you go about it? May I call on you, madam? Yes, the young lady sitting two rows behind Inspector Collis. In view of what I have said earlier, how are you going to sell millions of product A while the manufacturers of B go broke?"

"My name is Bettany, Mr Masters. Inspector Bettany."

"Thank you. Now what's your answer?"

"I believe, Mr Masters, that you will be substituting two criminal cases for your two boxes of chocolates very shortly."

"You read my mind, Inspector. Congratulations. But is this leading up to an answer?"

"Yes, sir. I can't improve the chocolates, any more than I can alter the crimes."

"Correct."

"But I can do something about what surrounds the chocolates. I think I would add a bow of ribbon to box A to make it more attractive to buyers."

"Excellent. Anything else?" As he spoke, Masters drew a bow on the top of box A.

"I would wait to see the effect the bow had on sales, but meanwhile I should be thinking up a more colourful wrapping perhaps."

Masters put polka dots of chalk on box A.

"And a selling slogan for my product. What could it be? Bettany's chocolates sweeten all occasions?"

Masters printed this carefully below the box. He turned to another male student. "Inspector Bettany touched on the next point I wish to make. Those two boxes are incident centres for similar crimes."

"Yes, sir."

"Observations, please."

"Box B is our standard incident centre, sir. Box A is that of the senior investigating officer who uses his private additional methods to enhance the value of the basic principles."

"Correct. Remember the box with the ribbon on, please, ladies and gentlemen. I would like you to hear just one example of how your methods can be enhanced—not necessarily in an incident centre—but within your own firms. My team and I were called to investigate the murders of three girls. Some weeks before their deaths a hut containing all manner of garden seeds had been broken into and the seeds mixed up. The local uniform branch was informed and judged it to be the work of vandals—youths—who would never be caught. They had apparently stolen nothing, and such incidents were happening a dozen times a day. The uniform men did not inform their CID—the case was too minor—and the CID people did not bother to read the incident book report. Six weeks later when I arrived, I had to ferret that fact out for myself and it gave us the clue to the murderer's identity."

Masters looked around. "Please make sure that everybody at all times is informed of crimes, however trivial, that occur in your area. A failure of communication in that particular force almost resulted in the escape of a triple murderer.

"I have mentioned this only as another example of how to put the bow of ribbon on the box. Students in Squad C will please prepare for me by next Monday, a paper on their suggestions for adding further ribbons to boxes. I don't want essays. I want lists with explanatory notes. As a guide, I shall need a minimum of six suggestions. There will be no maximum. There can be collusion between pairs of students.

No more than two to collaborate. Papers will name both collaborators should you decide to co-operate with a colleague."

Masters glanced at his watch.

"We shall shortly start a ten-minute break. Before we do so, however, I should like to warn you that after we reassemble we shall discuss, first of all, the part played by coincidences in detection, bearing in mind that, besides meaning exact correspondence between two events in substance, nature, character etcetera, the word also means contemporaneity as well as concurrence in things like opinions, sentiment, thought and so on. Please prepare your thoughts on the matter for when we start again.

"For the members of the senior course who are present, please make a note of this quotation. 'An air of comfortable commonsense, of dependability, which makes it seem natural to confide in him.' We shall discuss that also, but I should like a paper from each of you on that subject and how it applies to our handling of witnesses, suspects and the like. I will assure you that I do not consider it to be an airy-fairy subject, but one of the most important in the success of a policeman's working life. Please treat it as such.

"Now we can break. Please reassemble at ten-fifteen."

Masters stepped down from the dais. Locke rose to meet him.

"That'll larn 'em," he said.

"They'll get used to me."

"I hope so. I won't say what I think about your style or the content of your lecture, but I will just add that I have an appointment fixed for half past ten. I am about to put it off for an hour. I shall be back by the time you restart."

"That could be a compliment or an indication that you . . ."

"I'm too old to listen to many lectures, George. I shall attend as many of yours as I can. Make what you like of that. But come and see me at half past two this afternoon."

Locke left him. Reed came up. "Went well, Chief."

"Well?" demanded the man who had sat next to Locke. "Never a note in sight and you two put on a performance like

98

that! And I mean performance. Congratulations, Mr Masters. You're making them sit up and take an interest."

"Thank you."

The session was over at half past eleven. The students had a further hour's session from another lecturer before lunch. "Military Aid to Civil Authority." At one time nobody would have contemplated such an issue. In view of the trouble in Northern Ireland and, indeed, certain events in the streets of London, together with the possibility of having to ring centres like Heathrow with troops, the problem was now ever present. A thorny, ticklish problem which the police, with prime responsibility on such occasions, had to take very seriously.

By about twenty past twelve, Masters declared himself ready to return to the house. He invited Reed along for a drink before lunch. The walk took only a minute or two, but even so, Green and Berger had arrived before them.

"How did it go, darling?" asked Wanda. "I was keeping my fingers crossed for you."

"I felt quite satisfied," replied her husband. "Not necessarily with the content, but I think, with Reed's help, I managed to put it over in a somewhat different way."

"How d'you mean?" asked Green.

"He kept them on their toes," said Reed. "I don't know what they expected, but you should have seen Inspector Collis's face when the Chief asked for the number of the lipstick. . . . "

"Lipstick?" demanded Green. "Whose lipstick?"

"Inspector Collis is a woman," said Reed. "And there was a chap there who didn't know what colour socks he was wearing and the Chief had him standing on the table. . . . "

"Sounds like a kids' party to me," growled Green.

"That's what the Chief meant. As a lecture it was different."

"And everybody loved it, I suppose?"

"They lapped it up."

"I know. His nibs got up there and in his own inimitable way showed that lot that they are the biggest crowd of dim-witted numbskulls it would be possible to meet in a month of Sundays and they took it."

"Come to think of it . . . "

"It's his way, lad," said Green sadly.

Berger said, "The Chief's way or not, I'd have liked to have been there."

"No room," said Reed. "They were jam-packed. Extra chairs and standing room only."

"Sounds more like a pantomime than a serious lecture," said Green.

"William," said Wanda, "what's the matter?"

"Matter, love?"

"Yes. You're grumpy. Has something gone wrong?"

"Nobody's offered me a drink yet."

Masters moved across to the trolley that held the drinks. "Sorry, Bill. I'm falling down on my duty-steward's duties."

"Serve the drinks, darling," said Wanda, "but that is not what is upsetting William. He's umpty. He knows he could have helped himself to a beer, so what's causing him to be so fratchety?"

"Don't ask me, poppet."

"William?"

"I've had a bad morning," confessed Green, plonking himself in an armchair.

"Serious?" demanded Masters, handing him a tankard.

"Local rozzers," grunted Green. "Berger and I were using the car . . . " He gestured with one hand. "We were pootling, George. I had Berger drive along this entrance road here to see if anybody coming in the opposite direction could see who was at the wheel. You know how it is. Unless you've got X-ray eyes or something, very often you can't see through a windscreen. Not properly. Not to recognise people. Then we went out on to the road and tested those timings. Picking up, setting down, driving into the trees and so on."

"Doing a good job of work, in fact. Testing timings and distances and the like."

Green nodded. "Then the local filth swooped. They said they'd had us under observation for an hour and we'd been acting suspiciously." He looked up. "They're pretty desperate, George. They'd had plain-clothes blokes on motor cycles and

100

in cars keeping obbo on us and wirelessing everything we did to one another."

"Then what?"

"They took us in."

"They did what?"

"To a nick about three miles away. I can tell you I wasn't best pleased."

"But surely," said Doris, "you had your identity cards with you?"

"I didn't want to use them," said Green. "We're working undercover."

"What happened?" asked Masters.

Green flushed angrily. "A DS at that nick asked me if I liked little boys."

"William!"

"It's OK, love. But I was in a spot, you see. I hadn't been able to talk to Berger, because one of them was in our car. And when we got to the nick they separated us. So I had no way of telling what line the lad was taking, except I knew he would keep quiet about what we'd been doing."

"Was their line simply that you had been acting suspiciously?"

"I reckon so, but as I said, they're desperate. They threatened to fling the book at me and told me I'd make it easier for myself if I confessed and all that rubbish."

"Confessed to what, exactly?"

"Abducting a lad, murdering him and disposing of his body."

Masters stood up and took a restless step or two before saying: "Bill, I honestly don't get this. The boy disappeared several weeks ago. How could they possibly link the activities of yourself and Berger, this morning, with that event?"

"Search me, George. I suppose they've got the idea into their tiny minds that the murderer always returns to the scene of the crime."

"Even so, if they had been keeping an eye on you for as long a time as they said . . . "

"I think they had. They knew our movements."

"Right. Driving up and down the road immediately outside this house and then down on to the main road . . . "

"With me acting the part of the lad, Berger the driver. Picking me up, entering woods, setting me down, coming back. We went through it several times, working against the stopwatch."

"Could it have looked suspicious, darling?" asked Wanda.

"No," said her husband flatly. "Not in connection with the crime of some weeks ago. At least, not enough to take two people in for questioning and trying to bludgeon a confession out of them."

"William said they could give no very good reason for their actions. Wouldn't that be suspicious?"

Masters looked at his wife. "There, I must admit, I would have been interested. But that presupposes I had taken them in for questioning in the first place."

"And you wouldn't have done that?"

"No, because I would have had no reason to. I would have instructed my men to get detailed descriptions of Bill and Sergeant Berger, and of their car. I would have checked the ownership of the car—by its number—and continued to keep close observation, even following the car back to wherever it came from or was going to. In other words, I would have got far more information by not taking Bill and Berger in." He swung round to Green. "If they'd bothered to check the car, they'd have found that it was one of the Yard's unmarked vehicles. Did they do that?"

Green looked sheepish. "Sorry, George, it let the cat out of the bag. They threatened to do me for pinching a police car. So I then had to tell them we were Yard men."

"Not to worry, Bill."

"I'd thought up the story by then."

"What?"

"That we were out doing a recce for one of your lectures. Timings and so on for a case you were cooking up for the students."

"That sounds very reasonable," said Doris.

"Reasonable, love, but not very satisfactory to the locals."

"Why not?"

"Because they said I'd led them up the garden path by not saying straight away what we were on. They sounded off about if that was a sample of Yard co-operation how could we expect the public to co-operate? And a lot of bilge like that."

Masters grinned. "Had you given them a bad time when they were interviewing you, Bill?"

"Not so's you'd notice. I gave them my full name, age, address and so on, and I warned them I'd got a very good memory and demonstrated it by quoting back at them everything they'd said up to that point."

"But they ploughed on regardless?"

"George, I've always thought you went a bit over the score in your treatment of suspects. You're always preaching the gentle, courteous handling of people. Now I realise fully what you've been on about over the years. But I want the chance to make an exception to your rules. I can't take people in these days, since I'm technically retired, so couldn't you—as a kindness to me—think up some good excuse for bringing in that DS, and his mate the DC, and then letting me have a quarter of an hour alone with them?"

Masters grinned. "Sorry, Bill. The only kindness I can do you right now is to give you another drink and to thank you, and Berger, of course."

"Thank me? Why?"

As Masters poured the beer, he explained. "First for preserving, at some inconvenience to yourself, the true nature of your activities. Second, for the explanation about working for me on the Staff College solution of some hypothetical case. Third, for—in so far as we are to some degree in competition with them—getting to know how the opposition is operating and with how little apparent success. Fourth . . ."

"Go on," urged Wanda.

"The contact you have made and the treatment you have received gives me the excuse as senior officer of the team to approach them and demand to know what's going on. The form of approach can be anything we wish. Conciliatory, angry, up to the top . . . should we feel the need to get next to them we can do it any way we decide."

103

"You're saying I've put the mockers on them?"

"Shall we say you caused them to make a mistake and sometimes mistakes have to be paid for."

"I might have known you'd have seen some way to turn it to our advantage."

"Not too fast, Bill. It's an ace up the sleeve. It could be that there will be no need to play it."

Green shrugged and turned to Wanda. "Sorry to have been so . . . what was it? . . . umpty, love. I was feeling a bit miffed."

"I should just think you were, William. But the way you must look at it is that it demonstrates how very superior your methods are in comparison with those of other people. I suspect those involved are even now wondering what sort of a rocket they are going to get from their own senior officers—via George—for making such a bloomer as to take in for questioning two innocent members of an illustrious Yard team."

"Nice of you to say that, love. I could do with another . . . thanks, same again, please."

Because of the lengthy discussion with Green at lunchtime, Masters was late in setting out for his two-thirty appointment with Locke. As he hurried from the house into the College grounds proper and made towards the Administrative block, he heard his name called, and Inspector Woolgar, the quartering officer, puffed up to him from behind.

"You travel at speed, sir," said Woolgar, falling in alongside Masters and trying to match his long strides.

"When I'm in a hurry," admitted Masters.

"I wanted to see you," said Woolgar, "because Mrs Masters' car keys have been found and returned to my office."

"Good. Thank you for finding them so quickly."

"I didn't find them."

"Who did?"

"I don't know. They just appeared. We have a wooden filing tray in the general office marked FOUND in big letters. Everybody knows it's there and things that are picked up are just deposited in it. Mrs Masters' keys were there when I went in just before lunch."

"Well, whoever found them, I'm grateful. It has saved us having the bother of getting a new set."

They were approaching the main front door. "If you'd like to come along to my office now, sir, I'll get them out of the secure cupboard for you. I popped them in there for safety."

"Thank you, Mr Woolgar, but could I pick them up later as I'm already a minute or two late for a meeting with the Dean?"

Woolgar grinned. "Mr Locke won't mind, but the terrible Gertie will."

"That's exactly what I'm afraid of. I'll come along to your office after I've seen the Dean or, alternatively, if you have a free moment, you might phone Mrs Masters. She'll be very pleased and may come along to collect them herself."

"I'll do that, sir, straight after I've had a look at a ruptured downspout I'm supposed to inspect."

"Thank you."

Woolgar left him and made his way along the front of the building, presumably to see the damaged pipe round the end of the wing. Masters went through the swing door to report to Gertie.

"Sorry I'm late, sir," said Masters as he was shown into Locke's private office.

"Two minutes, George?"

"Three, actually," supplied Gertie as she closed the door on them.

"You see what I have to put up with, George?"

"Keeps you on your toes, Bobby."

"I'm past having to pirouette on other people's orders, but I suspect I'm also too old to start schooling Gertie. Have a seat, do."

Masters drew up a chair so that he sat at an angle to Locke's desk.

"I hear my missus and the Commandant's wife called on Mrs Masters."

"It was very kind of them to come and welcome her."

"It's the sociable thing to do, but from what I've heard

they enjoyed the visit. Duty call or not they found your lady delightful. And your son. I overheard them saying it's a pity you and your family are not staying longer."

Masters shrugged but did not reply to the compliment. Locke, apparently, didn't expect him to, because he immediately led off into other things.

"Your lecture this morning, George."

"Not what you were hoping for?"

"I didn't know what to expect. Nor, apparently, did some of the others present, or they'd have clued themselves up a bit beforehand. You disconcerted one or two of them."

"Is that a bad thing?"

"Not if it illustrates vividly a point you wish to put over, otherwise a sort of sheltered calm is most conducive to learning. The disconcerted mind is too busy thinking up what its owner should have done or said to attend to what it should be imbibing at the feet of the lecturer."

"Are we considering the teaching of theory or its practical application?"

Locke sat back and rested his elbows on the arms of his chair. "You've got a point. A good one. It was perfectly clear to me this morning that you believe strongly in the lively mind."

"Implicitly."

"As long as the lively mind doesn't run riot?"

"I'm not sure about that. I believe that senior police officers should have a strong sense of mental discipline which should prevent the worst excesses but never stultify the creative side of investigation. We urge our men to use their initiative. Initiative is a mental process, or the application of it. We should make sure we never cut off the top of the pyramid, because the point is what we are, after all, aiming for."

Locke considered this for a moment and then sat forward. "How long can you go on for? Talking like this, I mean?"

Masters grinned. "On my high horse, was I?"

"Shall we say astride a very sound animal? Your successes prove that, because you've passed the winning post first so very often. No, George, I was wondering if you could work up what you've just been saying into a presentation for a discussion group. I want other people to hear it."

"And then try to shoot me down?"

"Yes."

"Why?"

"Because I believe in testing concepts to the full. By using devil's advocates, if you like."

"To what end—with my particular views, that is?"

"Because, dammit," said Locke slowly, "you impressed me this morning and you're impressing me now. I liked the way you made people sit up and take notice, I liked your style and none of my team failed to notice that you spoke for the best part of two hours without a note. I, personally, found that amazing, because you were dealing with matters which most would say were mundane and so taken-for-granted that they—if dealing with them—would have exhausted each subject in two minutes flat. You made your subject assume an importance that very few people consciously accord it. That is the concept I am referring to. As you know, I was keen to get you here to help us to set up a new course in inter-force co-operation. That, too, is easy to say and most people would claim they do it, little realising that there is a mechanism to it, positive things to do other than just to pay lip-service to the idea. Now, after hearing you this morning, and this afternoon, I am seriously beginning to consider whether we should not add another dimension to our training programme. That of bringing along our young men to think and to encourage their ideas. To train them to extract every single drop of useful possibility out of every gobbet—however small—that comes their way."

Masters nodded. "We quite rightly insist on fact, fact, fact. But to me, that is the end product of thought eventually tested and found solid."

"Just so," said Locke. "That performance of your sergeant's this morning was unrehearsed, I take it?"

"Totally. In fact Reed had no inkling he would be called upon. Nor had I any prior intention of involving him." Masters grinned. "How could I? I didn't know the students wouldn't know what colour socks they were wearing."

"Just as a matter of interest, George, what would you have done if the man in question had known?"

"There'd have been something, Bobby. How many of them would have been able to give me the number of the car parked next to theirs in the car park?"

"And what would Reed have made of that?"

"Much the same. Remember he had no background information, no problem set. The mere fact that he was able to contribute at all indicates that his mind is tuned to go along any path, beating to either side, searching for hidden avenues. It takes time for someone not accustomed to doing it to become proficient, but I believe that any detective worth his salt could start making a useful contribution after very little training."

"I'd like to see you proved right."

"I had intended to demonstrate this more fully as part of the sessions you have earmarked for the moderator concept. But we can put in a preliminary session should you wish it."

Locke nodded. "I'd like that. I'll have to find the time for it." He made a note on his pad and then looked up. "That's that part of it, George. Now, Andriessen and the missing boy. Have you anything you can tell me about that?"

"A great deal, actually. No proof one way or the other, of course, as yet, but we discussed it very thoroughly yesterday afternoon, assembled our ideas and lines of investigation and have started work."

"May I know what you're about?"

"I came prepared to tell you, and to ask for your help in one or two places."

"If I can do anything. Anything at all."

Masters summarised the outcome of his team's brainstorming session, and then went on to say how Green and he had talked to Andriessen and how Green and Berger had been out on time trials.

"You move fast," said Locke. "You want me to provide lists of people here on both occasions?"

"Please."

"I can probably help with getting the Netherland's crime figures should you need me to."

108

"Thank you."

"I didn't know Andriessen had a wife and family. Hadn't thought about it in fact."

"It could be a point in his favour," said Masters. "But we can't count on it. There are aberrant characters about."

"Of course. Still . . . " Locke grinned. "You've cheered me up, George, just to hear you've started work."

"Please don't get too cheerful," counselled the Yard man. "You haven't heard everything yet."

"Trouble?"

"I don't think so, but you may be right."

"Meaning?"

"On the face of it there may appear to have been a bit of nonsense, but if we turn it to our advantage it could well prove to be of value."

"What happened?"

"Did you know that the College is, apparently, under constant surveillance by the local police?"

Locke sat up, sharply. "No, I did not," he said vehemently. "You mean they've got the place under observation the whole time?"

"Apparently."

"How did you find this out?"

"Green and Berger were doing some time tests for me. Using a Yard car and a stopwatch. Setting off from here and seeing, literally, into how many openings and rides into the woods they could get in the time available to Andriessen. Leaving the odd minute or two to stop, pick somebody up, kill them, dump them and then get back here."

"And?"

"Apart from the fact that it is fairly apparent that Andriessen couldn't have managed it, not to hide a body beyond finding?"

Locke said: "I'm glad to hear that, but this trouble you mentioned. Did the locals see them doing it?"

"Kept tabs on them for over an hour with a relay of cars and observers and then took them in for questioning."

"I don't understand. Were they breaking the law in any way?"

109

Masters shook his head. "Not even bending it ever so slightly."

"Then why were they picked up?"

"I have tried to decide that. I think the local police-mind—in its corporate version—suffered a short circuit. They have the College under observation which tells us they are suspicious about the place—presumably because Andriessen is living here. But instead of confining their attentions to one man, they appear to be ready to suspect whatever happens here, no matter who is involved or what their actions may be. Quartering the countryside in a motor car, watch in hand, may not be a usual occupation, but then neither are lots of lawful activities such as . . . well, carving large white horses on hillsides or getting married in an aeroplane."

"You did say Green and Berger were going down lanes and forest rides."

Masters waited for the Dean to continue, but the older man stopped after this observation. At last: "Are you saying, Bobby, that such activity gives grounds for suspicion?"

"There has been a murder round here and the body could be hidden down those same paths."

"Agreed, or rather, not agreed by our calculations. But what exactly did the locals suspect my two were doing? Visiting the scene of the crime?"

"Perhaps."

"Are you being serious?"

"You think they shouldn't have jumped to that conclusion?"

Masters sat back. "Apart from the fact that I don't hold with the old belief that a murderer always revisits the scene, I cannot see why any investigator should jump to any conclusion concerning Green and Berger. Would two murderers not know where they had hidden a body? Or were they suspected of having committed a further, similar crime?"

"Perhaps?"

"Perhaps? But they had no body with them. The locals knew that. They kept tabs on my two from the time they left here. So could they have been intent on hiding something,

110

although they were unable to make their minds up as to the exact hiding place? You know the answer to that, Bobby."

"Rubbish?"

"Just so. And yet they took my people to a police station nearby and advised them to make it easy for themselves by confessing to murder, asking, in the meantime, if Green liked little boys."

"Oh, no," groaned Locke.

"Oh, yes. And this can mean only one thing."

"What's that?"

"That they are desperate. That they haven't a clue."

"Grasping at straws?"

"Precisely. So our friend Andriessen could well be receiving their attention very shortly. In the situation the locals find themselves in they will feel they cannot avoid getting on to him, sooner rather than later."

"Despite anything I can say to them?"

"That is what I think. However . . . "

"Go on."

"They made a mistake this morning. And compounded it by their foolish treatment of Green. That gives me an excuse for approaching them and demanding to know what they're playing at. I could possibly make that approach in a conciliatory manner and try to head them off Andriessen."

"How?"

"Not directly, of course. But in the course of conversation I could offer my sympathy with their problem and, in a roundabout way, point out that the known timings appear to eliminate Andriessen. I could do nothing, however, about the witnesses who claim to have seen him in his car—or cars—at the vital times."

"That would cause them to hold off a bit longer, do you think?"

"It would me. But they're itching to lay their hands on somebody—anybody."

Locke nodded. "Is there anything I can do to help?"

"If we're to soft soap them . . . "

"Yes?"

"Could you invite the relevant characters round for a drink?"

Locke considered this for a moment. "Yes," he said at length. "I hesitated only because I felt I needed an excuse. I don't need one, do I? I can be quite open about it. I'll invite them in the first place in order to meet you and in the second to clear up the little misunderstanding over Green and Berger. They're certain to come with those reasons on the agenda and once they're here and we've cleared the air I can introduce the business about Andriessen. Not you, George. I'll do it and then appeal to you for your thoughts on the matter and you can trot out—off the top, as it were—the points you feel you would like to check if you were in their shoes."

"Excellent. Green will be a help there, too, even if on a somewhat more earthy plane."

"You feel you can do it?"

"I can try. Promises would be futile, because I don't know the men I'll be dealing with, but I know that if I were in their fix, I would take ideas from anybody. I'm certain of that because I do take hints from wherever they may come."

"That is what you were preaching this morning."

Masters nodded. "Some people, though, might consider it demeaning to take a tip from a Yard man. We shall have to see how your friends feel about such things."

There was a tap on the door and Gertie entered with a tray of tea. She stayed to pour them a cup each and then left.

"Tomorrow evening," said Locke, stirring his tea.

"What about it?"

"Drinks. I'll invite the locals over. Tonight would be too short notice, and in any case you're lecturing until seven."

"I am?" Masters was totally surprised. "There's nothing on my timetable about it."

"There should be." Locke got up to consult a large sheet pinned to the wall. He peered up at it for some seconds and ran his finger along one of the columns. "You're right, George. Your name hasn't been pencilled in. My mistake. Gertie wouldn't have put it in your timetable. You should have been on your feet at six in the lecture theatre."

"To say what?"

"Continuity of Evidence with the junior students. Not to worry. Skip it. I'll cancel the lecture."

"No, don't do that. At least, not unless it is part of a series on the same subject."

"It's a one-off."

"Then I should be able to manage to do that. Had it been part of a definite course I'd have had to prepare something to fit in, but I expect I can spout for an hour on that subject—if I make the students contribute their pennorth." He put his cup down. "Even so, it's getting on for four, and I would like to think about it for half an hour, so if you don't mind, Bobby, I'll push off now and make a few notes."

"To speak from?"

Masters shook his head. "Just to clarify the points to make."

Locke stood up. "Right, George. Sorry about that. I wouldn't have remembered at all except that I obviously had it in the back of my mind this morning and had resolved to attend."

Masters grinned. "Dinna fash, Bobby. No harm done, and I'm beginning to enjoy myself."

"I thought so. I'm glad you're enjoying yourself and, I need hardly add, we're enjoying having you. Now, off you go and do whatever it is you have to."

Masters left the office casually enough, but once clear he rushed away. Continuity of Evidence was basic and important. He had no wish to deal with it superficially and, contrary to the belief concerning the ease with which he could get up to lecture, he did, in fact, do a great deal of thorough preparation and thinking in readiness for the sessions he conducted. He thought about the subject as he went, and so immediately and deeply was he immersed in it that he completely forgot his promise to Woolgar to call in and collect the keys to the Jaguar.

Continuity of Evidence. Uninterrupted, unbroken sequence of information to establish each and every point in question and, further, coherence of every fact and point to prove the whole case presented in court, so that no skilled advocate

113

could find a chink in which to drive a defensive wedge. QED to be written at the end and the problem solved to the satisfaction of judge and jury . . . the tick for getting the business right. Like a sum. Not just the right answer, but the right working out to arrive at the right answer so that defence counsel could not use a red pen on it. A natural follow on, no jumps, no unproven conclusions . . . square it with circumstantial evidence . . . Masters didn't like evidence relating to or dependent on circumstances . . . adventitious, accidental, not solid . . . if this, then that . . .

He reached the house and was faintly surprised to find it empty. Green and Berger? Probably out and about on the trail. Reed, probably with them. But Wanda, Michael and Doris? They hadn't said they were going out, but the car had gone, so Wanda had probably taken the other two for a combined run in the country and shopping expedition. He wandered into the kitchen, intending to use the table as a desk. As he spread some books and papers preparatory to starting, he had to move one or two items—a small heap of newly laundered socks belonging to Michael, a half folded road map of the area, a pencil and shopping-list pad and a set of car keys for the Jaguar. It was as he was pushing this last aside that he remembersd his conversation with Woolgar. The quartering officer had obviously found time to ring Wanda and tell her the lost keys had been found and she had gone, herself, to collect them. With her own set now available, she had left his at home when taking Michael and Doris out in the car. Masters thought it was just as well he had forgotten to go to the office to collect the keys. It would have been a waste of time. He sat down, pad of paper in front of him and reached for a book of trials accounts. Somewhere here . . . he leafed through the index . . . was a case where continuity had broken down . . . what was it the judge had called it? . . . an elision? Or was it ellipsis? Anyhow, defence counsel had put his finger on the omission of something which would have been needed to prove the case completely. And the judge had stressed this. Ah, here it was. The evidence offered by the police did not satisfactorily connect . . . they had *assumed* that

114

because the dead woman had left her place of work at five-thirty she would have arrived home at ... defence had brought witnesses to say she frequently broke her journey ...

He ploughed on. A note followed by a few minutes of thought in which to think up a suitable illustration of the point. Something humorous? Bizarre, perhaps. If a woman is standing on a chair is she trying to swat a fly or escape from a mouse? It has to be proved. Dead fly on wall? Fly swat in hand? Holding her skirt close around her knees? Or has she had the unlikely experience of seeing a snake on the carpet? Signs? Proof?

He paid little attention to the time, but he had worked so conscientiously that by the time he had finished it was not yet a quarter to five. He didn't want tea. He'd had enough of that with the Dean. Fresh air? He'd spent the day indoors one way or another, and was about to spend a further hour in a stuffy lecture theatre. So fresh air it was. Just a quarter of an hour among the trees, quietly marshalling his thoughts for the coming lecture ...

He filled his pipe as he stepped out into the woods that came up close to the house. The bed of pine needles was soft to the feet. Sandy soil here, not ideal for the indigenous deciduous hardwoods. What was it he'd read recently about pine trees and their leaf mould? Acid rain! Yes, that was it. The experts who for so long had said that the acid rain which was killing fish in lakes and trees in forests was caused by industry allowing sulphurous fumes to escape into the air were being questioned. Now there was a new theory, backed by a deal of proof, that acid rain was caused by a lack of forest fires. In the old days, when forests were burned for clearing and before humans became so safety-conscious about causing fires, there was a plentiful supply of ash, alkaline in character, to neutralise the acidic properties of leaf mould. But now, rain which seeped through this mould became acid and then drained into lakes or was taken up by tree roots, doing damage formerly unknown when wood ash was there to neutralise it. The answer, said the new theorists, was not to spend billions of pounds to instal scrubbers in factory chimneys, but to spend a few hundreds scattering lime on forest floors.

He thought he could work that up as an illustration of the fallability of expert witnesses, of the possibility of conflicting proof—as both sets of theorists would claim to have proof to support their beliefs. He was musing on this, moving slowly through the trees perhaps a couple of hundred yards from the house when he heard, faintly, a car come up the approach road and then pull up. He guessed Wanda had returned home.

Slowly he started to make his way back, not hurrying. From time to time he stopped. Once to knock out his pipe and to make sure the embers were dead. A second time to examine a fallen tree and to consider the possibilities of coming out with a saw to cut it up for log fires in the house in the evenings. A third to stop and admire some early white flowers just beginning to peep through the thick floor covering. He wondered about them, not knowing what they were, or even that flowers grew in pine woods as bluebells grow under deciduous trees.

He glanced at his watch and then started to hurry back to the house. He had to inform Wanda that he was lecturing again at six and he felt the need to wash before his appearance in the theatre.

Chapter 5

"EXCELLENT," SAID LOCKE as Masters prepared to leave the lecture theatre a minute or two before seven o'clock.

"Thank you. I noticed you were sitting up high on the back tier this time, not within splashing range."

"Do you spit as you talk, George? I hadn't noticed it, but some do, you know. One chap we had here some years ago used to get little flecks of white foam at the corners of his mouth after he'd been going for a few minutes."

Masters laughed. "As far as I know I don't sprinkle even the front row."

"They wouldn't have noticed tonight even had you done so. Quite absorbing, made all the more remarkable by the fact that you had little or no time to prepare what you were going to say. I'm rapidly coming to the conclusion that you're a born lecturer, George, and that we could do worse than having you here permanently."

Masters shook his head. "You're doing just what I've been warning your students against. Jumping to conclusions."

"Erroneous ones, presumably?"

"I think so. You see, Bobby, for somebody like myself, a stint of a few weeks here is comparatively easy, if one is fairly capable of putting the stuff over. I am simply drawing on personal experience, and I can probably do so for the short time I am to be here. But ask me to prepare lectures for a year and I wouldn't be able to live off my fat. I would most certainly have to get down to a good deal of preparation. Reminiscing would not carry me through."

"I see what you mean, but the basic knowledge would still be there."

"I'm better doing my real job," replied Masters. "I prefer the practical work, much as I'm enjoying this break from it."

"You're right, of course. Your career opportunities would

be limited here, whereas at the Yard . . . what's the next step there, George? Commander?"

"I honestly don't know. It could be, of course."

"Meaning you expect to fly a little higher than that?"

"Meaning nothing at all. For the moment, administration does not appeal to me."

Locke nodded his appreciation of this point and then looked at his watch. "I've been holding you up, George. You'll be wanting to get back to your lovely wife and supper."

"Always that. But I also want to hear what Bill Green has to say. He hadn't got back to the house by the time I left to come over. We mustn't forget our other purpose for being here, you know."

"I'm really grateful for what you're doing. You know that. Now, be off with you. I'll see you tomorrow."

Masters walked to the house in the last of the light. He wished he could feel as sanguine as Locke appeared to be concerning Andriessen. He found it disturbing that the Dean should believe him capable of so solving the problem of the disappearance of two youths that, without any official involvement in the case, he could free Andriessen from suspicion. He felt that he himself had probably been guilty of leading Locke to believe that, somehow, it could be done. In fact, Green's investigations seemed to point to Andriessen's innocence simply because the Dutch policeman could not have committed the crimes in the time available to him. But would that satisfy the local crime squads? They would argue that his cars had been seen on both occasions. Wouldn't that, they might argue, counter the negative factor of time? If . . .

It was at this point that Masters had a thought that gave him a mental shock. The time available? To do what, exactly? What areas of woodland had the local police combed? All the discussions concerning the case he had heard so far had suggested that the areas combed were those enclosed by or cut through by public roads. But what about private woodland? There were acres of it here within the College grounds. He had himself, an hour or two ago, penetrated deep into thick woodland literally within a minute or so of leaving his house. And his house was not the only building closely neighboured by trees. Much of the place had been built that way, to blend into the countryside, with no garden fences or boundary walls to spoil the loveliness of nature. He cursed inwardly at the thought that Andriessen could have managed it: that there could be two bodies buried within a hundred yards of his own backdoor or of one of the other living-out quarters.

He went into the house grim-faced.

Wanda kissed him and then stood back, her hands still on his shoulders, to look at him. After a moment she said: "Darling, you've got a face like a thundercloud. Was the lecture such a disaster?"

"What? Oh, the lecture! No. That went off well enough."

"As we have come to expect," said Green from the depths of an armchair.

"Something has happened," said Wanda quietly. "Something to make you cross."

Masters managed a smile. "Nothing has actually happened. Sorry, darling, but it was thoughts."

"Pretty grim thoughts if they caused you to come home looking so angry. Can you tell us what it's all about?"

"Not . . . not fully, poppet. But I was thinking about those two boys, whether they were frightened, and whether they are lonely wherever they are."

"I understand," said Wanda quietly.

"I'm not cutting you out, my dear. But some thoughts are incommunicable. Somebody walks over your grave and you shudder."

She stood up on tiptoe to kiss him again. "I know. Some things come too close to home for comfort."

He stared at her for a moment or two. "That describes it in a nutshell," he said at last.

"You need a drink. We'll hold up supper till you've caught up."

"Gin and tonic?" asked Green, getting to his feet. "It will be my pleasure to mix you the best ever."

"Thank you, Bill. I'll have it and then go up to sluice before we eat."

"Oh, darling," said Wanda, "I put out a clean shirt for you. It's the one you don't like very much, but if you could manage with it just for tonight . . . "

"Not the one your mother gave me? The one with rosebuds on?"

"They're not rosebuds. They're pale pink geometric shapes. . . ."

"With green leaves."

". . . with pale green shadows."

Masters managed a grin. "I'll put a roll-neck sweater on over it."

"It's just that I haven't had time to iron the others since we got down here, and I packed in such a hurry that they got a bit crumpled in the suitcase."

"Have a snort, chum," said Green handing Masters his glass and holding out his hand to take Wanda's from her. "Same again, love?"

"Yes, please, William, as we're going to be a bit late with supper."

"I'll take it up with me," said Masters.

Green followed Masters to the foot of the stairs. "Anything I can help with, George?"

"Yes, Bill. I want to talk. After supper will do."

"Fair enough."

"Could you ring Reed and Berger and ask them to be here at nine. If you can't get them at their quarters they'll most likely be in the mess."

"Will do," said Green. "Do I tell them anything?"

"A talk session."

"I see. You've had an idea. Some bee has got into your bonnet. And from the looks of you when you came in, it had stung you."

"Something like that," said Masters, starting up the stairs.

The supper table had been cleared by the time the sergeants arrived. Wanda and Doris were in the sitting room discussing, among other things, a number of invitations they had received from individuals among the wives of permanent staff as well as the list of corporate functions which it was hoped they

120

would attend. Masters and his three colleagues sat round the table in the dining room.

"What's it all about, George?" Green was selecting a cigarette from a crushed packet, and did not look up as he spoke.

Masters replied: "I didn't get a chance to ask you how you got on this afternoon. I'd like to hear that before I tell you what's on my mind."

Green lit his cigarette. "We finished off what we started this morning before the local filth took us in. We stayed out until we reckoned we had completed a recce of every possible way off the main roads and into the woods within a radius that the time at his disposal would have allowed Andriessen to operate. The answer, George, is a lemon.

"We're talking about easy ways in, of course. A hell of a lot of the road has deep ditches or hedges, fences and so on. We disregarded those lengths, because of the physical obstacles they impose. We worked entirely on the assumption that the car would have to be taken off the road and hidden from passers-by if a dead body was to be offloaded and filed away. I say filed away, because the time at his disposal would not have allowed Andriessen to dig any form of grave."

"And what is your final considered opinion, Bill?"

"Assuming that the lad is dead and his body hidden in the woods?"

"Yes."

"Andriessen is definitely out. He could not have accomplished the job in the time. To go out, pick up the lad, drive him to a covered way into the woods, kill him and then dispose of the body would have taken a long, long time, even if you do not allow time for happening upon the lad, talking to him, restraining him, looking for a route into the trees and so on. We three tried it with everything laid on like a military operation, knowing exactly where to go and so on. With everything going like clockwork it took well over the hour using the nearest entrance to the wood and allowing no time to hide the body."

"Anybody disagree with that?"

"No, Chief," said Berger. "The only possible way

121

Andriessen could have been implicated is if he drove into the wood, alone that is, happened upon the lad there, in some ideal place for hiding a body, and then killed him on the spot before returning immediately to the College. He might then, have just managed it. But even so it would have been a tight squeeze."

"Agreed," said Green. "But you'd have to accept—apart from the coincidence of meeting the boy in the wood in the ideal spot for hiding a body—that Andriessen is the type of bloke who would stop his car, get out, and immediately kill the boy for no reason whatsoever. I know there could be such people, but I find it hard to believe of any man, let alone Andriessen."

"Thank you," said Masters. "So I can take it that that particular area of investigation is finished and done with, can I?"

"Nothing more we can do along those lines," grunted Green. "Unless you're going to suggest some similar ploy, that is."

"Not exactly the same," said Masters. "But I'd better tell you why I came home this evening with a few nasty thoughts in my head."

"Ah!" said Green. "Now we're going to get it."

"The Dean asked me to call on him this afternoon. Late on in our conversation I brought up the subject of getting the local officers in for a drink so that you and I could meet them, Bill. Locke agreed to the idea and I asked for the meeting to be arranged for the earliest possible moment. He suggested tomorrow evening because it was the earliest we could expect them to come and in any case I was lecturing this evening at six.

"Now that was news to me."

"Nothing about it on your timetable, Chief," said Reed.

"It had been missed off the master copy. Continuity of Evidence. One hour of it, down to me. When I heard that, I came back here to do a bit of preparation. It was almost four o'clock by then, and though I could probably have conducted the session at five minutes' notice, I feel that a lecturer owes it to his students and the establishment itself to present a properly prepared and illustrated exposition.

"Nobody was at home, so I got down to work, jotting down headings, getting them into a logical order, looking up a few cases and thinking of a few stories as examples of the points I was trying to make."

"I'd have said it was a bit of cake for you, George,"murmured Green. "You can jaw the hind leg off a donkey at any time."

Masters smiled. "It did go fairly well—the preparation, I mean—and by about a quarter to five I was satisfied that I'd be able to do my stuff. Everybody was still out and I felt like a breath of air, so I stepped outside the back door, and in a few strides I was among the trees. In no time at all I couldn't see any of the houses in this area or anywhere at all, and I am sure nobody could have seen me."

"Go on," said Green heavily.

Masters turned to him. "The College grounds are a private estate. There's a railing fronting the main road and I seem to remember fences and hedges round the other sides. But it is still woodland: woodland that can be penetrated almost anywhere within its boundaries with the greatest of ease, just as we penetrate it everytime we leave the road to reach the house. None of the ditches and hedges you found today."

They waited for him to continue.

"Two things, gentlemen. If Andriessen had brought a body back into the College grounds, dumped it, with no effort at permanent concealment, and then hurried back to the bar . . . "

"I think he could have just about done it in the time, Chief. That is, if he went back later to really conceal the body properly."

"It's a possibility," agreed Green. "His car was seen going out on both occasions. Let's assume the sightings were true-bill. Short journeys outwards on both occasions to pick up the lads . . . "

"Pure chance," said Reed.

"Not necessarily," countered Green. "Say he'd been out on a score of occasions on just such a mission. He'd struck oil twice. Once a few years ago, once a few weeks ago. How much of a lucky chance is that? Twice in twenty times, thirty times, maybe even a hundred times? A pretty low average success rate I'd call it and, therefore, all the more credible. But as I was saying, short journey out, quick pick up, straight back here, dump the body, straight back to the car park and the bar. Much later, when everybody is asleep, out to the spot where the body has been dumped and then dispose of it properly. Blows the time alibi to blazes and accounts for the two sightings of the cars."

"How did he dispose of the bodies?" demanded Reed.

"Buried them," said Green. "He'd be on foot, remember. He'd probably located a spade. That would be all he had to carry."

"And the grave? Wouldn't that be found very easily."

Masters came in. "That's my point, Reed."

"What is, Chief?"

"Did the local police comb private estates? Specifically, did they comb this one or did they give it a miss because they were short of time and labour and because this particular neck of the woods belongs to the police anyway?"

Green sighed wearily. "Here we go. I'll lay a pound to a penny they didn't search right up to these houses. That's what you mean, isn't it George?"

Masters nodded. "I couldn't tell Wanda why I was looking a bit grim when I came in tonight, but I'd suddenly had a vision of Wanda, Doris and young Michael going out there, the boy playing and running about among the trees, the girls strolling along or laying out a picnic . . . "

"Don't go on," growled Green. "We can all envisage them laying out the tablecloth on a grave."

"At best," said Reed. "At worst they might stumble across . . . "

"I said don't go on," said Green vehemently.

There was a short silence.

"I can understand you having dark thoughts, Chief," said Berger. "What's to be done, though?"

"You can give me a fag, for starters," said Green, holding out his hand.

124

As Berger offered his packet, Masters said: "Tomorrow evening we should be able to ask the local brass if they did, in fact, search close to the College and its houses."

"Which they didn't," grunted Green.

Masters continued: "But I don't want to give them ideas. By that I mean I don't want us to offer them on a plate a first-class excuse for taking up Andriessen, on the grounds that the time factor could be meaningless."

"But if he's guilty, Chief?"

"Then we want him, true. But I don't want the locals going off at half-cock. We need to be sure."

"Meaning we've got just one day," grumbled Green. "We can't comb these woods in that time. Not just three of us."

"Dogs?" asked Reed.

"Where would we get them from without letting the cat out of the bag? They'd need handlers, as well."

"Think it over," said Masters. He turned to Green. "Bill, would it be possible to do it theoretically?"

"Meaning?"

"If you were to get a plan of the College grounds it could suggest, to somebody such as yourself, a number of obvious alternatives."

Green mused over this suggestion for a moment or two. "It could just work," he finally admitted. "The time factor still matters. He'd have to get the car back to the park by some route that didn't take too long." He looked up. "Leave it to us, George, except for making sure that Woolgar produces the map for us."

"I'll tell him I'm planning a practical exercise based on the immediate area so as not to arouse his interest."

"Good. And that's it, is it?"

"I think so. Shall we join the ladies?" He looked at Reed and Berger. "If you two have nothing better to do . . . ?"

"If there's a jar of ale going free," grunted Green, "those lads will never refuse. Come to think of it, I could do with one myself."

They got to their feet and followed Masters across to the sitting room.

Masters was loth to mention his fears to Wanda. He had no desire to ask her not to walk in the woods with Michael because she was certain to ask for reasons which he was not prepared to supply. Not because what he might say would frighten her, but because the possibility of dead bodies being buried nearby might be so distasteful to her as to spoil the obvious enjoyment she—and Michael—were deriving from this brief break from routine. She would find it unpleasant to imagine her young son playing on a murdered boy's grave. Understandably so. But until he was sure his idea was the right one, there seemed little point in even hinting that the woods should be out of bounds to his family.

He tried to drive the disturbing thoughts from his mind and to concentrate on the conversation going on around him.

" . . . and they were exercising two horses in the field," Doris was saying. "Michael was delighted with it."

"Who was doing it?" asked her husband.

"Two men. I took them to be policemen. At any rate they were making a noise with a rattle close to the horses as they went past, to see if they reared or whatever the term is."

"Sounds like mounted police," admitted her husband, "but I didn't know there were any of them here. Did you, George?"

"They probably keep one or two horses here for students who want to ride. I imagine they school them like all other police horses. That would seem a reasonable thing to do as their minders are bound to be ex-police grooms and all animals on the strength would be looked after and trained according to the book." He turned to Doris. "Where did you see them?"

"We walked past the end of the residential block—at least I think that's what it is. We came to a playing field. . . ."

"Rugger and soccer pitches," said Wanda.

Her husband nodded. "I remember it from way back. That's where the horses were, is it?"

"No," said Doris. "In the next field. The one past the playing field. Just an ordinary grass field. We thought Michael would be better in there than on one of the pitches."

"And we were right," said Wanda. "We found the horses.

126

Michael loved them. Or at least he did until one nodded close to him."

"Nodded?"

"Yes. Lifted its head high and then lowered it, several times. It looked a bit fierce and the harness made a noise. Just a bit frightening. I had to pat the horses' head to reassure Michael. Then we had to stay to make friends again. That was why we were a bit late home for tea."

"This afternoon?"

"Of course."

"How did you drive to get there? I mean, Doris said you walked past the end of the residential block, and that's only just up the road. So . . . "

"We walked."

"The whole way? From the house?"

"Yes. What's the matter, darling?"

"Let's take this slowly, please," said Masters. "Did you go to the quartering office this afternoon?"

"No."

"Did Woolgar call here?"

"No."

"Did he ring you?"

"No, darling. What is all this about Woolgar, whoever he may be?"

"He is the inspector in charge of quartering."

"I think you had better explain."

Everybody else had stopped their private conversations and were listening to Wanda and Masters. Green said: "What's the mystery, George? It sounds as though you suspect Woolgar and your missus of some sheenanigans."

"Please listen, all of you. You will remember that because of all the chat about the local police taking in Bill and Sergeant Berger, I was a bit late setting off for my appointment with Bobby Locke after lunch."

"You went off like the clappers," said Green.

Masters nodded. "On my way, I ran into Woolgar, or rather he puffed up behind me to have a word. Without stopping to chat, he told me that the lost set of keys to the Jag had been handed in to his office."

127

"Oh, good," murmured Wanda. "Who found them?"

"That's just the point, poppet. He doesn't know. Evidently there's a desk tray in his general office kept specifically for the return of lost property, and the keys just appeared in it sometime this morning."

"Didn't you pick them up, darling?"

"I hadn't time, just then, but I promised Woolgar I would collect them after I'd finished my session with the Dean. That suited Woolgar who was, in any case, on his way to inspect a defective downspout at the time. But he did say, before he left me, that if he got back to his office fairly quickly he would ring you, Wanda, to let you know the keys had been found so that you could, if you liked, call in and collect them."

Wanda shook her head. "He didn't ring. At least not before we went out."

Masters grimaced. "And I didn't call in to collect them, either. Bobby Locke told me at about a quarter to four that I was due to lecture at six o'clock. I didn't know about it before because, by some mischance, it had been left off the programme that had been handed to me. As you can imagine, my one thought was to get back here to do a bit of preparation for the lecture. In fact, I forgot about collecting the keys."

"Never mind, darling, we can get them tomorrow."

"That's not the point, sweetheart." Masters turned to Green. "Here's the mystery, Bill. When I got back here, everybody was out. The house was empty and ... " he paused for a moment " ... the car had gone, too. It was not here. Yet Wanda didn't take it."

"We certainly didn't, Chief," said Berger.

"No. So there's mystery number one."

"You mean there's a second?"

"I do. When I sat down to work at the kitchen table, there was a set of keys to the Jag there. I had to move them to spread out my books."

"I left them there, darling," said Wanda. "We were going for a walk so I didn't need them. I left them on the table so that you would see them if you can home and wanted to use

128

the car. I locked the house up, so they should have been safe."

"Quite. And they were safe. They were there when I got home, but the car wasn't."

"What are you saying, Chief?" asked Berger. "That somebody lifted the keys from Woolgar's office and used the car?"

"I think not. Woolgar assured me the keys were in his safe-cupboard. Now I know safe-cupboards are only made of thin sheet steel, but they're too tough to break into easily and quickly and they have combination locks."

"Woolgar himself then," said Berger.

Masters shook his head. "Not Woolgar. He'd never pull a trick like that. He wouldn't do it, and he knows me. By that I mean that should the idea of borrowing the Jag ever occur to him, he'd forget it pretty quickly, knowing what my reaction would be were I ever to find out."

Green sucked his partial denture, the noise sounding unnaturally loud in the silence. Then he said: "So you are saying there is a third set of keys to your car."

"I am. Of course, we shall have to check with Woolgar tomorrow. But my keys—the set I lent Wanda—were on the kitchen table this afternoon, and the car was not here. Dammit, I heard the thing come back. I was out in the woods, a couple of hundred yards away, and I heard it pull up. That's why I started back. I thought Wanda had returned."

"And had she?" asked Green.

"Doris, Wanda and Michael were all here. They said they'd just got back, so I continued to assume, as I had done all along, that Wanda had taken the car out after having first picked up her own keys from Woolgar."

Green eyed him shrewdly. "You know what all this means, George. No, don't answer. Of course you do."

"I don't," said Doris. "Will somebody please tell me."

Wanda said, before anybody could reply. "The car was here when we left, and it was here when we got back. So if somebody took it, he didn't have it for long. About two hours at the most."

"If somebody took it?" queried her husband.

129

Wanda said: "There is just the possibility that you were mistaken, darling. You're not infallible, you know. You confessed just now that you forgot about the set of keys in Inspector Woolgar's office."

"True, my sweet. But this was a positive recognition of the absence of the car, not just an impression that it wasn't there. I noted that you, Doris and Michael were not here. I assumed you were all out in the car which was not visible anywhere near the house."

"I see, and I'm sorry if I doubted you, but it is better to be sure about these things."

"Infinitely better." Masters turned to Doris. "You asked a question a moment or two ago and nobody replied to you because the conversation took another turn. What Bill was saying is that somebody was in possession of Wanda's keys during the time we thought they were lost. Whoever it was took the opportunity to use our keys for the purpose of obtaining a further set. Then he returned the originals."

"Why go to the bother of getting a new set and then returning the old ones? If he'd kept the set he had found he would have had what he wanted, wouldn't he?"

Masters smiled at her. "Your mind isn't devious enough for this sort of caper, my dear. You are too honest."

"Am I? How's that?"

"If I were in his place I would do precisely what our car-borrowing friend did for at least three reasons. First, he would hope to allay suspicion by returning them anonymously to Woolgar's office so that we might forget the incident altogether and not be alert to the fact that there was a spare set sculling around presenting a constant threat of car theft. Second, by returning them he would ensure that both Wanda and I were in possession of keys. This would go some way towards protecting him from discovery as, indeed, it nearly did this afternoon."

"How?"

"If two people have access to a car that is missing from its usual parking place, it is odds on that each believes the other is using it and so doesn't report it stolen. If there is only one set of keys, the one holding them knows the other cannot be

130

using the car, even if it is missing, and so will start a hue and cry."

"I hadn't thought of it like that," said Doris.

"Thirdly," went on Masters, "I would get those originals back to their owners at the first practical moment, before they had time to exhaust the possibilities of finding them and go to the nearest agent for a new set. Agents might remember if one particular set were to be duplicated within a very few days."

"That won't do, Chief," objected Reed. "If he was worried about two enquiries about one set of keys, all he had to do was to hang on to the originals and not run the risk of a duplication."

"Granted, so long as you are willing to ignore my second point."

"No, Chief, because by hanging on to the stolen set he would know you would get a new set in a few days' time, so the three sets would be in existence, just as he wanted."

"True up to a point. But he couldn't know what I would do. He would want to be certain there were two sets of keys in this house, otherwise his plan would fall down. He would also want to give us a sense of being surrounded by honest people—as witnessed by the return of the keys—so that we should not be constantly on the watch for a car thief or—and this is even more important—so that I didn't have the locks changed as one does in a house if keys are lost. Jags are valuable cars and new locks are easily—if expensively— fitted. Door locks, that is. It would probably not be thought necessary to change the ignition lock."

"Satisfied, lad?" asked Green, addressing Reed.

"Entirely."

"Good. Well now we've got that load of dross out of the way, let's get down to brass tacks."

"Bill!" expostulated his wife.

"What, love?"

"You can't talk like that about what George said. He was answering my question, which was something you didn't bother to do."

"Sorry, love," said Green contritely, "but that really was

just a load of old explanation. There are more important points to be raised now."

Doris appealed to Masters. "Are there more important things to talk about?" she asked. "I would have thought knowing about your lovely car was almost as important as anything could be. I mean, you'll find out who's got the third set of keys, won't you? And then just take them off him?"

"Bill's right," replied Masters quietly. "You see, this may not be the first time our friend has obtained duplicate sets of keys."

"You mean he could make a habit of it?"

"Yes, love," said her husband bluntly. "He could make a habit of it and take out cars when he believed their rightful owners were otherwise engaged."

"But what for?"

There was a long silence, then Wanda said quietly to Doris: "I think I know what they don't seem to want to put into words. Mr Andriessen's cars were seen to be leaving the College on both the occasions when the two boys disappeared, but he swore he was doing other things both times and had not taken his cars out."

Doris put her hand to her mouth in a gesture of dismay. "And your car . . . this afternoon . . . did he use it for . . . ?"

"I think not," said Masters quietly, "otherwise we should have heard by now."

"But . . . but he could have been trying to . . . out looking for . . . "

"Forget it, love," said Green gruffly.

"Yes, please," said Masters. "We'll all have one last drink." He got to his feet. Reed rose, too. "Can I borrow the keys, please, Chief?" Masters looked at him. "Mrs Masters will let you have them."

Wanda took the car keys from her bag and handed them to Reed. Berger said, "I'll come and give you a hand."

"I can manage," said Reed

"What to do?" asked Wanda.

"I think the simplest thing would be to remove the rotor," said Masters.

"And two wheels, Chief," said Berger. "The spare and one

132

other. Rotors can be interchangeable, and with a bloke as organised as this one seems to be I wouldn't put it past him to carry a spare."

"But what about tomorrow?" wailed Wanda.

"We'll put the wheels back, Mrs Masters, and show you how to remove the rotor. I think you should do that every time you leave the car outside."

"I see. Is that all right, George?"

"An eminently sensible precaution," replied Masters.

"Are you lecturing today, George?" asked Green at the breakfast table next morning.

"Reed and I are in the middle of preparing our series, but I'm not actually lecturing unless there is some other mistake in my timetable."

"So you're tied up?" Green was carefully dissecting a kipper, lifting the backbone out in one piece and preparing to do a flip-over to allow him to remove the skin before starting to eat.

"Not necessarily. In fact I was about to suggest we all meet in my office after breakfast."

"More ideas?"

"Yes. And I don't want to air them here in the house. Last night was a mistake."

"Be fair to yourself. We had conferred in private. The business about the keys came up by chance."

"As it had to do, and Wanda had to be present to tell me she didn't use the car, but I'd rather not involve the ladies in the more macabre side of our theories. Today will, after all, be a continuation of last night."

Green grunted his agreement and concentrated on separating the fleshy body of his kipper along the natural break lines. Wanda was in the kitchen feeding Michael. Doris was there, too, brewing coffee after cooking her husband's fish. Masters appeared to be deep in thought and said very little when Doris came in to join them at table. He came to when Wanda appeared with Michael and said: "Watch him for me, darling, would you? Sergeant Reed has arrived to put the

133

car wheel back on and he's going to show me how to put the rotor arm back."

Masters picked up his son and sat him on a dining chair.

"Fish," said Michael, wrinkling his nose.

"Kipper," said Green.

"Fish," corrected Michael.

"All right son, have it your way. Kipper fish."

"Fish," reiterated Michael, satisfied to have won the round, and then, as a sort of sop to Green who was by way of being one of his friends, he added the gratuitous comment, "Smelly".

"Ta muchly," replied Green. "That's really made my breakfast for me. And I was enjoying this one-eyed steak."

"Bill!" said Doris, outraged. "You do nothing but teach that child bad manners and bad language."

"Now what have I said?"

"One-eyed steak."

"That's what they're known as in the northern fishing ports—or were, when we had any northern fishing ports. Tuppence a pair we paid for them in those days and I remember, before the war, one firm started to make kipper sausages."

"'Sidges," said Michael.

"That's right, old son. And very good they were, too, but I wonder what the EEC bureaucrats would make of them today when they can't even accept the good old British banger?"

Michael started to belabour a plate with a handy spoon. "Bang, bang," he said.

"Not that sort of banger, nibbo. Sidges bangers."

Michael looked at him wide-eyed and then gave him a heavenly smile.

"That's put things to rights," said Green. "You spoilt my breakfast but you've made my day. Now, if you'll let me have a cup of coffee in peace I'll be ready for anything."

Masters got to his feet. "Five minutes, Bill?"

"No you don't," said Green.

"What?"

"Go poking your nose in. Let Reed show your little missus

134

how to get her car back in action on his own. He'll enjoy it. You'd spoil it for him."

Masters shrugged. "When you're ready, then."

Just as at their previous conference, they met in Masters' temporary office in the main building.

"I think, gentlemen," began Masters, "that we are in a hurry. Not only to prevent Chief Superintendent Andriessen from being wrongly taken up, but also to discover the identity of the real murderer and to take him out of circulation before there is a third disappearance."

"To do that without involving the locals could still be sticky," said Green. "And I haven't forgotten what happened yesterday morning, so I don't feel happy at the thought of either approaching them or helping them."

"I haven't forgotten, either," replied Masters. "And because of that, I have changed my mind, somewhat. Last night I suggested that we should ask them if they had searched the environs of the College itself. On reflection I've decided that we will assume they didn't."

"Dicey, Chief," said Reed. "If they did search round here and did it well, we could be wasting a lot of valuable time, and you did say we are in a hurry."

Masters nodded. "It does sound a bit contradictory, I know. But I've tried to think it through, just as I expect the rest of you have. In fact, I'd be surprised if each one of you couldn't suggest a name for the man we think we should pounce on. But we've got to have proof, solid proof, before we can make our views known to the locals. What I mean is, we can't point to somebody and say 'There's your man' and then leave it to them to secure the proof, because they wouldn't know what had led us to suspect him.

"So, let us get the pattern clear in our minds and then we can proceed." He turned to Green. "Anything to say at this point, Bill?"

Green who was, for once, unwrapping a new packet of cigarettes, shook his head. "Not really. As you said, we'll all have thought it through, but I think we should hear your

135

appreciation first. After that, if necessary, we can add our pennorths."

"Fair enough." Masters looked at Reed. "I know I haven't really answered your objection yet, but I hope what I have to say will show my reasons for not discussing their search areas with the locals."

Reed grinned. "I expect it will, Chief."

"Here goes then. You three people have proved to your own satisfactions and, therefore, to mine, that in the time available to him, on both occasions, Andriessen could not have picked up and then disposed of the two youths outside the area of the College grounds. This supposition is proved if we accept that the local police have, as they claim, conducted a thorough search of the immediate areas roundabout.

"That must indicate to us one of two things. That the bodies are buried further afield or nearer at home than those areas you included in your timings.

"Whichever it is, the bodies still could not have been disposed of beyond finding within the time limits. So, in either case the bodies were dumped temporarily, to be finally dealt with later.

"Let us now consider the possibility of them being further afield. Your time trials suggest that only the most cursory efforts could have been made to hide them nearby at the time. That alone suggests the alternative nearby theory, but I imagine that by the time the killer went to pick up the bodies later, to convey them to a more distant burial spot, the hunt for the boys would have been on in just those areas where they had originally been dumped. This means that by that time they could have been discovered, if only hastily hidden, or the murderer ran the serious risk of being caught red-handed. Both those points argue against the further-afield possibility.

"The alternative, nearby theory has, however, much to recommend it, particularly to a man schooled in police work. The distances to be done in the possible time are much shorter. A simple out and back journey without the necessity to make a detour into the woods near a main road. You all agree that such a journey could be done in the time available.

Later, when the time came to dispose of the bodies finally, within these grounds there would be no risk of detection by search parties, no need to transport the bodies away and, therefore, no need to use a motor car. In other words, the victims could have been buried on the spot.

"I submit that the points in favour of the nearby theory so far outweigh anything the more-distant theory has to offer, that we are obliged to assume the former is the correct solution.

"Should we make such an assumption we must then go so far as to say the local police did not search the College grounds because had they done so, they must have found. I spent some time in those woods yesterday and I am strongly of the opinion that no man could have dug a grave and buried a body—by dark—on that forest floor without leaving very obvious signs of having done so. And I don't mean traces that could easily be missed. I mean definite signs."

"You're right there, Chief," said Berger. "Even piling up the soil from the trench would leave dirty great marks. Then there's trampling and breaking branches and twigs besides the disturbance of the leaf mould on the ground. Any man would have found it, let alone a trained dog."

"Thank you. That is why I propose that we should assume that the area of the College has remained unsearched. Any objections so far?"

"It sounds convincing," said Green. "Whether it is or not I'm not sure."

Masters was filling his pipe as Green spoke. As he closed the lid of the brassy Warlock Flake tin, he replied: "I'm not sure myself. But we are in a funny position—that of trying to win the game without taking part or, rather, without seeing the face values of any of the cards."

"It's a gamble, is what you're saying?"

"Exactly. But there's another pointer that leads me to believe we should adopt the view under discussion."

"The car sightings?"

"Right. Now I know you have a particularly poor view of the local force—with reason. But I think we might be as dunderheaded as they appear to be if we assume that everything they have done is wrong. It plainly isn't. And they claim that on both occasions cars belonging to Andriessen were seen leaving the College grounds at the relevant times and, even more important, similar cars were seen by their witnesses in the area of the crimes, again at the relevant times. These are stated facts, and we have little choice but to accept them particularly now when we have discovered a theory which fits the possibility of their use in the crimes. So we strengthen our belief of the nearby theory and, consequently, our assumption that these private grounds have yet to be searched.

"Our main objection to the use of those two cars was Andriessen himself, or rather his movements. But now we know that somebody round here could be a pathological and methodical car borrower, we don't necessarily have to consider Andriessen at all."

"Hold it, hold it," said Green. "If we discount Andriessen, the time factor, which after all was based on his appearances, goes completely by the board. The timings we did our work on could be much longer, and if they were, what you call the 'nearby theory' could have gone for a burton, too."

"Good thinking, Bill. And I can neither deny nor refute your point."

"But?"

"If we are going to put the car borrower in the frame instead of Andriessen, we have to assume that our man has used other people's cars on numerous occasions. You yourself, yesterday, said twenty, thirty, even a hundred times, and we are talking of a span of at least five years. Yesterday he pinched my car. I'm betting on that being the first occasion on which he has been found out, otherwise he'd either be away from the College with a flea in his ear or he'd have had his backside kicked so hard he'd never have attempted it again. In fact . . . "

"I know," said Green grinning. "Somebody would have connected his taking ways with the disappearance of the first lad and he'd be part way through a life-sentence by now."

Masters nodded. "So we can assume the car thief has never

before been spotted. That in turn suggests that when he does borrow a car, he takes care not to keep it out too long—otherwise he would have been caught. We can, probably, judge by the length of time he had the Jag yesterday afternoon. So, although the time factor can be lengthened until after Andriessen's known reappearances, I suggest there is still a limit within which our man had to work. That being so, could he have done a far away job, or would he, too, have been obliged to do a nearby one?"

"Nearby," said Berger, decisively.

"That's that settled," grunted Green. "No hesitation there, George."

"Is anybody going to argue?" asked Masters.

"Not me," said Reed.

Masters turned to Berger. "Reasons for being so adamant?"

"Lots of them, Chief. The locals have searched all the get-attable places round about with the exception, possibly, of the College grounds. That means the body is a good long way away, or it is close by. Andriessen's timings wouldn't even allow him the opportunity to hide a body in the area the police have searched, so even if you allow the car-thief a bit more time to play with, it's unlikely he could have operated far afield, therefore the odds are so strongly in favour of him having dumped his victim nearby that I feel pretty safe in suggesting there is no alternative to consider."

"Except?" asked Masters.

"How d'you mean, Chief?"

"It is one thing for us to discuss possible theories on the assumption that the local people did not search within these grounds, but before we can be entirely positive about our conclusions we have to be absolutely sure there was no search within the College woodland."

"Fair enough, Chief. Then the first job is to discover whether this area was searched."

Green said: "And after your experience of the local fuzz yesterday you're prepared to go and ask 'em if they covered this ground? Apart from telling them exactly what we are doing, you'll practically be accusing them of falling down on the job. They'll love that, and I don't think."

"We can get round it," said Masters. "If there was a search here, Woolgar would know. He should be aware of everything that goes on within the perimeter of the College."

"He lives here permanently," counselled Green. "It's ten chances to one he's got pals among the locals. We wouldn't want him passing on word of our enquiries otherwise the fat would still be in the fire. Why not ask Bobby Locke?"

Masters nodded. "I mentioned Woolgar because I've got to collect the Jag keys from him. I could do that now, with any luck. His office is in the main corridor of this building." Masters got to his feet. "While I'm gone, Bill, could you three get hold of the local phone book and get out a list of Jag and Volvo dealers. We ought to be able to get a line on anybody who has bought replacement keys recently. Don't ask around among the people here, though. You could be alerting somebody whom we would rather keep in the dark."

"Yellow pages," said Green to Berger. "Get a copy, lad. We could probably get the whole list from there."

"Or by ringing the area main dealers," said Reed.

Masters made his way down the main staircase and entered Woolgar's outer office. The girl clerk showed him into the inner office where the inspector was working.

"Good morning, sir. You've come for the keys?"

"Yes, please. I'm sorry I didn't call in yesterday afternoon as I promised, but I was suddenly saddled with giving an extra lecture before dinner last night so I had to rush away to prepare it."

Woolgar grinned. "I heard about it. All the typists have been twitting the Dean's secretary about it. She doesn't reckon to make mistakes, you see. . . . "

"The infallible Gertie?"

"That's her. She's by the way of being the senior of the civvy office girls—the Commandant's PA being a woman sergeant, of course—and she gets a bit sniffy over mistakes in others, so when they heard she'd made a dog's dinner of your timetable they saw their chance to make a few remarks about it in her hearing. You know how it is. Girls will be girls."

Masters smiled. "There was no real harm done as it turned out, but yesterday wasn't really my day."

"No, sir? I heard that your lecture yesterday morning was a great success."

"Oh, that! I was referring to two of my team being taken up by the local police."

Woolgar opened his eyes wide. "I heard there'd been a bit of trouble, sir. What happened?"

"DCI Green and Sergeant Berger were doing a recce for a practical problem I want to set the students later. They were darting about in a car with a map and a stopwatch and the locals descended on them."

"But surely . . . I mean a simple explanation . . . "

"I'm sorry to say the locals weren't open to simple explanations. They'd got well into their stride of accusing my people of abducting the local boy until the information that they were using a Yard car came through."

"They're crackers," expostulated Woolgar.

"They kept them under observation for an hour. Which means they were probably in the College grounds at the beginning."

"Doing what, sir?"

"I didn't know. But it seems they could have a regular watch on you."

Woolgar grimaced. "I've heard about Andriessen. He's the one they're hoping to get something on, I suppose?"

"But surely they searched the College grounds when the boy first went missing?"

"In a way, I suppose they did, sir. The woods inside the perimeter, at any rate."

"Then why sit at your gate?"

"I've no idea, sir, unless they've codded themselves into thinking there could be another abduction."

Masters shook his head. "They can't afford to look ahead until they've cleared the track behind them."

"In that case, search me, sir."

Masters sat on the corner of the desk. "But if they searched thoroughly inside the College . . . "

"Only the wooded areas sir. The area behind the senior officers' houses where your quarter is, and the area to the west and north of the playing fields. To the east, where the Commandant and Dean live the ground is more open."

He got to his feet. "Here's a large scale map, sir. The green areas are woods. To the south—that's the front of the main building—there's just isolated copses. I think that was formal gardens and park at one time."

"Between the house and the main road to the east of the present drive?"

"That's right, sir. They had dogs and search squads in all those areas."

Masters continued to gaze at the map. "It's funny, a property of this size having only the one entrance."

Woolgar put out a finger to point to some of the buildings behind the main block. "A lot of these have been put up in the last forty years, sir. The lecture rooms and single quarters, dining room and so on. They were just built, sir, using the ground, if you follow me. They were put up across the old back track as well as to both sides. Partly I think because at first, I believe, they put up old army huts, and the area of the track was clear of growth and offered harder standing for throwing them up quickly. Just like they built air raid shelters on side roads in the war, or so I've been told. Then when they came to build properly, they ignored the fact that there'd been a back way out. The result was the back track was never used and got grown over. It was only a track after all. It's not shown on the plans now because really it doesn't exist except that they take the horses out that way sometimes and a local farmer's tractor comes in to take the hay once a year."

"I see. There's a gate then?"

"On this old side road, sir. It was a five-barred job, but I had to put a new metal one in a few years back. It's padlocked."

Masters laughed. "The horses have to jump it, do they?"

Woolgar grinned. "I'd like to see them do it with some of the novice riders we get here. No, sir, we keep the keys in the outer office. A couple of them. Anybody who wants to use the gate just collects a key and returns it later. We're not too fussy about them, because anybody who wanted to get in

142

would only have to climb over. A three year old could manage it." He turned to face Masters. "You're not suggesting a body might have been brought in that way, I hope, sir?"

Masters shook his head. "Not at all. But you know how it is with active investigators like myself. As soon as a problem appears we can't help getting a bit nosey even if it isn't our problem. Actually, I hadn't given the thing a thought until Green and Berger were picked up yesterday. Then I got a bit angry at what seemed to me to be a ham-fisted way of carrying on and began to wonder what the hell the locals were up to, sitting round here instead of getting out and about." He turned away from the map. "However, as I said, it's no business of mine—unless they arrest the rest of us, that is. So now, Mr Woolgar, if I could have my car keys . . ."

"Of course, sir."

When they'd been delivered to him, Masters thanked Woolgar and started to leave. Then he said: "Oh, by the way, have you a couple of those large scale maps you could lend me. They would be useful when planning my exercise."

"You've taken your time," accused Green when Masters rejoined his team. "What happened? Did Woolgar forget his combination?"

"A certain amount of idle chatter, to say nothing of the retrieval of the lost keys and the acquisition of two large scale plans of the area as requested earlier."

"Great," grunted Green, taking a plan and opening it out. "I always feel I know where I am when I've got something like this to consult." He put a thick finger on the top right hand corner. "Not too old, either. Surveyed a couple of years ago. We should be able to quarter these woods as easily as . . ."

Masters gave a warning cough before saying, "Bill, there's something you ought to know before you do too much planning."

Green looked up at him. After a pause, he said: "Don't tell me. The locals have combed the College grounds."

Masters nodded. "Using dogs."

143

"Blast! There you are, young Berger. It's like the man said. Unsafe to count your hens."

"So we're scuppered," said Reed.

Green sat staring at the map for some time, then he said, suddenly: "Are we?"

"Are we what?"

"Scuppered, lad."

Masters stared hard at Green who stared back.

"Are you saying, Bill, that our theories are not necessarily worthless?"

"That's exactly what I'm saying."

"Perhaps a word of explanation wouldn't come amiss."

"I'm working on it," grunted Green, whose frown of concentration was an indication that he was marshalling his thoughts. After a moment or two he looked round at each of his colleagues in turn and then started to speak.

"We've all agreed that the nearby theory, as his nibs calls it, and in the way he has put it forward, is the most likely one we can think of, bearing in mind we have satisfied ourselves the more-distant theory won't work.

"We assumed that the locals wouldn't comb the wooded areas of the College grounds and that made us keener than ever on the nearby theory. Right so far?"

"Agreed," said Berger, answering for everybody.

"That nearby theory was strengthened in our eyes by the recent revelations about the habit of some bloke in this set-up of pinching cars. What I mean is, in addition to all the chat we've had about those spare keys, there's something that's not been mentioned that strengthens the nearby theory."

"What's that?" asked Reed.

"The joker who borrows Jags and Volvos comes from this establishment." Green looked at Masters. "That's a safe assumption isn't it? It's not somebody from outside who nips in and pinches keys, is it?"

"I think you're safe in that assumption, Bill."

"Right. That definitely centres the problem on the College, to my way of thinking. So, though the local police have searched the woods inside this perimeter, it doesn't invalidate

144

the nearby theory. We've assumed the bodies were buried. What if they weren't?"

"How do you mean?" asked Reed.

"If the bodies are within the College perimeter, but not in the woods and fields, where are they lad?"

Reed stared open-mouthed. "You mean they're in the buildings somewhere?"

"Why not?" demanded Green. "We get bodies inside buildings more often than outside, don't we?"

"Yes, but . . . "

"But what, lad?"

"There are scores, if not hundreds, of policemen crawling all over this place, to say nothing of permanent staff and civvies."

Masters joined in. "We've all heard it said that the best way to hide anything is to put it in the most obvious place. Where better to hide a dead body—or bodies—that the police are looking for than in a police establishment? I think, Sergeant, that though I was wrong in assuming the local police did not comb the College woods, I'm certain they didn't search the College buildings. If they had done so, Woolgar would have mentioned it when I spoke to him. As it was, he said they combed the woods with dogs. He'd not have kept quiet about it had his beloved buildings been turned over."

Reed grimaced. "Still, Chief, think of the risks. People crawling all over the place. The smell of a dead body. Probably blood and guts on clothing or walls."

"A valid point," agreed Masters. "But not all homicides are accompanied by blood. Strangling for instance. Some head-crushing blows produce little blood. As for smell, well, bodies have been hidden in buildings for years without giving themselves away. In airtight cupboards, buried in cellars, to say nothing of being burned in furnaces. I don't think your objections are insuperable. However, I think the DCI was going to tell us a bit more of his idea when we interrupted him."

"It's the map," said Green. "Look at it." He pointed with a stubby forefinger. "Whoever did this put it all in. There's a gazebo here . . . new cricket pavilion here . . . old summer house here . . . and closer in to the buildings themselves there's the old boiler house, ruins of the vinery, old stables with new ones alongside . . . and so on. And I'd like to bet there are cellars in a wigwam like this. Cellars big enough to put down racks of booze and store fuel, but now no longer in use." He looked up at Masters. "I reckon hiding a body here could be a bit of cake, George."

Masters nodded. "I'd say it's a distinct possibility, Bill. In fact, I'd go a bit further than that because you have at least provided a solution—if not the solution—as to why the bodies have never been found. If we give the locals credit for having organised a very good search of all the surrounding wooded areas, near and not so near, it seems logical and—now you've pointed it out—obvious to suppose that the bodies are elsewhere. If not outside, then inside. Inside some building that is. Here at the College or . . . " He shrugged. "We can make no guess at the alternatives, but we can specify that such a building would have to be not too far away because the time factor limits the distance and, I suggest, the building would need to be deserted or at any rate not a place where many people go."

"On the grounds that bodies have a nasty habit of giving themselves away, Chief?"

"A lot of them seem to have that habit and so I can't imagine that a successful hider of corpses would run the risk of allowing them to declare their presence to anybody but himself."

Green grunted his appreciation of this support for his theory. Masters waited a moment before continuing.

"Bill, I can't help feeling that a character who can—as we think—successfully pinch car keys and then use the vehicles at intervals over five or six years without being discovered, will be just the man to have found some hiding place to which he alone has the key and, therefore, personal access only."

"Meaning he's got a locked area in some cellar which nobody else ever has need to use and for which there isn't

146

a spare key? Our man having pinched the only one in existence?"

"Something of the sort."

"Which means we can't get into it either."

"Maybe not. But I suspect you are envisaging a search."

"How else are we going to test our idea?"

"What I was about to say is that the search—the initial one at any rate—can be quite a simple matter."

"Oh yeah!"

"Yes. You merely go round looking for locked doors. You note their exact location and then you ask for those keys only. If they can be produced . . . well, you can open up for a look, if you like, but if there's a door for which there is no key . . ."

"Got it," said Green. "It could save a lot of time."

"There's just one other thing, Bill. Remember that the youths had to be taken to the place you will be looking for. Either on their own feet or as a burden. Whichever it was, the approach would have to be covered from other eyes."

"That wouldn't matter by night, Chief."

"I think it would. Say, for instance, that the cellars lead off the kitchens, as they often do in these old houses. I imagine the kitchens are locked overnight. Our friend would have to be able to get in there to get to the main cellar door. Not easy, I'd say, even though our friend appears to be proficient at providing himself with spare keys."

Green said: "Lots of these old cellars have external chutes, George, where they used to send the fuel down."

"If that is the case here, Bill, and one of them has been opened in the last few weeks, it could well show signs of having been used, as opposed to those that have rusted solid over the years."

Green nodded. "Anything else?"

"I don't think so."

"How do we get hold of keys for locked doors, Chief?"

"If you find any such places, then we shall be obliged to bring in the Dean and Woolgar. I'd rather not implicate them before we have to, however, because even though the secret might be kept, the suppressed air of excitement our

147

activities would engender could well alert somebody whom we would rather keep in the dark. Don't you agree, Bill?"

"Absolutely. Excitement like that engenders curiosity even though, as you say, nobody knows what it's about. And curiosity leads to guessing, and if I'd got two corpses stashed away I'd be guessing all sorts of things."

"In that case, Bill, we'll try to get ourselves a cup of coffee and have it while we talk over the tactics of the search."

Chapter 6

"ARE YOU AND Reed going to help us?" asked Green as they started to arrange the proposed search.

"We're far enough ahead with our preparations for lectures to give you a few hours," conceded Masters. "That's if you would like us in the team."

Green put down his coffee cup and turned to the map. "I don't know anything about the foundations and cellars here," he said, "but even if there are none, there's enough work to keep four of us busy for the rest of the day. Count yourself and Reed in, George."

"Fair enough. I'll leave it to you to allocate the areas."

"Work in twos," replied Green. "The only question is whether you and I should work together, close in, and let the lads do the running about round gazebos and such or whether we should take one of them each and divide the job in some other way."

"Whichever you like, but I'd have said the College buildings proper would take more time than the bits and pieces."

"There's a hell of a lot of outbuildings to the College itself," asserted Green. "There always is in this type of old building. So there'll not be much difference. We'll divide the usual way. You take Reed, I'll take Berger."

"Fine. How do you want us to divide the territory?"

"I'll do inside," said Green. "You do outside. Will that suit?"

"Admirably."

"Chief," said Berger, pushing his cup and saucer away, "you touched on one point earlier, but since then we've not heard any more of it. You said each one of us could probably put a name to the villain."

"True."

"Why didn't we discuss our thoughts on that point?"

149

"For no great reason. Probably I thought it would be a waste of time to start bandying names about with no proof to substantiate the guesses."

"Leave it, lad," Green counselled Berger. "If we dredge up names it could mean we'll no longer be open-minded about this caper."

"You think so?"

"I'm sure of it. As we stand at this moment I could, for instance, make out a much better case against Andriessen than the local rozzers, and look where they are. On the point of pulling him in. Which we reckon is a mistake because they've seized on his name and can't forget it, even though they did decide to collar you and me yesterday morning. They're not being open-minded because they've got a fixed idea. We'll try to steer clear of falling into the same blob-hole."

Berger shrugged. "Anything you say. Are we ready to go?"

"The old vinery, Chief," said Reed. "Looks like an ordinary glasshouse to me."

"Basically it is. But you see those holes, low down on the sides?"

"In the brickwork below the glass, or where the glass used to be?"

"Those were for the vines to come in. They planted them outside and then trained them to come through the holes to grow and produce their grapes in the hot house. Don't ask me why."

"It could be that the roots like to be cool, like a clematis, while the rest of the plant likes heat."

"Very likely—as I seem to remember that clematis does actually mean vine-branch. Same genus probably. And I knew one old gardener, when I was a boy, who had charge of vines in the grounds of a largish house, and I can still remember him telling me that he always put rubble on the soil round the vine roots. I didn't know why and he didn't tell me, but I think it could have been to keep the roots cool in the same way as ordinary gardeners put a slab of stone over a clematis root for that reason."

Reed had penetrated further into the long glasshouse. "There's heating pipes under this grill, Chief, but I can't see any form of . . . yes, there's a chimney stack here, at the end. But it's blind. There's no fireplace."

"Try outside," said Masters. "Yes, at your end."

Reed climbed out through the empty frame. "Little boiler house, Chief."

It was merely a sloping roof with two side walls and an old rickety door not tall enough to admit a man without stooping. Reed levered and tugged to open it. "This hasn't been opened in years, Chief," he puffed. Inside was a flight of three steps down to a level where an ancient, coal-fired boiler stood rusting away. Though small, it filled the space except for a few square feet of brick flooring in front of the fire box. This area was covered with rubble, but as Reed stirred it with his foot he uncovered a small layer of coal slack. "Nobody's been in here since they stopped growing grapes, Chief. And there's no room to hide anything." He picked up a brickbat to use as a lever for opening the little fire door. A trickle of fire ash and dust fell out. "No bodies here, Chief."

"We ought to have had a torch," said Berger. He was on his hands and knees alongside the bottom flight of stairs. He had opened a door about eighteen inches square and was peering inside.

"Light a match, lad," commanded Green.

"Nothing but dust," said Berger, getting to his feet and dropping the spent match. "Mark you, it would be a good place. It's obvious nobody's ever been in there or even looked in since this new part was built. Shoved up against the narrow end a body would be well out of sight of anybody not specifically looking for it."

"The stink would give it away, lad."

"Usually, I agree. But there have been bodies put in dry warm cupboards and they haven't rotted. They've been discovered after twenty years, all wrinkled up and full of grub holes."

"Thanks," retorted Green. "Any more tasty little stories like that? If not, let's get down through that door marked

151

Basement and see what delights await us there. There should be electric lights somewhere."

"If the door is open," said Berger.

"It isn't," replied Green in a disgusted voice, "but hang on a moment. This is some sort of lift." He had moved to a small opening covered by a folding canvas door. "Press the tit lad and see what happens."

Berger drew the door aside to display the grills. "Service lift," he said, "for ground floor and basement only." He pushed the call button. The utility car rose into view and they entered the unpainted metal chamber.

The basement was divided into cages, each with a pad-locked door carrying a notice.

"One for each department," said Berger. "It's their storage space for old files and such. This one is labelled 'Psychology'. I didn't know they taught that sort of thing here."

Green merely grunted in reply to this observation, and passed on down the row of cages. "Woolgar's got two," he observed. "One for office stuff and one for more practical bits and pieces." He pointed to a number of white finger boards on short stems and heavy round bases. "They use those when they have some sort of public jamboree here, I suppose. And those . . . those boxes are marked Christmas Decorations. Friend Woolgar has a pretty varied job here what with defective drainpipes, Christmas tree fairies and lost car keys to think about."

"Nothing here," said Berger decisively, "unless some of those paper sacks contain a body."

"Which they don't," said Green. "Every one of these cages is padlocked and I'll bet each department hangs on to its own keys like grim death. I know these places. Every department is as jealous of its allotted space as a lioness of her whelps."

"Meaning our friend wouldn't get a chance of gaining entry to deposit a corpse."

"Not unless he's the holder of one of these keys, and though we can't rule anybody out, I can't see any head of department, who has to send members of his staff down here from time to time, filing away a body in his own cage."

"These are the new basements," said Berger, as they

returned to the lift. "Under the old part of the building things could be different."

"Old laundry," said Masters. "And very nice, too."

"For its time perhaps," agreed Reed. "But today you've got to have washing-machines, tumble-driers, spin-driers and all the rest of it."

"Of course. I wouldn't want my missus up to her elbows in tubs of clothing every day, particularly with a child who creates washing on a seemingly endless production belt. But look at those two sinks, there, side by side. They're the best part of a yard deep."

"Why two, Chief?"

"Rinsing. That left-hand one has only got a cold tap over it. The other has hot and cold."

"Chief?"

"Yes?"

"These sinks are white porcelain. I always thought sinks as old as this were those old stone things people now use for making miniature rock gardens."

"You're making a very common mistake," said Masters. "For some reason, younger people in this country think that the British people lived like cavemen until after the last war. Nothing is further from the truth. TV commentators and the like never have a thought above the industrial back-to-back houses of the old days. Admittedly those were terrible. But even then, this country had more baths per head of population than any other country in the world. And it still has. In houses other than the bad areas, you would find porcelain hand basins and sinks installed certainly as long ago as the last century."

"I didn't know that, Chief."

"When I was in hospital recently," continued Masters, "my mother-in-law came to visit me. Whilst she was with us, she was reading a book written by a woman who is now middle-aged and, consequently, was alive during the thirties. The author stated categorically that, before the war, women had only lisle stockings, bust-bodices, woollen knickers and generally unattractive underwear. My mother-in-law was both amused and angry. She, in her youth, had worn silk stockings, cami-knickers, French knickers and so on and so forth. I asked if those were only available to the favoured few. Her answer surprised me."

"What did she say?"

"She said she bought her stockings at sixpence a leg in Woolworths and made her own French knickers out of off-cuts of oyster-coloured slipper satin which could be bought for next to nothing on any market or direct from the factories which sold remnants. She said she could make a dozen pairs of pants for five bob. Those were her actual words. I was so surprised that I checked up—or rather my wife did—with several elderly women and they all bore out what she'd said."

Masters shook his head. "I've long believed we've allowed those who've had the ears of this nation to sell us short in every possible way. Your remark about these sinks shows how right I was."

"Makes you think, Chief, seeing we invented the best part of most things in the past."

"We don't do too badly in the present either." He looked up at the ceiling. "I see the plaster has come down close to the back wall."

"A square yard of it."

"The joists are pretty deep. Nine inches or more."

"You reckon a body could have been pushed in between two of them, Chief, through the hole?"

"I think we should make sure one hasn't been stashed away up there. Find something for me to stand on, would you."

Reed was gone for several minutes. "Sorry to have been so long, Chief, but I went to the car for a torch." He set down a high stool. "I borrowed this from the main kitchen. Will it do?"

"Admirably."

Masters took only a minute or so over the search between the joists. "Nothing," he said as he descended from the stool. "We'd better return this to the kitchen."

They wandered around the building, prying into what

remained of the old outhouses. Eventually, between the west-end main wall of the old building and the east end of the new gymnasium, they discovered a six-foot wide alley which led to an old brick building, single storied, which blocked the end of the way.

"What's that, Chief?"

"On the plan it's called 'Cutters Shed', whatever that means. But it explains why the two buildings are separated in this way. Somebody thought it wise not to knock that shed down. We'd better take a look."

"I'll go, Chief. You won't want to climb over that heap of sand."

"Builders' materials," said Masters. "That probably explains why the shed is still standing. It was probably used as a works' office when the new buildings were put up."

The sand referred to was a large heap, probably three feet high in the middle and sloping off towards the walls of the buildings. It had obviously been there for some time as several roots of grass and groundsel were springing from it. Masters led the way over it despite what Reed had suggested.

"Why leave it here, Chief? It's an inconvenient spot."

"Oh, I don't know. The alley is blind. Nobody—that is students—will need to use it. My guess is that they kept it here either to use when the paths in the College got icy in bad weather, or they dumped it here to spread over tar when they sprayed the car parks and roads once a year. That habit seems to have died out now, thank heaven."

Masters reached the far side of the heap and stamped his feet to remove the sand that was clinging to the welts of his shoes. Reed followed suit and together they walked the last few yards to the shed.

A dilapidated notice painted in red on a small white board, barely discernable from more than a few feet away, said "Keep Locked Shut". Below the words was the little zig-zagged arrow sign showing that the notice was displayed to indicate the presence of electric current.

"It's a sub-station of some sort, Chief."

Masters was looking through the window. "I think not. There are cupboards in the walls of the buildings on each floor with danger notices stating how many hundreds of volts are sculling about inside. This, I think is merely a storeroom for old electrical equipment and the notice is bogus. One our friend, ex-Sergeant Rimmer, found lying about spare somewhere and which he had put up as printed protection for his bothy."

Reed had now joined Masters at the window. "There's a bench in there, Chief, so I suppose he does some repairs when he's not feeling too idle."

"I imagine most of what he does in here will be recovery—cannibalisation of useful bits and pieces. It's amazing how many plugs and bolts and lengths of flex one can rescue from electrical goods these days. I know to my cost as a householder that some little part very often gives up the ghost before the item they're part of has the shine off it, but repairs are so expensive its cheaper to buy new if you're not an electrics buff capable of putting the thing to rights yourself."

"I'll tell you something else Rimmer does in here—if it is Rimmer's place, that is—and that's brew up. There's an old electric kettle there, Chief, and a power point up there on the right." Reed peered more closely. "Yes. There's a pack of tea and a couple of tin mugs." He rubbed the window in an effort to get a better view. "He's even got a tin tea-tray on his bench. A couple of those old cast-iron garden chairs, too. I reckon old Rimmer holds tea parties. . . . " He broke off as Masters edged him aside. "What . . . what's up, Chief?"

Masters didn't reply for a moment, then he said quietly: "We shall need this key." Reed noted the quiet decision in Masters' voice.

"Straight away, Chief, or shall we wait till . . . ?"

"Now, I think." He thought for a moment. "What's the best way of going about it?" He looked up. "We shall have to be careful."

"Somebody has got to know if we want the key, Chief."

"True. Look, we must not be seen here, otherwise we could do a lot of harm. The best thing is for us to get out of this alley. We're too conspicuous. Come on." Masters led the way across the sand heap, saying as they went: "I shall hang about and smoke a pipe, keeping the entrance in view. You find the DCI and Sergeant Berger and ask them to join me wherever I am out here."

"And tell them what, Chief?"

"That I'd like their help please."

Reed stopped. "About the key, Chief . . . "

"Yes."

"I think Sar'nt Berger and I could open it."

"It's not a spring lock to be forced with a cheque card."

"An old-fashioned mortice, Chief. One that has a biggish key, but very simple for all that. Berger and I could do it—with your permission, of course."

Masters nodded. "What would you need? Heavy wire?"

"Perhaps. Maybe only the set of Allen keys from the car. We'll bring them."

"Right. Make it quick."

It was almost a quarter of an hour before Green appeared alone. He strolled quite casually up to where Masters was standing under the trees opposite, but forty or so yards distant, from the end of the alleyway.

"I've taken my time coming, George, because young Reed said you didn't want anybody to see us prancing about with excitement."

Masters grinned. "I'd like to see you doing it, Bill."

"Like Hitler in Paris, you mean?"

"If you say so."

"The old devil actually did skip about in front of the *Arc de Triomphe* after Paris fell in forty. The silly old bastard was in jackboots and full Nazi fig, too. It was then we finally knew he was a clown. A wicked clown, but a clown nonetheless."

"I didn't know that."

"And I don't know why you sent Reed to find us."

"I think we've struck oil, Bill. Only think, mind you, but the idea seemed to leap into my mind so readily, that I felt we couldn't ignore it."

"And?"

"We have to keep it quiet, so I thought the sooner we all got together so that I could hang my idea on you and then do something about it . . . "

"Fair enough."

"Do you mind if we wait for the sergeants, before I start spouting, Bill?"

Green shrugged and took out a, by now, battered packet of cigarettes.

"Did you come across anything worthy of further investigation?" asked Masters as the DCI lit up.

"Nice of you to ask. The answer is no. Not an emphatic no, because there are so many nooks and crannies that anything could be hidden there, but there was nothing to make us actively suspicious. And as you reckon you've struck oil, it's not likely that what we're looking for was in our search area. So . . . " He shrugged again. "So you've got the body or bodies, we haven't."

"I haven't discovered them," replied Masters quietly. "I haven't a clue as to where they are."

"Then what the hell?"

"The sergeants are coming, Bill. We'll have a chat before lunch and decide whether I'm on safe ground and, if so, how to play it."

Reed and Berger strolled up. "All fit, Chief," said Reed laconically.

"Thank you. I'd suggest we went indoors for this chat, but I want everybody to hear, and at the same time I want to keep watch on the alleyway that runs between the gymnasium and the old building. Please don't look round or stare at it, but the mouth of the alley is straight opposite us, and when you do see it, casually, you will see that there is a large dump of sand not far from the entrance. At the far end of the alley is an old brick-built shed with a door and a window. The door is locked, so one can't get in, and there is an electricity warning notice which I believe is bogus.

"The window is pretty scruffy, inside and out, but after we rubbed the outside it was just possible to make out some of what was in there. It is, I believe, the store room for pieces of old electrical equipment. Perhaps not an official one, but Woolgar probably turns a blind eye if any member of his staff rescues old items and dumps them there for cannibalisation of still-useful parts."

158

"By any member of his staff," grunted Green, "you presumably mean Rimmer, as he's the electrics buff round here."

Masters nodded. Reed protested: "When I wanted to say something like that an hour ago you read me a lecture about not naming names in order to keep an open mind."

"Quite right, lad. But circumstances change. That was before we'd got anything positive to pin on any one person, despite what we might think. Now His Nibs has come up with something that has to do with a load of electrical junk, and as Rimmer is the sparks round here, that constitutes a positive pointer towards him. So he can now be named."

"Since when have we been so almighty cagey about naming names?"

"Steady, lad. It's an old saying, 'No names, no pack drill.'"

"Rubbish. Mrs Masters' car went missing from the Chief's quarter as soon as she got here. She'd only got out of the car and walked about fifteen feet to get into the house. And only one person came near the place in between her arrival and the keys going missing. It must have been Rimmer who nicked them—off the table as he passed through the kitchen or wherever it was she'd put them down. I know it, you know it, we all know it. But everybody has been fighting shy of saying so. Why?"

"Because we'd no proof, lad. Don't take this the wrong way, but you were there, too. What you've said about Sergeant Rimmer could apply to Detective Sergeant Reed. We know that you didn't pinch the keys. But put the circumstances of their going missing in front of the crowd that pulled young Berger and me in yesterday and tell me what they'd have said."

Reed, disgusted, merely murmured, "That lot!" and let the subject drop.

Green turned to Masters. "You were saying, George?"

"I confess I jumped to the conclusion that the shed would only ever be used by one man. That notice he had put up suggested to me that he was pretty keen on keeping it private and I assumed—thinking I knew some of his tricky habits when it comes to keys—that he would have possession of the only key to the door. It seemed to me he could claim there would be no reason why anybody else should ever need to go there."

"Fair enough. But could he dump the bodies there?"

"There was no sign of bodies as far as I could see."

"Then what the hell are we talking about?"

"I think that his shed was his spider's web."

"You mean he lured the lads there and then knocked them off?"

"Yes."

"How?"

"You'll see it all more plainly when we go in there, but this is what I think."

"So what do we do?" growled Green, after Masters had finished his explanation.

"You and I stay this end of the alley to guard against unwanted interruptions or spying, and the sergeants force the door."

"As soon as you like," grunted Green. "And if I happen to see that bloke Rimmer . . . "

"You'll ignore him," said Masters. "You'll play the waiting game, as we all will."

The lock took some minutes before yielding to the attentions of Berger who seemed the more proficient of the two sergeants at this type of exercise.

"Once we're all inside we'll be more or less invisible except to a close-comer," said Masters, "so nobody need stay or watch."

They stood in a crowded group inside the hut and looked around carefully.

"Just as you said, George," grunted Green.

"Make sure we're right in everything," said Masters to Berger, "but oblige me by touching nothing."

They waited for some minutes before Berger said quietly, "It's all here, Chief."

"Thank you. Now, can anybody think of anything we have overlooked to satisfy ourselves that there is reasonable and defensible evidence of what we think took place here?"

"Short of dusting for prints, nothing, Chief," said Reed.

"Everything's here," growled Green. He turned to Masters.

"It's an execution chamber right enough, George. We'll be able to show that beyond doubt. The problem is now to prove it was ever used."

"And that means finding bodies."

"Does it, Chief?" queried Berger.

"I think so. I know we don't have to produce bodies to prove murder, but it is easier if we do."

Green nodded his agreement. "Makes the job a lot harder without bodies."

"I think we could leave the finer details for the moment," said Masters. "It's fairly obvious we shall have to have an expert here to inspect and report and, if necessary, give testimony in court. But we can't get him here. It's not our case and we must touch nothing until it has all been examined at the request of the local force."

"You're going to call them in straight away are you, George?"

Masters looked at Green. "Well, now, Bill, we have no proof of any crime having been committed here, have we? If we had proof . . . "

"Like a body or two?"

"Exactly. If we had overt proof of crime it would be our duty to report it. But I can't see that a force, widely deployed to find the body of a missing youth, would take even a passing interest in the junk shed of a jobbing electrician. They could even think we were being frivolous in drawing their attention to it—with no solid proof to back up our theory."

"Just so, just so," murmured Green, catching the mood. "The locals could even accuse us of being obstructionist. I mean to say, after they said what they did yesterday because I did not immediately claim to be from the Yard, they could even believe I was trying to get a little of my own back."

"I get it," said Reed. "We're going on to get the lot before we show our hand. Is that it, Chief?"

"Well now," said Masters, glancing at his watch, "time for a little smackerel of something, I think. But I don't think we can leave this place unattended."

"I knew it," said Reed. "You want us to dust and photograph . . . "

161

"Not dust. Photographs only. A complete pictorial record, please. I suggest that Berger fetches the camera from the car. No flashes. I don't want to attract attention. . . ."

"There's not much light, Chief. I know it's a bright day, but . . . "

"Can you do it without attracting attention?"

"Only somebody going across the end of the alley could see it, Chief, and if Sergeant Reed keeps his eye open and tells me when I can or can't use the flash . . ."

"Right. I'll leave it to you. When you get back with the camera, Reed can get you both some sandwiches from the mess. Remember, leave everything as it is. The DCI and I will be back at two."

"Come on, George," said Green. "They're itching to get rid of us."

Masters nodded and looked down at his side pocket to make sure he had his copy of the large scale map in his pocket. Green noticed this. "We shan't need that to find our way home for lunch."

"I want another look at it," said Masters cryptically.

"Any special reason?" asked Green as they left the hut.

"Yes."

"I thought there might be. I mean you're not the sort to want to sit scanning just any old map through the lunch hour if there wasn't something you were looking for."

Masters laughed. "I see you've got your copy in your pocket." They turned right round the front of the gymnasium and then struck off at an angle towards the house. "You don't credit me with much professional zeal, Bill."

"And that's where you're wrong. You do more homework than most, but you regulate it better. You wouldn't go home for lunch with Wanda and young Michael and then bury yourself in some document unless the need was pressing or it could pay dividends in some other way."

"True. With a family like mine, I should be a fool to ignore them."

"That's what I'm saying. So why the anxiety to look at the map?"

162

"I'd have done it out in the open, Bill, but for obvious reasons I'd prefer to study it under cover."

"You think the hut you've found isn't enough? That you've missed something or there's something still to come?"

"Still to come? Yes. A body or bodies. As to what I'm missing, well, I think the answer to that is that I could do with a drink. And, I suspect, so could you."

"Not 'arf. There's some large bottles of beer, George. Ones you can really fill a tankard from. Not these little cans made to go into phoney little European sized glasses that they give away free with petrol. Ghastly, they are. Straight sided and so narrow you can't get your nose into the froth like you can with a pint mug."

"Screw-topped bottles, Bill?"

"That's right. When I went shopping and saw them, I thought they're the things for us. I tucked them away for an occasion. I reckon you finding that hut is an occasion."

"Fine, but keep the news from the girls, please, Bill. I'd rather we kept a happy atmosphere for them in the house."

"You're right, but they'll have to know sooner or later."

"Of course, but I would prefer it later, and if the locals happen to make an arrest, well, we won't know much about it, will we?"

"Humbug," growled Green. "And while we're talking about the locals, how are you proposing to tell them you've cracked their case for them without even trying. It's going to be tricky."

"It's got to be done."

"I know. But I asked how."

"We'll discuss it this afternoon, Bill. Ah! There's Doris with Michael waiting at the door for us."

"There's nothing I like better than a sweet violet," announced Green as he helped himself to the fare on the luncheon table.

"Violets, William?" queried Wanda, accepting a chunk of fresh French bread from her husband. "I didn't know you were particularly fond of them."

"Pay no attention to him, dear," said Doris. "The fool

means pickled onions. He'll eat the dishful if you don't watch him."

Wanda smiled. "They're here to be eaten, of course, but so many? People will be aware of him from yards away."

"He revels in that sort of thing," said Doris. "I've even heard him refer to them as halitosis pills, and as for what he calls radishes . . . "

"Burp pills," interrupted Green. "What's wrong with that. You and Wanda use the word. When you wanted the choker here to bring up wind, you talked about burping him."

"That's not the word I meant," said his wife. "You call them eructation aids. And I remember when I first asked you what you meant you said they made you belch better than Henry the Eighth. Disgusting."

"Maybe," said Green, "but you did ask."

"What's that got to do with being disgusting?"

"Seek and ye shall find, ask and it shall be belched forth unto you."

"He grows worse," said Doris to Wanda.

Wanda grinned. "I've noticed . . . "

"You've what?" demanded Green.

"I've noticed that when you've discovered something, William, or are feeling mighty pleased with yourself, you indulge in a load of inconsequential twaddle."

"I like that!" exclaimed Green, his mouth full of cheese and pickle. He swallowed the food and turned to Masters. "Did you hear what your little missus said?"

"Inconsequential twaddle," said Masters with a grin. "A fairly good description of your conversation at table so far, I'd have said."

"That's what I'd expect from you, but from Wanda, never. Still, as I keep telling her, it comes from living with you. She's picking up your bad habits."

"No you don't," said Wanda.

"Don't what, love?" asked Green innocently.

"Try to change the subject and head me off. I said you were feeling pleased with yourself. Very different from yesterday at this time. I know yesterday you had been subjected to treatment which would make anybody angry.

But you recovered your equanimity quite quickly and were more or less on an even keel. Now you're being garrulous, which shows us that today something has happened to cheer you up."

"Garrulous now, am I, love? I'd have preferred you to refer to my lunchtime conversation as . . . pass the cheese board, George, would you? Tasty bit of mousetrap, this. What we used to call sore cheese when I was a lad. You know, the sort that makes the inside of your mouth tingle. Thanks. I'll put it down here, just in case I need it again."

Doris had listened patiently to this typical wodge of circumlocution from her husband. When it was over, she said: "As what?"

"I beg your pardon?" asked Green.

"You said, before you got greedy for the cheese . . . "

"Greedy? You mean like a hungry rodent?" He bared his teeth and glared at Doris, who ignored the interruption and continued, " . . . that you would have preferred Wanda to describe your nonsense as something or another."

"Airy persiflage," said Green, selecting another pickled onion.

"Airy what?"

"Persiflage, love. It means light banter."

"It also means," said Wanda, "a frivolous way of treating a serious subject, I think. Doesn't it, George?"

"I imagine so, though it is not a term I use myself. As far as I can remember the only memory I have of it is a reference by the one and only W. Schwenk Gilbert, famed librettist and creator of ludicrously incongruous plots, the words of which, as he so rightly claimed, were not entirely without merit—as compared to his collaborator's musical score, that is."

"George," said Wanda seriously.

"Yes, my darling?"

"You're at it now. You and William are conspiring to keep Doris and me in the dark concerning your case which, it is apparent from your attitudes, has taken a turn for the better. We should like to know what has happened."

Masters gazed at his wife for a moment and then said:

"Bill and I are feeling a little happier about things in general. So much is true. But for you to attribute it to a great success would be wrong. We have not solved the problem, nor have we discovered a body or bodies. However, as you know, we are nibbling round the fringes of this business and treating it as a mental exercise rather than a practical investigation, because we have no standing in the matter and, therefore, no opportunity to be totally active."

"I know that."

"The four of us confer, as you also know. And that has yielded a number of good ideas which we feel could well be relevant and which—more importantly—we feel we can investigate surreptitiously. I confess we are quite excited by the prospect. But they are only ideas, and ideas are fragile things and, in this case, only partial and quite nebulous. To recount the conversations we have had and what has come out of them would be pointless until we have tested them. I say this, because they are technical and we need to seek advice because we don't fully understand them ourselves. But the mere fact that we have opened up a few more avenues has cheered us up. That is the situation. What I have said leaves you two ladies little the wiser as to facts and details, but we have none of these to offer up at the moment. When we have . . . well, if the situation permits, we shall let you know."

"Thank you," replied Wanda. "A nicely-put brush off."

"Not so, darling. Merely a deferment of the news you naturally wish to hear. I hope you will accept what I have said, because we have nothing for you yet."

Wanda smiled at him. "Of course I'll accept it. We're very lucky to be privy to what you and William and the sergeants do so often in your cases. The trouble with having privileges like that is that they encourage one to want more. And to ask for it."

"Like me with cheese," said Green.

"I expect so, William. Sorry to have been so . . . so importunate."

"No need to apologise, love. I'm nosey myself, so I know what it feels like when I think I'm missing out on things. Can

166

I have a pear from the bowl? Fingers will do. No need to pass the lot. Ta!"

After lunch, when the dining table had been cleared and the two men were alone, Green said: "Right, George. What's all this about the map?"

Masters drew the folded plan from his pocket and put it on the table, still unopened.

"I've been thinking, Bill."

"For a change, you mean? Do you ever do anything else, George?"

"Whilst we were having lunch, I mean."

Green waited. "I said I wanted to consult the plan again, because when I had it open at first, I noted the old vinery, the old laundry, old stables and so on, and I noticed that the place we have just visited is called 'Cutter's Shed'."

"Cutter's?"

"Yes. See for yourself." Masters opened the sheet fully and put his finger on the map spot.

"Cutter's," repeated Green. "What does that mean? Wood cutter's shed?"

"That's what I thought, originally, though I couldn't see that a building such as that would be much of a fuel store for a property as big as the original house, here. Inconvenient, too, to get big stuff in for sawing and chopping, I'd have said."

"You're right there. Wood sheds were open-sided, with enough room for a chap to work and stack his cut timber besides the big stuff he'd need in there for drying out. But if not for wood cutting, what was its purpose?"

Masters sat back and started to pack an after-lunch pipe. "I think—or I hope—I've got the answer to that, although the plan doesn't help except in one way."

"What's that?"

"Why should builders—or an architect—leave a rather inconvenient blind alley running between what are, after all, the two large buildings that form the front elevation of the College? The old house and the new gymnasium. I could understand it if that alleyway were to have been left there as an unblocked walkway between the two buildings, to save a

167

long trudge round one or the other to get to the back of those buildings or to the car park and living quarters. But it has Cutter's Shed across it and that leaves it as nothing more than a dumping area for heaps of sand."

Green waited for Masters to continue.

"I know I suggested that the builders might have found the shed useful as a works' office, but I can think of no reason why, when the extensions were finished, it wasn't pulled down and the walkway established."

"So?"

"So I have two queries to answer. Why waste valuable building ground by not butting the two buildings together or, why not demolish the eyesore hut which, as far as I can see, has no aesthetic value and merely serves as an inconvenient block to what could be a useful route between the buildings? Now, while Reed and I were searching this morning, we came across a number of tumbledown outbuildings which, in my opinion, could usefully have been demolished. But at least they were tucked away round the back, not in anybody's way and, I suppose, are capable of reclamation at some time for some purpose. But a small hut to the front of the buildings? I thought there had to be a reason why it was left there."

"And you're now going to tell me why."

"Yes. The result of my cogitations over lunch while you were engaging the rest of the company with airy persiflage. I came to the conclusion that the area of ground that constitutes that alleyway was considered by the architect and surveyor as unsafe to build on."

"Unsafe? Why?"

"Because it wouldn't take the weight of the end wall of that huge gymnasium."

Green stared at him. "How in hell's name can you possibly have known that? George, have you gone off your trolley?"

Masters spread his hands, deprecatingly. "I haven't said I knew it—or even know it. I've concluded it."

Green scratched one ear. "Just like that! You've concluded that a small area of ground has been left vacant because it won't take the weight of the end wall of a building?"

"Yes."

"Because an alleyway has been left open and a little old brick shed left standing you claim that the ground is . . . what? Likely to cave in? Subsidence, is that it?"

"Precisely."

"But you have no grounds whatsoever for assuming any such thing."

"I didn't assume, I concluded."

"You mean thare are reasons behind what you have thought up?"

Masters nodded.

"This Cutter's Shed. We're both agreed that it is unlikely to have been the place where the woodcutter worked."

Masters nodded again.

"So who worked there? A cutter of what?" demanded Green.

"Ice."

Without a word, Green started to get to his feet. "You just stay there, George. I'll get Wanda and then ring for the doctor . . . "

"Sit down, you silly ass, Bill."

Green slowly complied. "Ice," he snorted. "An ice-cutter's hut. What sort of a joke are you trying to pull now, George?"

"No joke, Bill. It's obvious you've never heard of ice-cutters. But they still exist. Not in this country perhaps but certainly in South America for example. They have men there, whose sole livelihood comes from taking a few donkeys, everyday, up into the Andes to the face of the nearest glacier. There they cut out huge blocks of ice, wrap them in straw and matting, load them, two to each animal, and bring the ice down into the local towns—to the markets and drinking houses. The ice is cut into smaller pieces and sold to keep the fish, meat and booze cold, much the same as happened everywhere else in the world until comparatively recently."

Green grimaced. "I can remember ice lorries delivering dirty great blocks to fishmongers," he agreed. "And I know trawlers went to sea with holds full of crushed ice. And the ice-cream men. They had big wooden boxes full of broken ice, with just a little metal cylinder in the middle for the hokey-pokey itself."

169

"Hokey-pokey?"

"Hokey-pokey, penny a lump, it's the stuff to give you the hump," quoted Green. "Where were you brought up, George? Ice cream—the old custard sort—was known as hokey-pokey."

"I see. But to get back to ice cutting. In the old days, before domestic refrigerators or their forerunners, the great ice-houses at fish docks and the cellars at the old Billingsgate market, big houses such as the one which is now the foundation of this College, had need for ice, particularly in summer when there were hordes of guests to be entertained, wine to be cooled . . . "

"I've seen some of the old wine coolers," broke in Green. "I bid for one once at an auction. A long wooden trough, lined with zinc or lead, perhaps, and standing on splayed legs. A lovely bit of furniture, built for a great dining room, of course. I thought Doris would like it for plants."

"Did you get it?"

"Did I heckers-like. Too pricey."

"Hard luck. But where do you think the ice came from for troughs like that in, say, the middle of the last century?"

Green shrugged. "I suppose I'd better say the ice cutter provided it, and then you'll ask me where he got it from when it was ninety in the shade and melting the parasols and croquet balls."

"Right. Where did the cutter get his ice from? The answer is he made it in the winter and kept it for when it was needed."

"And how did he do that?"

"In his ice-pit."

"Pit?"

"Underground chamber in which ice was stored for preservation throughout the year. It was built with non-conducting walls. By that I mean they applied non-conducting materials to the stone they constructed the pit of. I'm not sure of my facts here, but I think they used a good deal of straw or rushes, made to adhere with cow dung. Some I suppose used the ordinary chalk or lime daub of the day. . . ."

"And they kept their domestic ice in it."

170

"Harvested ice, they called it, but I'm sure they had bowls and cloths to keep it moderately hygienic, and they probably washed it before putting it in lemonade or hock and seltzer or in their iced puddings, which I believe they ate a lot of."

"Wait a moment, George. This cutter bloke. He wouldn't be overworked, would he? I mean he could get this harvested ice when the weather was freezing. Where did he get it from? The duck pond?"

Masters laughed. "Despite their way of cladding their walls they paid some attention to cleanliness. The cutter had a variety of vessels—pans, tubs and the like—which he would fill with water and put out overnight in cold weather. Some, I believe, were merely shallow pans an inch or two deep for use in less severe weather, but they had big wooden troughs—with sloping sides so that the ice would fall out when overturned—and that would give them the huge chunks that would refrigerate the chamber itself, without melting. Little broken pieces or thin layers would tend to disappear gradually—to evaporate rather than melt—if the great chunks were not there."

Green nodded his head. "I've seen wooden tubs like that. When I was a kid women round our way used to wash clothes in them. They had a dolly tub for poshing the clothes—that was like a metal dustbin. But for scrubbing they had these wooden things with sloping sides. One end was always more sloped than the other and they used to kneel down to scrub clothes on that end. Like they used to use those ridged boards in skiffle groups twenty or thirty years back."

"Actually, I've seen one of those tubs in a little museum," replied Masters, "and it was more or less exactly what I imagine the ice cutters used." He straightened up. "So, chum, I reckon that alleyway was not built over because the surveyor's soundings told him there was some sort of cavity below it. So he moved the gymnasium wall out a few feet and left the hut. He did that, I imagine, because he either felt the alley would not be strong enough to take much traffic or he discovered the entrance to the ice-pit and thought it best not to destroy the old place, just as he didn't destroy the vinery, laundry and stables."

171

"So," said Green, "you reckon there's a pit under that shed."

Masters nodded. "There was a mat on the floor, I seem to remember."

"A rubber one," said Green. "An old darts strip cut in two, with the halves laid side by side. I remember thinking Rimmer had probably scrounged it from the mess bar at some time."

"Under that, then."

Green took out a cigarette. "The lads will have discovered it."

"I think not. I told them to touch nothing."

"So what do we do? Call the locals to open it up?"

Masters smiled. "What do you suggest, Bill?"

"They've got to be told."

"Of course. But what if we're mistaken?"

"If you're mistaken, you mean."

"Whichever."

Green looked up. "We've got to make sure ourselves. Not that I've any doubts. Then, we've got to tell them, though I honestly wouldn't like the job myself."

"Of opening the chamber or of telling the locals?"

"Telling the locals. However well you put it they're going to be niggled, even if they are grateful. I mean, how do you go up to the local DS and say, "Oh, by the way, when I came down here three or four days ago I heard you'd been trying to solve a little problem for the past five years. So I've sorted it out for you in between preparing and delivering lectures?"

Masters grinned. "Put like that it does sound a little condescending. But we owe these people a bit of a jolt for the way they behaved to you and Berger, so I'm not concerned to wrap it up too diplomatically for them."

"Nice of you to remember young Berger and myself, George, but you needn't bother if it's going to cause difficulties and red faces all round. Getting a bit of our own back would be nice, I know, but . . . "

"Cut it out, Bill. If you hadn't been personally involved in that fiasco yesterday morning but the two sergeants had

172

suffered the treatment, you'd have moved heaven and earth to do something on their behalf. I believe you would even have complained to the AC Crime. Me, I'm making no harsh complaint about them, in fact I'm being very kind. I'm handing them the solution to an intractable problem on a plate. How's that for co-operation? A kiss for a blow."

Green grinned. "It all depends how you propose to hand them their solution, and in what terms."

"As to that," replied Masters, "I'll tell you as we go to the hut. The sergeants will be getting a little bored by now."

"And you wouldn't by any chance be in a hurry to make sure there's an ice-chamber below that hut, would you?" asked Green, getting to his feet. "With two dead bodies in it just as a bonus?"

"It will be rather nice if all our surmising turns out to be correct."

"And if it does?"

"We touch nothing, and I go straight to see Bobby Locke."

"To tell him?"

"Perhaps not. That's what I want to talk to you about, Bill. Come on, let's not keep Reed and Berger waiting any longer."

As they left the house, Green said: "Right, George, fire away. How are you proposing to break this to the locals?"

"Do you know what I'd really like to do, Bill?"

"Tell me."

"To present the whole thing as an object lesson, here in the College, as an example of what Bobby Locke wants me to introduce."

"The use of a Moderator?"

"Yes. I'd like to get Fred Pollock up from Truro, brief him, and then get him to run the session, with the four of us on the panel with a forensic man and one or two of the local characters who have been so ungainfully employed on this business either recently or over the last five years."

Green pondered this for a moment and then looked at Masters walking beside him. "Be honest with me, George. Are you proposing the Moderator session to fulfill your obligation to the College, to show them how it should be done, or are you intent on doing it to get your own back in public for the way the locals treated young Berger and me?"

"Both," said Masters without further explanation.

"In that case," said Green, "all I can say is I'd like to see old Fred Pollock again if he can get away from Truro for a day or two."

"Am I to take that as agreement with my plan?"

"Why not? If you can swing it on Bobby Locke and the locals. That's going to be the difficult bit. Getting them to agree whilst withholding the news that we've already sewn up their case. They could turn nasty later on, George, if they wanted to. A senior Yard detective holding back vital information could be the basis of a very serious complaint."

"Quite. But I have no vital information. Only surmise that what I've seen in the Cutter's hut would lead me to come to certain conclusions that might or might not be borne out were we eventually to discover that there is a chamber containing bodies below that building."

"You mean you are not going to open it up?"

"Not if we can do the Moderator stunt on them."

"No, George. You've got to complete the case. Then in, say, a week's time, you can put on your Moderator session, showing how it was done. Nobody will object to that, not even the locals. Their guv'nor might even be pleased to send his chaps along to co-operate and learn something."

Masters shrugged. "That's your advice, Bill?"

"It is. I'm not having you play a dangerous game on my account. You could ruin your career or at least set it back. It's not worth it, just to show the locals up or pay them back. We go ahead as if this was a normal case. You report—if there's anything to report—to the locals tonight when they come to Bobby Locke's drinking party."

"You're threatening me, Bill."

"That's right, and if you don't do as I say, I'll blow the gaff myself."

Masters turned and grinned. "Thanks."

"What for?"

"Keeping me in line. Ah, there's the alley. Skirt the sand if

174

you can, I don't want us to leave too many footprints over it to warn you-know-who should he see them."

"Shouldn't he either be taken in or put under observation?" demanded Green.

"As soon as we have solid cause." Masters opened the hut door and stepped inside. Reed was alone.

"Berger?" asked Masters.

"Gone on a bit of a recce, Chief. To locate Rimmer and see what he's about. I expect he'll be back in a minute or two. We've been looking at everything in here, Chief—without touching. Nothing of much note except that there's a dirty great hook on the central joist above your head there, and an old block and tackle in the corner."

"Just what we wanted to hear, lad," said Green.

"Pull the other one," said Reed. "I was only talking to the Chief . . . "

"The DCI was not joking," said Masters. "Would you be good enough to roll up those two bits of rubber mat, please, and let's see what you can discover to warrant the use of a geared pulley fixed immediately above them?"

Reed did as he had been asked.

"Heavy metal trap door, Chief. Just like the ones outside pubs for letting beer barrels down to the cellars."

"Can we lift it by hand, or do we need the block with tackle?"

"It's heavy, Chief. If you could lend a hand . . . "

The two younger men strained to lift the large iron plate while Green stood by ready to insert bits of old electrical goods as wedges as soon as gaps appeared. Even with so much strength deployed, it was a slow job to raise and lay the cover back.

"No wonder it was bloody heavy," said Reed. "It's lined with two-inch oak."

"That's why there's a hook in the ceiling and that block, lad," said Green. "If you look at it closely you'll see there's a pulley system in it. The ratio will be such that one chap could lift this plate and let down whatever went below."

"You mean bodies," said Reed.

"I mean ice, lad, blocks of ice. Where's your general knowledge? Haven't you ever heard of ice-pits?"

Masters smiled. Half an hour earlier, Green himself had been unaware of the old fashioned ways of preserving ice.

"Down there's a dirty great refrigerator, lad, a couple of hundred years old," went on Green. "This iron lid isn't an original, I'd say. Probably it had stone slabs up to the late eighties." He rattled this off knowingly. "And if you'll take the trouble to look in the hole, lad, you'll see that only half the stairway is steps, the other half is a ramp for running stuff down on." He turned to Masters. "They probably sent the stuff down on rush mats, wouldn't you say, George?"

Masters entered into the game. "Rush mats, Bill? Maybe, but I'd have said hurdles. Although that ramp looks as if it had been worn smooth, I think some of the little protruberances would soon have worn through rush matting. Hurdles would be harder and cheaper to make."

"Quite right," agreed Green. "These things were a bit before my time, so I never actually saw one in action." He sighed exaggeratedly. "But nowadays these youngsters have never even heard of them. I often wonder if they ever read anything or were taught anything at school other than the five- and ten-times tables so they can count the metric money."

Reed was standing agape, looking from one to the other, not quite sure whether to take them seriously or not. He was spared the embarrassment of asking by the arrival of Berger who stopped, stared down the hole and then said: "Somebody's been busy. It would have taken a gang of a dozen men a month to dig that in London. Longer if they hadn't got a mechanical shovel."

"Where's Rimmer?" demanded Green.

"He's putting a new strip light up in one of the offices. He's not too happy because he's having to move an old one, and the ceiling is concrete. That means he's got to drill and also he's got to run the cable in conduit. It'll take him an hour or two at this rate, I reckon."

"Nevertheless," said Masters, "you'd better keep watch up here. Outside, I think. I don't want him coming up to the

176

hut and seeing this place open. If he does come, and you can't head him off by fair words, or if your mere presence looks as though it had given the game away, arrest him. Both of you, I think. The DCI and I can go down there and see what there is to see."

Berger asked: "How did you know the cellar was there, Chief? The floor didn't sound hollow when we were in here before."

"It wasn't meant to," said Reed airily. "The flap is heavily lined, as you can see, and there was a thick rubber mat over it. In any case, it isn't a cellar. It's an ice-pit. I'd have thought you would have known that. In the old days, when the DCI was young . . . "

"Out," growled Green. "Hand me that torch, then get git. And shut the door behind you."

"Use both hands, Bill," warned Masters, who was leading the way. "These treads are not very wide. One hand on the wall and one on the ramp if you can reach down."

"That cutter chap would have used the pulley rope as a hand rail, I suppose," puffed Green, going down, crabwise. "Not too fast with the torch, George."

A minute or so later they were standing in the small chamber. Long and narrow, little more than a wide passage, it had a stone sill, eighteen inches above the floor, down both sides and across the far end. It was at that end on the sill, one on either side, that the two bodies lay, fully clothed.

"Poor little sods," murmured Green. "Still lifelike, aren't they? I mean, there's practically no deterioration."

"And no smell," agreed Masters looking closely at the hands of the boys. "This place is so well insulated there's been no corruption." He raised his voice slightly. "Up you go, Bill. There's nothing we can do down here. The forensic buff has to see them first and then it's up to the locals." He swung the torch beam towards the steps. "It should be a bit easier going up."

Masters called Berger in.

"Still got a camera handy?"

"Yes, Chief."

"Go down there and take a couple of quick shots."

177

"Bodies?"

"Yes. At the far end. Here, you'll need the torch to see your way Don't be long about it . . . "

Berger was back very quickly. "Just two flashes of each, Chief. That enough?"

"Plenty. Now, please give me a hand to get this plate back."

When all was restored to normal, with the rubber mats down to cover the metal grid, Masters said to Green. "I want a quick wash, Bill. Then I'm going to ask Bobby Locke to grant us an immediate interview. You and I, that is. Reed and Berger will have to keep an eye on this place."

"And Rimmer," grunted Green.

"There's a loo with a washbasin on the ground floor of the office block, Chief. Liquid soap and an electric hand-dryer."

"Thank you. You and Reed know what to do?"

Berger nodded.

"I don't know when we'll be free."

"We'll still be here, Chief."

"You'd better be," grated Green.

Chapter 7

"Hello, George. Gertie said you insisted on seeing me."

"This is Bill Green, Bobby. Former DCI, now SSCO at the Yard."

Locke shook hands with Green, and invited him to sit. But he had little time for the courtesies, because of his anxiety to learn the reason for Masters' demand to see him.

"Good news, I hope, George?"

"Good? Serious I think would be more appropriate."

Locke looked alarmed. "Andriessen . . . ?" he asked sharply.

Masters shook his head. "He's in the clear, definitely and finally. We can prove that now."

"Thank heaven for that. George, I can hardly tell you how grateful . . . "

"Please, Bobby," interrupted Masters. "Hear us out first. We've cleared Andriessen, as you wanted, but in doing so . . . well, it's a sordid business. We are here to report. I think you may wish to have the Commandant present."

Locke stared at him. "The Commandant lives in a bit of a rarified atmosphere, George."

"Then he'd better come down to earth, quick," grunted Green. "Policy and admin and whatever else he does is going to have to wait for a bit."

Locke paused for a moment, scanning their faces, and then lifted the internal phone. "Very well," he said. "I'll have a word with him."

Two or three minutes later Masters and Green were being introduced to the Commandant in the latter's office on the first floor.

When they were all seated, Highett said: "We've not met before this, Mr Masters, but I've been kept abreast of your activities among us by Bobby Locke here. I was expecting to meet you for the first time tonight at the drinks party. But I understand that events have overtaken us. What have you got to tell me?"

Masters, with some help from Green, gave a comprehensive account of their work over the preceding few days. It took over twenty minutes, during which time neither the Commandant nor the Dean interrupted. Both men, middle-aged and accustomed to long years of academic authority, which usually tends to engender the habit of putting questions at every opportunity, sat as still as music lovers listening to a favourite symphony exquisitely played.

"That is the situation, gentlemen. The bodies of the two missing youths—as yet unidentified, of course—lie within the purlieus of the College. We believe we know how they were killed, but that is a problem for the local forensic team. We also believe we know the identity of the murderer— unfortunately one of your employees. And finally, though I didn't mention it in our report, I believe that Green and I can supply a motive—always supposing our suspect, after further investigation by the local forces, turns out to be the one they arrest for the crimes."

"I think we are safe in assuming that will be the case," said Highett quietly. "Thank you, gentlemen. You will have set many minds at rest by your good work. Not least those of the Dean and myself, for even though the suspect is employed here, the effects of that, from the point of view of the College, will be far less traumatic than had one of our foreign students become involved by police error."

"Hear, hear," said Locke, thankfully.

Highett continued. "Now we have to decide what is to be done. I obviously cannot explain to the local CID officers, over a telephone, all you have told me this afternoon, but without such an explanation I cannot ask them to come and arrest Rimmer. But the man must be held. Do you agree, Masters?"

"He must certainly be kept under close observation, sir. I think that as yet he has no inkling that we are on to him, but he could presumably take it into his head to visit that hut, and though we have been very careful, I cannot guarantee that everything there is exactly as it was, and a man in Rimmer's situation would immediately be aware that somebody had been inside if something was slightly out of place. A sort of sixth sense would tell him so, just as a woman will know if her dressing-table drawers have been turned over in her absence even though nothing is missing."

"So you think we ought to take him up?"

"Only if he makes for the hut," grunted Green.

"I agree with that, sir," said Masters. "In the meantime, could I suggest that you phone the local CID and say that you have what you believe will be vital information for them in the missing boys investigation and that you would appreciate an immediate but unobtrusive visit by the senior officer on the case. I feel sure you know somebody of sufficient authority to arrange that."

Highett nodded. "I can do as you suggest quite easily. And do I leave Rimmer at large?"

"If the proposed visit can have the appearance of a low-key, routine call, sir, I would leave him under observation. If, however, our colleagues arrive with sirens blaring and tyres squealing, our man would almost certainly be warned that there could be trouble."

"I can stress the need for normality."

"In that case, sir, Green and I will be on hand when you receive them. I think our best plan is simply to show them what we have found and then hold ourselves ready for questions and explanations after they have done what they have to do at the scene. Then Rimmer will have to be taken in."

Highett turned to Locke. "Any suggestions, Bobby?"

"I concur with what Masters has suggested, sir."

"Good. Sorry about your party tonight, but our guests will understand why you will have to cancel."

Masters said: "I wouldn't cancel the party, sir. Green and I could probably tell our story better in a relaxed atmosphere, and there will be nobody there who shouldn't . . . "

"Only a few of us and a few of the interested local officers,"

181

agreed Locke. "If you really feel you can make it—literally—a working party, so be it."

"Good," said Highett. "Now, gentlemen, the sooner I get on to the local CID, the better."

"Detective Inspector Kendon, Detective Sergeant Welch and Detective Constable Smail," said Highett, introducing the local officers who had arrived within half an hour of his phone call.

"We've met," grated Green, "Under unhappier circumstances."

Masters came in hastily to prevent Green saying too much more about the circumstances referred to. "We have some information for you, Mr Kendon."

"You have, sir? I thought it was Mr Highett . . . "

"DCS Masters is the man," said the Commandant. "I was merely the messenger boy. I would advise you three gentlemen to put yourselves entirely in his hands."

"If you say so, sir."

"I do say so, and I have been at pains to inform your DCS that I was about to advise you to do so, and he has concurred." He turned to Masters. "So, if you will take over, George, please, I'll leave it to you."

"Thank you, sir." He said to Kendon: "If you will all three come with me, we will talk as we go."

The mutinous attitude plainly visible on the faces of the locals began to disappear as Masters told them he was escorting them to the site of the two bodies they had been seeking for so long.

As they approached the opening to the passage, Reed appeared. "Rimmer is still busy, Chief. Sergeant Berger has him under observation."

"Thank you." He turned to Kendon. "We are going into a very small shed. With two of us and three of you we shall be overcrowded. I suggest DC Smail stays with DS Reed."

Disconsolately, Smail acted on the suggestion of the Yard man, though Kendon said nothing.

The cover of the ice-pit was soon open. Masters said to Kendon. "DCI Green and I have already seen what is down there, so I suggest you and DS Welch take a look for yourselves. Have you a torch?"

"Yes, sir."

"Good. Off you go, then, and for heaven's sake take care on those steps. They are narrow and worn and there's no hand hold."

Two or three minutes later the two local detectives reappeared.

"Are they the two you have been looking for?"

"Yes, sir, and I think you have some explaining to do."

"Don't adopt that tone with me, Mr Kendon. If there's any explaining to be done it is you who will have to do it. You've been looking for one of those two bodies for over five years. I've been down here less than five days and have produced them for you. There are those who might question your efficiency in view of such a discrepancy."

Kendon brazened it out. "Just because you happen by chance upon a hole in the ground and find two bodies in it . . ."

"Watch it, lad," growled Green. "There was no chance about it. The DCS investigated this case—in his spare time—and came up with the answer. Investigated it, lad, and was able to lead us straight here as a result of detective ability and thought on a plane so high you wouldn't even know it existed."

"In that case," replied Kendon, "perhaps Mr Masters could tell us how those lads were killed—before I call in our forensic people."

"Didn't you see how they died?" demanded Masters.

"See? It must have been poison. There were no marks."

"You mean you didn't see any marks?"

"I did not. And I'd like to remind you, sir, this is not a guessing game."

"If it were, Mr Kendon, I fear you would be way down the class for marks. The boys were not poisoned. They were electrocuted."

"Electrocuted? There's no burning or charring."

"Quite right, and that probably accounts for the fact that you seem to favour poison. But in case you don't know too

183

much about electrocution, Mr Kendon, let me tell you that there is a phenomenon known as the electric mark and, very often, that is all there is even when cases are fatal. Sometimes both entry and exit points are minute. Had you looked at the fingers of the right hands of both boys you would have found small areas of pale, hardened skin, slightly depressed with a raised rim. In fact, very like a localised deep burn which I suspect every one of us has experienced at some time.

"I didn't examine the bodies further than that, because I wanted to leave them exactly as they were found—for your benefit. But I think you can accept that the fingers were the entry points for the current which killed both boys. The exit points could be anywhere, but I would think they were most likely somewhere on the left hand side of each body. Hand again, maybe, or even some part of the leg, from the buttock to the ankle. I say this because it is as well for you to know that it is current which passes through the body across the chest that is most dangerous. Say from hand to hand or from right hand to left leg."

Kendon looked unconvinced. "And from noticing a barely discernable mark on each lad's fingers you can deduce they were electrocuted, can you, sir?"

Masters ignored the enmity in the tone. "I didn't 'notice' the burns, Mr Kendon, I expected to find them; and I didn't 'deduce' that the boys had been electrocuted. I knew that is how they had been killed before we discovered the bodies."

Kendon sneered. "You knew before you'd discovered the bodies. Just like that!"

"Oh yes, Mr Kendon. I knew who, how and where, long before the bodies came to light. However, as you appear to doubt my competence in this case, I shall say no more until we have a forensic report to substantiate what I have said. We shall now leave this business to you, as you seem to resent our help. But at least you cannot deny we have found the bodies for you—something you appear to have been unable to achieve over a period of . . . how long? Five years, was it?"

Kendon made no reply. As Masters turned to the door, Green said: "Whether you like it or not, lad, I'm going to give you a bit of advice. Don't touch a thing until the boffins have had a look."

"They'll be called in straight away."

"Good. Shall we see you at the party tonight?"

"Party?" growled Kendon. "What party?"

"The one the Dean laid on yesterday so that Chief Superintendent Masters could tell your guv'nors—over a drink, like—that he'd solved your case for them."

Kendon's face reddened with anger. "Yesterday? Laid on yesterday? You mean you've been sitting on this evidence for over twenty-four hours without informing me?"

"No, no, lad," said Green soothingly. "It was only yesterday the problem was mentioned to us. When we heard about it we reckoned it would take us about a day to sort it, so the party was laid on for tonight. There's no point in hanging about when these things crop up, is there? And don't look so angry, lad. We can't all be . . . "

"Bill," interrupted Masters. "I think we should go and leave Mr Kendon to get on."

"Right, George." Green turned to Kendon. "One thing I forgot to mention. Pay particular attention to the fuse in that point on the wall and to the one in the main box that controls this shed. I reckon you'll find somebody will have put a six-inch nail in both of them. Stands to reason, doesn't it, that ordinary fuses might blow when . . . "

"Bill."

"Coming, George."

They were invited for six o'clock. Highett, the College Commandant, Bobby Locke, Chief Constable Ernest Ballyn and DCS Sandy Feaver from the county force, Masters, Green, Reed and Berger. The last two added at the last moment by Master's request. They gathered in Bobby Locke's sitting room precisely on time, all there at the outset because of what they knew and not wanting to miss a word of the discussion they sensed would take place.

Locke asked the two sergeants if they would be kind enough to preside over the drinks. It was a reasonable gesture to

185

make, yielding his own prerogative to make the two junior ranks feel more at home among so much top brass.

"Gentlemen," said Highett, just a few minutes after they were all assembled, "as you must all appreciate by now, the tone of this little get-together has changed somewhat from what was intended when Bobby Locke first issued his invitations. Then we were being brought together so that we might all become acquainted with each other and to laugh off, if I can put it that way, a slight misunderstanding between some very zealous local officers and Bill Green who, with Sergeant Berger, was subjected to durance vile yesterday morning. I think that by now tempers on both sides will have cooled somewhat—to a degree, I hope, where we can all forget or at any rate regard the business as an unfortunate mistake."

Green grunted what could be taken as an assent to this suggestion, while Sandy Feaver said: "Agreed, sir. But I won't allow my people to forget it in a hurry. I'd like the memory to cause a few red faces every time the chaps concerned think about it."

"Thank you, both of you. Now, just one more point. Another purpose of this little party was to allow you, Sandy, to meet George Masters and his team in a semi-official sort of way. It seemed to Bobby and myself that as we were fortunate enough to have a complete Yard murder squad staying here in the College that it would be sensible—and courteous—for them to meet their opposite numbers in the local force. As I said, not officially, but to give both sides the opportunity to discuss problems should they wish to do so. I had little doubt that a certain amount of shop would be talked.

"Bobby and I were very keen for this to happen because, as you all now know, a student at the College began to emerge as a suspect in a serious case which your people were investigating, Sandy. This troubled us so much, for many reasons, that when we found ourselves lucky enough to have George Masters come here as a temporary lecturer we mentioned our fears to him. Quite properly, he took the view that he could in no way interfere in your case. However, he said he would keep the business in mind, and if anything

186

occurred to him he would bring it to your notice as a gesture of the co-operation he felt you should expect from the College. Yesterday's incident, the one we have agreed is now forgotten, did, however, bring the business to the forefront of his mind and he got down to thinking in earnest. You will have heard the results of his thinking already. DI Kendon, I take it, has reported to you, Sandy?"

"He has," agreed Feaver. "The forensic buffs are on the job now. In fact, I'm hoping our man, Dr Daggett, will be reporting soon. I took the liberty of giving him this address in case he should have something for the Chief Constable and myself within the next hour or so."

"Excellent. Now, as I said, the tone and purpose of this meeting has changed somewhat. I believe we all expect it now to develop into a report from Mr Masters and his team as to how he came to discover the bodies—the inferences that led up to his finding them and the facts that put him on the right path. For your benefit mainly, Sandy, but we are all, I feel sure, as interested as you are."

"Quite right," said Feaver. "DI Kendon is, despite any suggestions to the contrary, a good copper. But he lacks the ability to assimilate anything out of the ordinary. And what he can't assimilate, he can't believe in, so you can imagine that what we've heard from him about this case is virtually nothing—or nothing coherent."

"That lad's trouble," said Green, "is that he won't listen. So he only gets half the facts. But that doesn't stop him jumping to conclusions. And he gets nasty if anybody tries to put him right. It wouldn't have surprised me this afternoon if he hadn't tried to run George in—as an accomplice—simply because he'd found the bodies."

"I apologise for that," said Ballyn. "I think that worry causes Kendon to lose his temper. It's fairly obvious that—as far as big cases are concerned—he's reached his ceiling. Some things are just too much for him."

"He certainly lacks understanding," agreed Masters, "and the common courtesies are a closed book to him. I agree that unless and until he changes his attitude he should be given some job where he can do a little more good and a lot less

187

harm. That sounds presumptious of me, Mr Ballyn, but when a senior officer cannot even call forth co-operation from people like Bill Green and myself, he's unlikely to draw it out of people other than policemen, and that is a serious defect in a detective. You cannot bludgeon facts out of witnesses, you have to wheedle them out."

"Agreed," said Ballyn. "And I take no offence at what you've said, George. After all, you could be sitting on his next promotion board—should he ever get another chance to be called in front of one—and you'd say the same thing then. Better to hear it all now than see it in writing later on."

Highett stepped in. "George, I think we should hear from you."

Masters set down his glass. "Right, sir. I think there are enough pews, so should we all sit down? I think it would be better than just standing round . . . "

"Of course. Sergeant Berger, would you see everybody is topped up and then we can sit and listen without interruption."

When the party was settled, Masters began.

"In the afternoon of the day I arrived here, Bobby Locke mentioned to me the disappearance of the boy for whom you, Sandy, have been looking. I had not heard of the business because I'd been in hospital at the time the lad had gone, and when one has an arm in a sling it is difficult to manage newspapers, so I had read nothing of the incident.

"Bobby mentioned it to me as a friend, not as a policeman. As a friend because he was worried and not as a policeman because I am here only as a temporary lecturer and not as a murder squad detective.

"As you all know, Andriessen was Bobby's worry. I sympathised with Bobby over the possible diplomatic repercussions there would certainly be if a senior officer of a foreign police force were to be taken up by your people, Sandy, but I stressed that even so, if Andriessen were guilty, he must be subject to the full force of British law like everybody else. Bobby, of course, agreed with that, but he was fearful of the damage that could be done if Andriessen were taken up and then found not to be guilty.

188

"I won't enlarge on that. But—and I stress again, as a friend—I promised to give the matter some thought, based only on what he could tell me of your investigation. I felt that I could in no way approach you for information." Masters grinned. "Having met DI Kendon, I think I was not only right to make that decision, but lucky as well.

"I did think about what I'd heard, which was simply that five years ago you had a similar disappearance and that on that occasion, as on the recent one, Andriessen's car had been seen leaving the College grounds about the time the boy had disappeared. Also, that on both occasions his car had been seen in the vicinity of the places where you believed the boys to have been picked up. That to me, and obviously to you, seemed a significant fact that pointed straight at Andriessen.

"But my further information was that Andriessen claimed not to have left the College at the relevant times, and it was also proved that on both occasions he was inside the College buildings within something like half an hour of the time his car had been seen leaving."

"That's what held us back," said Sandy. "That and the fact that we found nothing in his car this second time. We didn't examine the first car, of course."

"I thought that would be your thinking."

"You had a different way of looking at it?"

"Slightly. It struck me that both cars were the sort that would be noticed. They were left-hand drive, they carried Netherlands signs and plates and so would not be anonymous. An experienced detective such as Andriessen, I felt, would be aware of this were he planning some criminal activity. So I assumed he did not use the cars. But you had evidence to show that the cars had been used. So if not Andriessen, somebody else must have been driving. Somebody who would take the opposite view from Andriessen in that the fact that the cars would be easily remembered by other road users would be what our advertising friends call a plus point. It is difficult, indeed, always to recognise who is driving a motor car. Light refraction, shadows, glare and so on all obscure the view of witnesses, but because they are acquainted with a certain car and its owner, many witnesses will simply assume that the rightful owner is driving it."

"We didn't take that into account," admitted Sandy. "Our witnesses seemed so sure . . . "

"Naturally. But each of us has encountered this non-recognition of the occupants of a car on many occasions. I personally have often been told that I've simply walked past people I know who have waved to me from cars. What I am saying is that if you don't know the car, you often don't recognise the driver, but if you do know the car, you don't necessarily recognise the driver."

"True enough," said Ballyn. "And it's so common an occurrence that I don't suppose we ever give it a thought."

"We ought to have done," grunted Sandy Feaver. "I ought to have done and Kendon ought to have done. It's bloody basic."

Bobby Locke waved his glass in the air. "Don't be too hard on yourself or Kendon," he said. "I attended a lecture given by George yesterday morning in which he showed that senior detectives didn't know what colour socks they were wearing, and they had only put them on an hour before. There were lots of other similar things he brought to light— even showing that a woman inspector didn't know the shade code of the lipstick she'd been using solidly for at least five years."

"Ah," said Ballyn, "but I'll bet George suggested very strongly that these people should have known these facts."

"Of course. But the point is everybody overlooks something, whether they're detectives or lay witnesses."

Masters continued.

"So I was considering the possibility of somebody other than Andriessen having been the driver of the cars which had been positively identified. My conclusion was that there were certain difficulties in the way of this theory. As, for example, why had Andriessen not said to your people when they examined his car that he had lent it to somebody on the evening of the murder.

"So I left that point and considered, in great detail, with

190

the help of Bill Green and our two sergeants, the mechanics of the crime as far as timing was concerned.

"It seemed to us, in conclave, that having no access to your files, we should have to divide the countryside into different areas."

"To search, you mean?" asked Ballyn.

"No, sir. Your people had searched. We knew that. And we had every confidence in your oganisation, just as we accepted that your reports of witnesses sighting the cars and so forth were all irrefutable."

"Besides," grunted Green, "what could four of us do in hundreds of square miles of woodland where four hundred searchers had failed?"

Nobody commented on this observation, so after a moment Masters went on: "As luck would have it, I was planning an open-air exercise for my students, and I roped in Bill Green and Sergeant Berger to do some of the leg work for me. Distances, timings and so on—an area in which I have found we are sometimes quite unsure of ourselves as investigating officers. So many people refuse to believe watches, maps and other yardsticks that I thought I should bring it home to my students that they must accept such aids." He grinned. "It was while Bill was preparing the ground for me that he was taken up—stopwatch in hand—by your watchers, Sandy. I had warned the two of them that their operations had to be secret as I didn't want the students to be forewarned of what I was preparing for them. Hence their reluctance to divulge what they were about to your people."

"However, as was said earlier, the action of your people caused the four of us to concentrate more closely on your case. Not only because of what we regarded—in our anger—as totally unwarranted interference with our blameless activities, but because it showed us, quite clearly, that you had the College under surveillance and were maintaining a constant presence in the neighbourhood. Quite simply, we wondered why. And when we began wondering, we began to discuss reasons and to provide probable answers.

"The upshot was, as I said earlier, that we began to divide the countryside into different areas, probably because we were, at the time, involved in doing a time and distance problem.

"Time and distance. Time to drive out, locate, pick up a boy, drive to a lonely spot, commit murder, dispose of the body, drive back to the College, and then to reappear among his colleagues in no state of disarray. All in something like a little over half an hour. Because that is what Andriessen would have had to do if your sightings and witness reports were correct.

"Bill's timing exercise convinced him that this couldn't have been done if your search for the body had been thorough, and we were prepared to accept that it had been—totally thorough."

"Thanks for that at any rate," said Ballyn. "But what's this about dividing up the territory?"

"It was a gradual process, sir, but we divided it up, initially, into two circles centred on the College. We named the inner circle, 'nearby', and the outer circle, 'more distant'. 'Nearby' was the area you had searched. 'More distant' was the area beyond it. Basically, there was no time for a murderer to complete his operation in either area if the figures were right."

"We're talking about Andriessen now, are we?"

"Yes. He just could not have got out and back again from the more distant ring. But he didn't use the nearby ring because your searches proved that. So how could he have cut his operations down and saved time? Our answer to that was that he did not completely dispose of the body immediately."

"How do you mean?" asked Feaver.

"Say he just left here, picked the lad up and brought him back to the College, dead."

"And?"

"And then went about his normal business until after everybody was in bed and then took his time to dispose of the body. Not in the likely area of search in the nearby ring . . ."

"Further out, you mean? Way beyond the scope of any likely search?"

"Why not?"

"We were covering roads by then, but ... hell, yes he could have got through, I suppose."

"With luck, you mean?"

Feaver nodded. "It takes time to make an area of any size absolutely watertight. Anybody who looks at the map book in his car thinks there's just a few motorways, A-roads and the odd B-road, but get an Ordnance Survey map and you'll see there are as many tracks and lanes big enough to take a car as there are hairs on the back of your hand. We have a drill to cover main roads and, depending on circumstances, we can do it within minutes. But there's the whole force area to cover for normal policing. To get men concentrated in a ring five miles in radius, centred on just one point takes time. There can't be a drill because you don't know where the centre point is going to be. It could be Reading, Aldershot or merely a spot in the middle of nowhere. So just how soon that ring was tight, I don't know. We didn't know the lad was missing until nearly eight that night. Then there were the necessary initial moves—checking with his pals and so on. We can't go to the expense of mounting a vast operation before we know it's necessary. So ... yes, he could have slipped through."

"But you have your doubts?"

Feaver nodded. "If he left it very late, yes."

"That is what we thought. But say he had brought the body back here, and had slipped through your net, he could then have hidden the body well beyond your likely area of search."

"In the distant ring?" asked Locke.

"Quite. Remember, please, that I am trying to give you a synopsis of our thoughts. Having got so far, we had to make presumptions." He held up his hand as Feaver was about to expostulate. "Hear me out, please. We gave you, Sandy, and your people, the credit for ensuring that the nearby area did not contain the body, otherwise you would have found it. We also gave you credit for not allowing our man to escape further afield. So our two initial areas—we presumed—were non-starters. That was presumption one. Now, Sandy, you can object to that at this point if you wish."

Feaver shook his head. "I'd be a bit of a Charlie to fault you four for trusting us."

Masters grinned. "That's what I thought you'd say. Now for our second presumption, which I hope you will find equally acceptable. If not the nearby or distant areas, then where? The answer came to me, Bobby, yesterday afternoon when you suddenly informed me I was due to give the early evening lecture—one I didn't know I was down for and for which, consequently, I was not prepared."

"Pleased my mistake was of value," said Locke.

"I sat at my kitchen table to make a few hurried notes," went on Masters, "and then, because my family were not back from their afternoon outing, I stepped outside to assemble my thoughts in the fresh air. As you know, those particular quarters are very pleasantly built, actually within the woodland, so as soon as I stepped outside the back door I was in among trees and undergrowth and within two minutes was out of sight of the houses or any passers-by along the road. Between that moment and my walk back from the lecture about an hour and a half later I had come to question whether the local police had searched the private woods within the College boundary and those belonging to other houses round about. I felt that such areas could have been lacunae, overlooked in an otherwise meticulous search."

"They weren't," said Feaver. "We did the lot."

"So I discovered, later," replied Masters. "Inspector Woolgar, who is the chap responsible for the College, told me you had searched the grounds. But that was information we only got this morning, so before that we were presuming that in addition to the nearby and distant areas there could well be a minute cell, like the eye of the storm, which had been overlooked. Our problem then, was to find this small spot."

Masters turned to Highett. "I hope you will forgive me when I tell you that we all immediately assumed that the spot we were looking for lay within the purlieus of the College."

Highett nodded to show he had taken no offence.

"Our choice seemed justified," said Masters, "because the two peccant cars seemed to have originated from here. We

194

couldn't disregard that fact, nor had we any other fact to lead us elsewhere."

"Reasonable," agreed Highett.

Masters smiled. "Then we had our stroke of luck."

"Ah!" breathed Feaver. "You'll admit to luck?"

"I often do. Ask Bill Green. He says I'm the jammiest copper alive. But I'll tell you about our particular bit of good fortune.

"Because my arm was heavily bandaged, my wife drove me down here in our own car. Both of us have keys to the car. Wanda, naturally, used her own set on the journey down. After all the fuss of moving into the quarter, checking inventories, settling in our young son and so on, Wanda suddenly discovered she had lost her keys. She thought she had put them on the kitchen table when she first arrived, but a very thorough search failed to unearth them.

"We informed Inspector Woolgar of the loss. In his outer office he has a lost-and-found tray and he told me that small items like keys, pens, gloves and so on were always being found and returned and he had hopes that Wanda's keys would soon turn up. So I decided to give it a few days before having new keys cut. Yesterday afternoon, when I was on my way to an appointment with you, Bobby, rushing because I was a minute or so late and having visions of Gertie giving me a rocket because of it, I met Woolgar. He told me Wanda's keys had appeared in his lost-and-found tray and that he had personally locked them in his cupboard for safety. He offered to get them for me there and then, but as I have said, I was already late for an appointment and Woolgar himself was going in the opposite direction, so we agreed I should pick them up after my visit to you, Bobby or, alternatively, that if he had returned to his office more quickly than expected, Woolgar should ring Wanda and invite her over to collect her keys should she wish to do that."

Masters looked across at Feaver. "Your men didn't have this particular bit of luck, so I must admit that my colleagues and I had something of an unfair start. It was this way!

"Bobby sprang on me the information that I was due to lecture last evening. I was in so much of a hurry to get to my

195

quarter to prepare what I was to say, that I forgot to call into Woolgar's office to collect Wanda's keys. But when I got home, my family and the car were missing. Nothing odd in that, because my wife often goes off shopping or takes our son for a ride in the country. So I was not surprised to find the car gone, nor was I surprised to find a set of car keys on the kitchen table when I sat at it to write my notes."

Feaver said: "You assumed your missus had gone to Woolgar's office to pick up her set of keys after having received a phone call from him?"

"Quite right. Then, as I told you, before the family got back, I finished my notes and stepped out into the woods for a breath of air. I was, I suppose, a couple of hundred yards from the house when I thought I heard the car draw up or the rasp of the handbrake or something—I forget exactly what—that told me it was time to return and greet the family. So I turned back towards the house. I was in no great hurry, so I took my time, smoking a pipe and looking about me as I went. When I got home, there was the family and there was the car.

"I think I was entitled to suppose that the two had arrived together. In other words, that my wife had been using the car. Later on last evening, after supper, Doris Green—Bill's wife, who is staying with us for a few days—mentioned that she, Wanda and Michael, my son, had been out for a walk in the afternoon.

Masters looked round. All his listeners were gazing at him solemnly.

Green said: "George called it luck. I call it good, professional detective work to pick up the word 'walk' and to go on from there as he did. He established that the family had indeed not used the car and that Wanda had not heard from Woolgar about the return of the lost keys, nor had she, unbeknown to Woolgar, picked them up from the office. Don't forget there was a set of keys on the kitchen table, there was a set in Woolgar's safe and—because it was out and about—there must have been a set in the car."

"Unbelievable," said Highett. "Really unbelievable."

"It's not, you know, sir," said Green.

"But somebody must have . . . "

"Too true. Stolen one set the first day George was here, used them as a pattern to get another set, and then returned the first lot—anonymously—as having been found within the College."

"But why get a new set if you've already stolen . . . "

"That's the way it would have to be, sir," said Feaver. "If you left the owners with only one set, only the one that held them could use the car. If there were two sets and the car was absent, one would naturally assume the other was using it and so wouldn't report it as stolen. That's it put simply. It's slightly more complicated than that, of course. But if George would carry on . . . "

Masters smiled. "There's little more to be said on this particular point. We reckoned that if there was somebody round the College willing to go to those lengths to borrow my car, he was probably an inveterate user of cars that were not his. His technique argued experience in the business of transport borrowing. So perhaps he had borrowed Andriessen's cars, not only recently, but also five years ago. Borrowed them for specific jobs because they would be noticed on the roads as foreign."

"Where yours, being a Jag, would also have been noticed, you mean?" asked Locke.

Masters nodded. "It is highly probable that our friend always favoured, as his weapon of choice, a car that stood out from the common ruck. But that is by the way. He borrowed my car yesterday afternoon, in my opinion, because he saw the keys had gone from the lost-and-found tray in the office, and he therefore assumed that they were once again in our possession. He did not know Woolgar had put them in the safe-cupboard.

"I imagine he saw me go to visit the Dean, and then saw my family set off on their walk. The coast, in fact, was clear for him to have a run in the Jag. He returned it—as I heard whilst I was in the wood. Between that moment and my own return a few minutes later, Wanda, Doris and Michael got back to the house. He had run it mighty fine. Why, I can't say. But the logic behind his reasoning was borne out.If

197

Wanda hadn't left her keys where I could see them, on the kitchen table, and if, indeed, we had recovered the other set from Woolgar, nobody would have suspected or guessed that the car had been borrowed.

"As you can imagine, we guessed at the name of the culprit. Somebody who had been to the house on that first day, and somebody who could wander in and out of Woolgar's general office at will—to return the keys surreptitiously and then, later, to see that they had presumably been claimed. Ex-Sergeant Rimmer, the staff electrician, was the only person other than my immediate family and Sergeant Reed to enter the house after our arrival that first day. He brought a stock of new light bulbs, installed them and then let himself out."

"Passing through the kitchen to get to the back door," growled Feaver. "With the keys on the table and nobody to see him nick 'em?"

"Quite right. So," continued Masters, "what it boiled down to was that we reckoned the body would be in the College— either the grounds or the buildings—and the man we wanted was Rimmer. The two suppositions supported each other. So this morning we thought our ideas were worth putting to the test."

"I'll say," grunted Feaver. "Why didn't you call us then?"

"I would have liked to, but I had no solid fact to offer, and in view of Kendon's attitude—previously and subsequently— I am sure I was right to hold off until we had exhausted our own resources."

Ballyn turned to Feaver. "I think it is time it was pointed out to Kendon that courtesy and co-operation could solve more crime than his rather doubtful investigative powers."

Feaver nodded glumly. Masters continued his account. "We suspected the body would be within the College bounds, but we had no clue as to whether in the grounds or the buildings. Whilst I was borrowing a couple of large-scale plans of the property—on the pretext that I wanted to set up an exercise—Woolgar mentioned that your people, Sandy, had searched the grounds."

"Something you thought we had overlooked, eh?"

"I confess I thought you might have missed it on the

grounds that it was police property and we cops don't make a habit of turning over our own nicks when searching for missing persons."

Feaver waved his hand to show that he accepted the point.

"It was a piece of good news for us," continued Masters. "With only four of us to do the work—well, the College buildings themselves were enough of a task to keep us occupied for a bit. Bill Green and Sergeant Berger tackled the main buildings—looking for cellars and so on. Reed and I took on the outbuildings, of which there are quite a lot remaining from the old days.

"To cut a long story short, we had no luck until Reed and I found a small brick shed left standing at the end of a six-foot alleyway between the old house and the big new block. The sign on the door and those contents of the shed which we could see through the windows showed that this must be the electrician's junk store. And Rimmer is the staff electrician."

"Ah!" breathed Highett. "So you decided to concentrate on that."

"You could say that, sir, but the door was locked and I suspected there would be only one key, and that in Rimmer's possession."

"Tricky," agreed Feaver. "What did you do?"

It was Reed who broke in. "It was what the Chief saw through the window that decided our course of action, sir. How he noticed what he did, I'll never know."

"What was it he saw?" asked Locke.

"A tin tray bolted to the bench," said Reed.

"You what, lad?" asked Feaver.

Masters said, "A tin tray on the bench was not a strange thing in itself. Anybody who strips old electrical goods might have one for catching small screws and washers and so on. But this one had a large coach bolt in the middle of it. The bolt ran through the wood of the bench and protruded underneath it, far enough to take two nuts."

"Of what significance is that?" asked Highett. "You have me totally bewildered."

"Hanging close to the nuts on the end of the bolt," said Masters, "were two heavy wires, both ending in large spade terminals. The largest spade terminals I'd ever seen. I suspect they had been specially cut out of a sheet of metal."

"Is that it?" asked Locke.

"No," grunted Green. "That was just George having one of his flashes of imaginative invention. He reckoned one of those spade terminals was intended to go between the nuts on that bolt, and he wondered why the hell anybody should want to send a dirty great current of electricity into a tin tray."

"So what did he do?"

"He sent for me," grinned Green. "And young Berger. The lads picked the lock and we went inside." He looked at Feaver. "Don't worry, Sandy, we didn't touch anything. We looked around. There was an electric kettle and a teapot there and . . . a tin mug."

"Go on."

"There was also a metal chair—one of those old Victorian cast-iron ones—with all the paint rubbed off."

"So what happened then?" demanded Highett.

"We went for lunch," said Green airily. "George wanted time to think, you see."

"About what?" demanded Feaver.

"There wasn't a sign of any bodies," explained Green, innocently. "We reckoned that Rimmer could have been running his own version of the execution shed at Sing Sing, but we had no proof. And proof—in the shape of bodies—was what we had to have."

"I see that," said Highett slowly, "but . . . "

Masters cut in. "There was a large rubber mat on the floor of the shed, sir. As you've heard, we touched nothing, so we didn't look under the mat. Perhaps we should have done. But the plan gave us our clue. It named that shed. 'Cutter's', it was called. We wondered about that. It was obviously the work shed of a member of the household staff in the old days. We reckoned it couldn't have been used by a woodcutter, not so close to the building. Then we wondered why the builders of the new block had avoided that eight feet of ground and left a useless alleyway leading nowhere except to a tumble-down hut. We guessed they must have had some reason, and

200

rightly or wrongly we came to the conclusion that that area was avoided because the ground wouldn't take the weight of a big new building. To us that suggested some sort of cellar or tunnel below ground, probably approached through the hut. It was then that the penny dropped. An ice-cutter's hut with its refrigerated storage cell below ground."

"Just like that, eh?" asked Feaver. "Of course I've heard of such ice-houses, but that idea would never have occurred to me."

"There's no reason why it should have done," said Masters. "You would—as investigating officer—have lifted the rubber mat. We fought shy of doing that before lunch. But after lunch . . . "

"You lifted it, of course."

"Yes. To reveal a large metal plate which obviously gave to a cellar. The plate was fastened to a wooden lining by short screw bolts—thick, large headed jobs. If you look closely at one in the corner of the plate you will see it has been removed and greased, with lanolin I think. And as you know, lanolin is the stuff one uses on car battery terminals to get a good connection with the leads."

"What you mean," said Feaver, "is that the second spade terminal had been connected to the metal plate by that screw bolt."

Masters nodded. "That was our reading of what we saw. An electric circuit between the metal tray and the ground plate. Sit somebody on the metal chair on the plate and invite him to have a cup of tea in a tin mug placed on the tray . . ."

"After having been careless enough to splash a drop of water about as you brewed up," said Green

"Circuit," said Feaver. "With the current running through the body from the hand, glued by the power of the tin mug as soon as the handle was touched, and down to earth through the chair to the metal plate, whether the drinker was wearing rubber-soled shoes or not."

"Right," agreed Masters. "I imagine Rimmer put very strong fuses not only in the plug in the hut, but also in the internal fuse box and I suspect he counted on the first jolt—

201

as soon as the cup handle was grasped—causing the muscles of the holder's arm to jerk, thereby spilling the tea all over the tin tray and thus heightening the effect."

"That's what an electric shock does," confirmed Ballyn. "Electricity either throws you clear or it causes muscle contractions which cause the victim to hold on to the source of the current. That's devilish, Masters, because those contractions could cause a victim—especially a youngster—to suffer bladder contractions which would cause him to urinate immediately, thereby increasing the ease with which the current would flow between the body and the chair . . . "

Ballyn stopped and reddened. "Sorry, I didn't mean to take over."

"It's a valid point, sir," said Green. "The forensic people could well bear you out when they inspect the clothes, and in case you're feeling just a bit squeamish about mentioning that, you've got to realise that our murderer probably took hold of the lads outstretched arm to hold it down so that the tin mug kept in contact with the tray. He could do that quite safely, you know, if he had rubber-soled boots on."

Ballyn nodded miserably and Feaver asked: "What next, George? You opened up and found your ice-cellar?"

"We did. We also went down and found two bodies. After that we wasted no time in calling you in."

Feaver nodded and said: "Thanks. And I mean that."

"You've still got a lot of work to do, Sandy. Preparing the case and . . . "

There was a knock on the door and DI Kendon poked his head round. He looked across at Feaver. "You said you wanted to see Dr Daggett when he'd finished his preliminary inspection . . . sir."

"Show him in," said Highett, "and come in yourself if you can spare time for a noggin."

Daggett accepted his drink gratefully. "This sort of caper gives one a thirst. The only consolation this time is that the bodies are in a fairly reasonable state." He turned to Feaver. "I take it you know you've got two cases of electrocution here?"

"I know, Doc. What can you tell us?"

"Very little at the moment. Most of it will be post-mortem evidence. But I've found what we call the electric marks—the sites at which the electricity entered the bodies and then exited. Sorry to say they were in the most dangerous positions. The currents passed across the bodies, in both cases, from right hand to the left leg area."

"That's the most dangerous route?"

"Definitely. There seems to have been no resistance to the current, so I imagine there was a lot of fluid about. Dryness increases resistance and therefore reduces the danger, you know."

Masters looked at Ballyn to make sure the Chief Constable had noted that his contribution had been upheld

"As for causes of death," went on Daggett, "well, gentlemen, we'll have to see, but the most likely cause is ventricular fibrillation. Then there'll be respiratory failure, of course. Paralysis of the muscles of respiration, you know. I don't expect any central nervous system damage as that is usually due to the source of the electricity being in contact with the head, and that wasn't so in these cases. There's been no obvious bleeding, but we'll see when we examine the bodies. Though that's a bit of a waste of time, really, because internal evidence in cases like this is usually sparse and often non-existent. There could be some damage, of course, to the walls of the blood vessels along the path of the current. But little else, I imagine."

"Is that it, Doc?"

"No. We shall have to examine the set-up, of course. I'll have to tie it all in with the infernal machine this electrician set up. He may have changed the fuses for smaller ones by now, but we'll match the pattern of the handle of the mug to the burns on the fingers and so on. There'll be no difficulty in establishing the evidence, I imagine." He held his glass out to Berger for a refill. "What's the chap's motive for all this?"

Masters turned to Reed. "I think you can best answer that, Sergeant."

Reed did not hesitate.

"Rimmer is a crank, of course. A pathological case. Mentally abnormal, in other words. But the abnormality rests on an emotion, or a passion, rather, that isn't all that uncommon these days among quite a number of people. Especially people getting on a bit in years who usually sum up their feelings by saying the country has gone to the dogs. That's as far as most of them go, thank heaven, but there's still a tidy number who want to bring back birching and hanging and some form of corporal punishment for kids who go off the rails. We know that's true because we hear it often enough. But if you get these beliefs, held strongly by someone who not only thinks he can do something about it, but actually sets out to do whatever it is he has in mind, then you've got trouble.

"Most of the old 'uns who want more and severer punishments are too old to be able to act. But Rimmer—well, he knew he'd got the means. Not bodily strength any more, but electricity. He told me that the DCS and I weren't proper cops because we'd never felt the collar of a man who was hanged as a result of our arrests. Rimmer claimed he had and the country would be better if the same were happening now.

"However, as I said, Rimmer had electricity to help him see off a few of the guilty. I believe that though he would prefer judicial hanging, he thought the American electric chair would be a good substitute. A substitute which he could contrive for himself and use, even if only in secret."

Reed looked at Masters. "I reckon, Chief, that we're lucky only to have had two deaths to deal with. It's my guess that Rimmer has tried more often than just twice, but has failed to get the kids to go into his hut for a cup of tea. Most of them would accept a lift perhaps, but nothing more. That's by the way, though. Both the kids who have been killed were young tearaways. They'd done a lot of damage to cars, committed theft and so on and got away unpunished by the courts. Rimmer thought that was wrong, and wanted to put it right. He set out to identify them, learn their movements and then went out, time after time, to try to pick them up. He never knew when he'd be successful, that's why his gear had to be there, ready for use. Twice to our knowledge he has been successful. And he'll be proud of that. All we can do is be pleased he hasn't had more cases to be proud of."

There was a moment of silence after Reed had finished speaking, then Masters thanked him.

Dr Daggett said: "It'll be up to the trick-cyclists to put all that in their own jargon, of course, gentlemen, but what we've just heard is a fair enough lay explanation of the man's motive. I reckon you could proceed along those lines."

"Is Rimmer in custody?" asked Highett.

"He is, sir," said Kendon, assertively. "With any luck we'll have him charged tonight and up in front of the magistrates tomorrow morning." He turned to Daggett. "We'll need to know all that about voltages and cycles and milliamps that you were talking about a bit ago."

"You'll have it. The danger factors. The ordinary domestic supply is lethal enough, so there'll be no attempt by the defence to claim it isn't. In fact, the lower tensions around two-forty can be more dangerous than really high voltages." He looked around. "Now, gentlemen, if you'll excuse me . . . thanks for the drink . . . any more and you'd be asking me to breathe into one of your little bags."

As Masters and his companions made their way back to the quarter for a belated supper, Green said: "How much do we tell the girls, George?"

"Now? Nothing except that the bodies have been found within the College. The matter is *sub judice* now as a man has been arrested and charged. I know that is slightly specious, but we'll lean on it."

"And your demonstration of the moderator principle of investigation, Chief?" asked Reed. "The same applies. You won't be able to use this case."

"I've suddenly gone off the idea altogether," said Masters. "I think I'll try to suggest that we've completed what I was really brought here to do."

"And go back to the Yard, Chief?"

"As soon as I can wangle it, yes. Just so long as my missus doesn't mind. If she really likes it here, I shall stay. She was partner to the agreement, after all."

"Get her to attend one of your lectures," grunted Green, "then she'll agree to get out of here fast enough."

"She'd want to stay for ever,' said Reed. "Once she heard the Chief speak, Mrs Masters would never leave here."